BENEATH THE SECRETS

A BEST FRIENDS OLDER BROTHER ROMANCE

SHANDI BOYES

COPYRIGHT

Editing: Swish Design & Editing

Editing: Mountains Wanted Publishing

Cover Design: SSB Covers & Design

DEDICATION

For my crazy family.
Chris, Haidyn, Clayton, CJ, Mason & Mackenzie
Thanks for putting up with me.

WANT TO STAY IN TOUCH?

Facebook: facebook.com/authorshandi

Instagram: instagram.com/authorshandi

Email: authorshandi@gmail.com

Reader's Group: bit.ly/ShandiBookBabes

Website: authorshandi.com

Newsletter: https://www.subscribepage.com/AuthorShandi

ALSO BY SHANDI BOYES

** Denotes Standalone Books*

Perception Series

Saving Noah *

Fighting Jacob *

Taming Nick *

Redeeming Slater *

Saving Emily

Wrapped Up with Rise Up

Protecting Nicole *

Enigma

Enigma

Unraveling an Enigma

Enigma The Mystery Unmasked

Enigma: The Final Chapter

Beneath The Secrets

Beneath The Sheets

Spy Thy Neighbor *

The Opposite Effect *

I Married a Mob Boss *

Second Shot *

The Way We Are

<u>The Way We Were</u>

Sugar and Spice *

<u>Lady In Waiting</u>

<u>Man in Queue</u>

<u>Couple on Hold</u>

Enigma: The Wedding

Silent Vigilante

<u>Hushed Guardian</u>

<u>Quiet Protector</u>

Enigma: An Isaac Retelling

Twisted Lies *

Bound Series

Chains

Links

<u>Bound</u>

<u>Restrain</u>

<u>The Misfits</u> *

Nanny Dispute *

Russian Mob Chronicles

Nikolai: A Mafia Prince Romance

Nikolai: Taking Back What's Mine

<u>Nikolai: What's Left of Me</u>

<u>Nikolai: Mine to Protect</u>

<u>Asher: My Russian Revenge</u> *

Nikolai: Through the Devil's Eyes

Hotshot Neighbor *

<u>The Bobrov Bratva Series</u>

Wicked Intentions *

Sinful Intentions *

Devious Intentions *

Deadly Intentions *

DEAR READER,

I know you have fallen in love with Hugo from the *Enigma* series and that you know and love him as he is now, but Hugo didn't become the man he was overnight. Certain events and people in his life influenced the man he has become today. So, in saying that, I feel it's important to show you how Hugo became the man he is. To do that, we need to go back to the very beginning. Only by showing you who he was in his past will you truly understand why he made the mistakes he has made and the consequences that followed his massive decision.

Are you ready? Because it's time to dive beneath the sheets and learn about the real Hugo. The Hugo Marshall only those closest to him know.

I hope you enjoy his story.

Cheers,

Shandi xx

ONE
HUGO

Ignoring the roach devouring the crust of a sandwich on the cracked vanity in front of me, I loosen my tie in the mirror. With my failure at securing a job today, I may very well be scavenging for food alongside him next week.

My desperation to find a job had me arriving for an interview at a piece-of-shit club on the outskirts of New York City. Calling this establishment sleazy would be an understatement. Its walls haven't seen a coat of paint since the day I first breathed air, the bathroom is more outdated than my grandma's petticoat she wore on her wedding day, and that roach isn't the first one I've seen, but I'm so desperate to add a few more digits to my scarce bank balance that I'm open to *any* opportunities available.

When your options are limited, you take what you can get.

Unfortunately for me, even a crack dime bar in the middle of nowhere is too dignified for an ex-Air Force sniper.

After a brief chat with a guy who looks like he stars in seventies pornos, I was told there were no suitable positions available for a 'person like me.'

I drove over an hour to be blown off in five minutes. Even my brother would have lasted longer than that.

Laughing off the fact I've been rejected by a Ron Jeremy wannabe, I amble out of the bathroom. My black wingtip boots click along the cracked, uneven floor as I cross the room. I throw my jacket onto the counter then sit on the grime-covered barstool for a beer. I might as well down a cold beer while waiting for the peak-hour traffic to ease before heading home.

The bartender with a sleeve of home-botched tattoos on his left arm nods at my request for a Bud Light as he sets down a scotch on the rocks in front of the gentleman next to me.

"Leave the bottle," my nameless companion requests.

When the bartender doesn't blink an eye at his demanding tone, I toss back half the beer the bartender sets down before lifting my eyes to the grainy image on the small television hanging from the ceiling. The picture is so blurry, I can't tell if it's the LA Dodgers or the Chicago Cubs playing.

Deciding the eye strain isn't worth the hassle of knowing the score, I shift my focus to the dance floor. Although the bathrooms are severely outdated and the beer isn't as cold as it could be, there are still a handful of patrons crammed onto the four-sizes-too-small dance space.

After tipping my beer in greeting to a trio of girls at the side of the dance floor, batting their eyelashes at me, I sling my eyes back to the television. Even dolled up in pretty dresses and wearing more makeup than Prince dons on stage, their demeanor screams stage-five clinger.

Since I do not want and am not looking for *any* type of relationship right now, bed companions who are reluctant to leave in the morning are *not* on my radar.

My focus is on securing a job. Once I achieve that, my motivation will return to washing away the two years of hell that still plague my dreams every night.

"Are you a regular?"

As I shake my head, a chuckle escapes my lips. "Normally, you wouldn't catch me dead in a shithole like this." I swing my eyes to the voice interrogating me. The more my gaze roams over my drinking comrade, the more my brows join. "You?" I ask, even though I already know the answer to my question.

It's not just his expensive Hugo Boss suit, polished dress shoes, and one-hundred-dollar haircut that gives away the fact he's a fly-in visitor. His expensive watch is the biggest sign. That piece, no doubt, costs more than I made my entire time serving in the Air Force.

After shaking his head, Mr. Trust Fund throws back a three-finger serving of scotch before he pours himself another generous helping. When he locks his eyes with mine, the uniqueness of their coloring gathers my interest, but it's the secrets hidden in their darkness that holds my attention. "I was considering buying this place."

"Why?" My tone is blunt and straight to the point. "If you want to throw your trust fund into an empty pit, toss it this way."

He smirks against the rim of his dirty glass before downing another nip. After dragging the back of his hand across his mouth, he mutters, "Unless you look past the surface, you'll never find the diamond hidden beneath the rubble."

"Hey, I'm all for finding a diamond in the rough, but this place isn't it. Even if you throw a bucketload of money into this project and have her sparkling like Mariah Carey in a sequined mini dress, you'll still be throwing money away."

He dumps his glass onto the countertop and angles his torso to face me. "Why?"

"For one, the demographic is all wrong. The average age in this region is twenty-five to forty-seven. Even if they haven't been tied down with the standard two point five kids that most people in this county have, they're either unemployed or financially strangled by the housing market. Before the stock market crashed, house prices in this area were astronomical. People went nuts, buying any parcel of land they could get their mitts on. Once the market crashed, so did the land value. You may get people walking through the doors, wanting to escape the misery of life for a few hours, but they'll be the patrons who arrive drunk and leave once the buzz wears off."

I wave my hand around the space. Even with fifty-plus people on the dance floor, including the mysterious stranger and me, only four people are gathered around the bar, ordering drinks. "This place will be nothing more than a money pit. In my opinion, you'd be better off investing in another fancy watch than this dump."

My scotch-drinking comrade gathers his suit jacket hanging on the back of his chair before he places a hundred-dollar bill onto the counter, then he shifts on his feet to face me. "Do you have any plans tonight?"

I grin behind the rim of my beer before taking a swig. "I'm sorry, but you're not my type." I nudge my head to the ensemble of girls standing to the left of us. Their lips pucker when they notice they've secured our attention. "I'm sure walking up with one of them on your arm will give your mommy dearest the shock factor you're after."

My focus is pulled from the pretty brunette in the middle of the group when a low chuckle rumbles out of my drinking companion's mouth. "I'm not gay, but I can assure you if I were, your long-haired, Mills and Boons romance cover appearance you're *trying* to pull off isn't tickling my fancy."

My mouth gapes, surprised by Mr. Trust Fund's witty comeback.

I knew there was something hidden in his eyes, but I had no clue it was a personality.

He puts on his suit jacket and adjusts his gold cufflinks before his gray eyes lock with mine. "So, what do you say, Fabio, five hundred dollars for an hour of your time?"

I leap off the barstool. "Hell, if you'd mentioned the five hundred dollars at the start, I wouldn't have made you buy me a drink first."

After winking farewell to the women floundering near the bar, I follow the smirking stranger to an awaiting town car idling at the curb.

"Corner of 57th and Welsh," he instructs the driver as he gestures for me to slide into the back seat before him.

Forty minutes later, we pull into a nightclub on the other side of the city. Since Mr. Trust Fund isn't the talkative type, preferring to interact with his cell phone than the real-life person sitting next to him, the trip was made in silence.

"Go inside and have a look around. I'll meet you in there in a few minutes," he instructs.

I nod, acknowledging I heard him before exiting his vehicle. My lips twist when I raise my eyes from the cracked white pavement. Although not as rundown as our previous establishment, this club has still seen better days.

After the driver of the town car has a quiet word with the rake-thin gentleman standing at the door, I'm ushered inside the building, forgoing the moderate size line waiting to enter.

With poor lighting, dark furnishings, and black carpeted floors, it feels like I'm entering a seedy strip club more than a dance club. Although the bar is crowded, the dance floor is nearly empty. Only once the jukebox music alters from a slow, lazy song to a club-thumping beat do partygoers emerge from the dark corners of the room like vampires coming out after sunset.

Once I've used the clean but stark bathroom facilities, I make my way to the bar. Partway there, I spot Mr. Trust Fund sitting at the very end. His suit jacket is removed, the sleeves on his light blue business shirt are rolled up, and a twenty-five-year-old bottle of Craggan-more scotch is sitting in front of him.

He raises his brow in silent questioning when I approach him.

"Is this another potential purchase?"

He lifts a crystal glass to his lips while curtly nodding.

My eyes drift around the space to drink it in with a more adept eye. "It's better than your last selection. What's your aim? More profit or better clientele?"

He hides his smirk beneath the rim of his glass. "You tell me."

"Approximately eighty percent of the crowd are college-age students. College kids are ideal for a nightclub, but they're cheap drunks, rarely spending over ten dollars a night on drinks. This club could benefit from charging an entry fee. That way, you get the ten dollars out of them before they walk in the door, easily doubling your profits because they'll still spend their stingy ten on drinks once they enter. At this age, their focus is on the head in their pants, not whether they will have enough money to pay the heating bill."

Mr. Trust Fund leans over the counter and snags a glass from the wire rack. Remaining quiet, he pours a generous helping of scotch into the fresh glass before sliding it across the counter to me.

I dip my chin in thanks before downing the significant serving in one hit. A fiery warmth slides down my throat and settles in my gut, but even knowing they charge over thirty-five dollars a nip for Cragganmore, my taste buds can't tell the difference between its high price tag and a standard bottle of scotch.

"If I were to charge an entry fee, what would the impact on the clientele be?"

I shrug. "I'd say maybe sixty-five percent would continue to come here even if a cover was charged, but you'll easily gain back the lost clientele within months. Currently, the ratio of females to males is sitting at around forty-sixty. If you get rid of the cheap drunk, the female ratio will increase, which will bring back the more reputable male clientele. Girls expect guys to buy their drinks, not spill their drinks on them or puke on their shoes."

Mr. Trust Fund's smirk forms into a half-smile. "Business major?"

"Nope." I shake my head. "I just frequented these types of places a bit during my college days." *And now,* but I keep that snippet of information to myself.

Nodding, Mr. Trust Fund pulls a leather wallet from the back pocket of his trousers. After removing two business cards, he hands one to the pretty blonde barmaid, oblivious that she's making kissy gaga faces at him. "Have the owner contact me. I want to purchase this club."

The bartender's teeth munch on her bottom lip as she nods. Ignoring the sex kitten who wants to purr at his feet, Mr. Trust Fund slings his eyes to me. While tucking a business card into the pocket of the long-sleeve dress shirt I rummaged from the back of my closet this morning, he orders, "Call me tomorrow morning. I want you to join my empire."

With that, he pivots on his heels and stalks out of the building without a backward glance. When I remove his card from my pocket, I discover his name is Isaac Holt, entrepreneur and founder of Holt Enterprises. It's only when I notice his business address is for a bum-hick town over two hundred miles away does it dawn on me I'm stranded in the city with no ride back to my truck.

Fuck!

While mumbling incoherently under my breath, I make my way outside while logging into my internet banking. I am praying like hell I'll have enough in my account to pay for a cab ride back to my truck.

My brows furrow when I notice my truck parked at the curb when I step onto the sidewalk outside the club. Upon seeing my shocked expression, a gentleman with a thick silver mustache pushes off the back-quarter panel of my truck and heads my way. Even though his pistol is hidden, I can tell he's carrying a weapon just from the way he walks.

He has the recognizable swagger of a police officer.

"Hugo," he greets me.

I nod, masking my surprise that he knows who I am.

"Mr. Holt requested me to give you this." He smiles while handing me a sealed white envelope. I don't need to open it to know what's inside. My nose can sniff out freshly printed Benjamin Franklins from a mile away. "I look forward to working with you," states the unnamed gentleman before he enters the passenger seat of a black town car idling at my right.

The black Lexus pulls into traffic as slowly as the back passenger side window glides into place, concealing the curious gaze of Mr. Isaac Holt, aka Mr. Trust Fund.

In that instant, I know my life is about to change.

I just have no idea it will be so fucking mammoth.

TWO
HUGO

Six weeks later...

"Are you sure you don't want to purchase a new one?"

My sister, Jorgie's, cornflower blue eyes stray from gazing outside to me. She snarls, bearing her teeth before she shifts her focus back to the storm forming outside.

For most of the day, a scattering of clouds pummeled the dry land of my hometown with much-needed moisture. Although the wind that intensified throughout the day dispersed the clouds to the horizon tonight, the threat of rain is still prevalent. After spending months living in the unbearable conditions of a hot desert, I'm relishing the cool change the rain brought, but Jorgie is more a summer girl. She loves hot, humid days and steamy nights.

Jorgie is a year younger than me and the baby of our family, which earns her the coveted title of 'Baby Girl.' Her real name is Marjorie, but like every family member, she hates her christened name, so we call her Jorgie. Although she's tall for a girl, standing a little over six feet tall, she's a stick of dynamite—feisty and full of life. Her hair is as dark as the clouds she's eyeing, which makes her blue eyes stand out even more on her pale beige skin.

For years, she rebelled against everything and everyone who tried to ruin her plans to escape the clutches of Rochdale and live her life how she envisioned. She didn't want a nine-to-five job or a house with a white picket fence.

She wanted freedom.

She craved adventure.

She wanted to live.

All her big plans came to a halt when I introduced her to Hawke, my college roommate. We were members of the Kappa Sigma Phi fraternity. Even with our age difference, we became blood brothers from the moment we met. Girls, partying, and hitting the club scene were how we spent the first two years of our newfound kinship.

Watching the sparks fly between Jorgie and Hawke was like watching fireworks in a pitch-black sky. It was explosive. But I wasn't having it. For one, Hawke was two years older than Jorgie. He played the field nearly as much as I did, and he also had every intention of leaving Rochdale in the wake of his dust. As much as Jorgie wanted to escape the stranglehold of her dreary existence in Rochdale, it is her home. She was born and raised here. Although our parents were strict and never let us get out of line when we were younger, they're the glue that ensures we remain a close-knit family.

Jorgie rebelled more as she not only had Mom and Dad's stringent rules to adhere to, but she also had Chase's. Chase is five years older than me and the eldest sibling of my family. If you thought my aversion to Jorgie and Hawke dating was harsh, you should have seen some of the elaborate ruses Chase pulled.

Not many men can make Hawke nervous, but one wry look from Chase, and Hawke quivered in his boots like the earth was shaking beneath his feet. But Jorgie is as stubborn as a mule, and when she wants something, she never gives up. She fought tooth and nail for Hawke, and in the end, she won.

Now I can't comprehend what my original objection was about. Jorgie is glowing. She is the happiest I've ever seen her, and lives in a cute little house nearly smack bang in the middle of Rochdale. She has a steady job as a bank teller, and she and Hawke are getting married in three weeks.

He balanced out her rebellion by instilling the discipline she fought so hard against in her teens. Mom always said one day the right man would swoop in and calm the raging storm of Jorgie.

Hawke was that man.

He's her serene.

I slide out from beneath the motor of Jorgie's beloved 1969 Chevrolet Chevelle SS. It's a piece-of-shit rust bucket she purchased over eight years ago, but she loves it as if it's her own child. After nagging me relentlessly for the past three years to assist her in restoring it, I squeezed in a couple of hours this afternoon to replace the carburetor.

My time is more flexible since I returned from my second tour in Afghanistan. Since I'm unemployed and unable to sleep, I have more hours in the day than ever before.

Sleep has never been a close friend of mine, and when I joined the Air Force, it became an even more distant acquaintance.

"By replacing the faulty carby, it should be drivable again, but you have a heap of other issues you need a mechanic to look at before you can even consider getting behind the wheel." I wipe chunks of black grease from my hands with an old rag before hanging it over the radio antenna. "Does Hawke know you're trying to get Baby back on the road?"

Jorgie stops peering at the storm clouds on the horizon to glare at me. Her button nose is screwed up tightly, and her lips are pursed, but she remains as quiet as a mouse.

My lips tug high when I see the guilt marring her face. "You know Hawke doesn't want you driving this around, Jorgie. It isn't safe for you or your bun in the oven." I jab my index finger into her rounded stomach.

"Ouch." She rubs the area I poked, feigning injury. When her blue eyes lift to mine, they're glistening with the mischievousness that forever sparks them. "He never complained about me driving it when we took it to the Mt. Louis lookout during summer break."

I inwardly gag. The last image I want in my head is my little sister making out in the back seat of a car with my best friend. Some images you can never wash from your mind.

When she notices my scrunched-up face, her faint giggles bounce around the dingy garage.

"You do know there's only one way this baby got inside my belly, don't you, Hugo?" she jests, her tone thickly drenched with cheekiness.

"Yeah, I'm fully aware." I roll my eyes while fighting not to gag again. "But that doesn't mean I want to hear the explicit details coming out of your dirty little mouth."

Her giggles increase as she bounces on her heels. Jorgie and I are close, and I don't mean solely by our difference in age. We're two peas in a pod, both rebels cruising through life one adventure at a time.

Although she found her Achilles heel and is expecting her first baby in a few months, her cheeky antics keep Hawke on his toes—even when he's on the other side of the world.

Hawke is currently deployed to Iraq. He's on his second and final tour as part of the First Battalion. With troops being pulled from Iraq by the end of the year, it's the perfect time for him to leave the service.

My suspicions pique when Jorgie scratches her brow. It's a nervous trait she does every time she's either in trouble or is creating it.

When I cock my head to the side and arch my brow, the corners of her mouth twitch as she tries to conceal a smirk.

"What are you up to, Jorgie?" I release the latch on the hood of her car. The loud crack of heavy steel clanking back into place rumbles through the quietness of the late afternoon.

Jorgie's teeth gnaw on her lower lip as she fiddles with the oversized button on her shirt. "You don't have any plans tonight, right?" Even though she's asking a question, she continues talking, not waiting for a response. "Because I'm cooking that chicken dish you love, with a side of ribs, mashed potatoes, green beans—"

"What are you up to, Jorgie?" I ask again, overemphasizing her name in a thick drawl that relays I'm not buying her bullshit offer of cooking me a free meal. She only ever cooks when she's scheming or sucking up after her last failed scheme.

Her already large eyes widen, making them stand out more than normal. "Ava is coming over for dinner."

While struggling to ignore my increasing pulse, I cringe. "That's nice. I'm sure you'll enjoy the company."

I move to the corrosion-riddled driver's side door to crank the engine. I smile when the motor kicks over on the first crank of the ignition. I've never studied to be a mechanic, but I picked up some useful skills during my wild ride from rebellious teen to even more insubordinate man.

I rev the engine, trying to drown out Jorgie's ramblings, but I still catch portions of the pleas she's declared a minimum of once a day since I returned from my tour in Afghanistan.

"She's the perfect match for you, Hugo. She has a well-paying, stable job and owns a three-bedroom apartment in that fancy new building on the river. I went there last month, and the views are to die for. Mom and Dad already know and love her, and even Helen has given her approval. And you know Helen, you have to be valedictorian four years in a row to get the smallest smidgen of attention from her."

I rev the engine more. It's not a requirement to check the capabilities of the motor, but it does successfully drown out Jorgie's incessant blubbering. Everything she's saying I've heard a million times before. Ever since Ava moved back to town, Jorgie has made it her mission to force us together. She gathers since she's marrying my best mate, I should marry her's. In her head, it makes perfect sense. She just failed to get the memo that I'm not interested in dating anyone right now, let alone getting married.

When Jorgie stops jabbering long enough to inhale a much-needed breath, I release the heavy compression of my foot on the accelerator.

She crosses her arms in front of her chest while glaring at me. "Deny it all you want, Hugo, but you can't fight fate. One day, you and Ava *will* be together, and you'll have me to thank for it."

A grin curls my lips. Jorgie's favorite quote since the day she met Hawke has been 'you can't fight fate.' I'll admit they met in unusual circumstances. Most saw it as luck, but Jorgie saw it as fate. "What have you got against Ava, anyway?" She steps closer to me. "You were close when you were younger."

What she is saying is true. Back in our teens, Ava and I were close. It was a weird kinship only a handful of people were aware of, but circumstances change. People change. I've changed. I'm no longer a teenage boy who can't control his cock around a beautiful girl. I'm a grown man whose skin crawls when anyone mentions the dreaded M and C words—marriage and commitment.

When I crank my neck, I catch Jorgie's murderous glare, word-lessly demanding an answer to her question. I give her the same excuse I've given the past two months. "For one, Ava is a dentist. You know I hate dentists."

Jorgie scoffs and rolls her eyes, not buying my pitiful excuse. "You'll never have a cavity," she remarks, her tone smug.

I cock my brow. "Two, she probably still *smells* like a dentist."

Jorgie's bottom lip tucks into one corner as she tries in vain to stifle a smile, but she doesn't refute my claim because she knows as well as I do Ava most likely smells like every child's worst nightmare —the dentist's office.

Ava's last two weeks of high school saw her interning at a fancy dental practice downtown. I swear to God, a week after her visit, I was still smelling that ghastly dentist surgery smell.

Jorgie pledges Ava only smelled like that because her employer made her spend a week sterilizing the equipment at the local training hospital for being insubordinate, but I'm not convinced. Ava always followed the rules to the most stringent detail, so I can't comprehend that she'd suddenly rebel against anyone, much less someone as important as her employer.

"And third, but not at all least, she's too... *innocent*." I choke on my last word.

Don't construe this the wrong way. The last time I saw Ava, she was no doubt attractive. Although she's always been a little nerdy, and her head never left the inside of a book during her academic career, she could garner the attention of any hot-blooded male she feigned an interest in—myself included.

She was the first and only girl I've ever lusted over. One flash of her killer smile, and I wanted to drop to my knees and kiss her fucking feet. My infatuation only ended when she left for college. Unlike Jorgie and me, Ava attended a university on the other side of the country. Although we kept in contact the first two years, all contact stopped when I joined the Air Force. The last time I saw her in person, she was walking into the airport with a flood of tears streaming down her face.

An eerie silence intrudes the garage as rain falls from the sky. Big drops of water sizzling on a sun-heated steel roof make Jorgie's silence even more paramount. The only time she's quiet is when she's telepathically communicating with Hawke or fuming in anger.

After placing a dirty rag onto a rickety wooden shelf at the side of the garage, I pivot on my heels. Jorgie's hands are spread across her expanded hips, and her brows are tightly knit. "Are you seriously condemning Ava because she kept her legs closed during high school?" Even with a pleasant breeze blowing in from outside, the room is roasting from the furious heat pumping out of Jorgie. "Would you prefer she opened her legs for any man who feigned an interest in her?" Her lips purse as she screws up her nose. "Perhaps like Victoria Avenke." Spit flies out of her mouth when she sneers Victoria's name.

I smirk. I should have known she'd heard about my *arrangement* with Victoria. Vicky and I have been on a handful of dates. By dates, I mean casual hookups. No strings attached. No false promises. Just two consenting adults happily sticking to the no-commitment requirement of our agreement.

"Vicky knows what she's getting."

Jorgie huffs. "Yeah, with you and at least another ten guys."

"Cattiness doesn't suit you, Jorgie."

Her eyes snap to mine. "It's not being catty when it's true. Vicky puts out more rides per year than the Ferris wheel at the state fair."

I try to hold in my laughter, but my chuckle rumbles through my gaped mouth when I spot the repulsed mask slipping over Jorgie's face. Jorgie has always attracted men once she passed the awkward puberty stage. When she was younger, her legs were too long, and her body was as straight as a board. It was only once she filled out did Chase's and my big brother's protective mode kick up a gear.

Vicky was the equivalent of Jorgie's schoolyard bully in a nasty prom queen bitch way. Vicky was one of those girls who had the attention of every guy in school, including the male teaching staff.

Even back in the day when Vicky and I first messed around as seniors, Jorgie was disgusted.

It's safe to say, no matter how much time passes, Jorgie and Vicky will never be classed as casual acquaintances, let alone friends. Jorgie still holds a grudge against Vicky from when she called her a giraffe in junior high.

As much as Vicky's taunting words hurt Jorgie, it was true. In her pre-teen years, Jorgie was tall, lanky, and had the hugest pair of wobbly knees. She was the very definition of a giraffe.

"You won't be laughing when you catch something from her," Jorgie mumbles, her snarky tone barely audible from the rain hammering the steel roof.

"Very mature," I remark.

While she sticks out her tongue, I head to the other side of the garage to pack away the tools I used. A grin carves on my mouth at the anal cleanliness of Hawke's garage. He's so meticulous about his man cave, each tool has its rightful spot.

Like Jorgie, Hawke also collects vintage cars, but unlike Jorgie, his are valuable. One of his beauties is a 1969 Chevrolet Camaro Z28 SS Coupe. I've known Hawke for seven years, and I've only driven his Camaro once. That was only because he was too drunk to drive and refused to leave it at the college dorm where we were attending a party.

As fond memories trickle into my head, I drift my eyes to the other side of the garage. Even hidden under a protective car cover, I can recall its shimmering dark blue paint with thick white stripes and fat-rimmed tires.

Just the thought of its 500-horsepower aluminum V-8 engine rumbling through my ears as I cruise down the highway has my pulse quickening and my palms sweating.

Noticing my appreciative glance, Jorgie cozies up next to me. "Stay for dinner, and I'll show you where Hawke hides the keys." Her voice is barely a whisper like she's afraid Hawke will hear her in Iraq.

My eyes rocket to hers. "You're that desperate for me to stay for dinner?"

A vast grin stretches across her face before she nods.

"Deal," I say, thrusting my hand out in offering.

Bile burns the back of my throat when Jorgie spits on her palm then wraps it around my hand before I have the chance to protest about her childish prank. "You've always said 'a deal means nothing unless it's been sealed with a spit shake or a pinkie promise.'"

"I haven't said that since I was ten, and if I knew I had a choice, I would've chosen the pinkie promise," I grunt out while running my spit-coated hand down my jean-covered thigh.

Jorgie's giggles resonate over the heavy downpour of rain as she makes her way into the three-bedroom weatherboard house with me following closely behind. She's grinning smugly, looking victorious. Little does she know I would have agreed to date Ava exclusively for a month if it meant getting behind the wheel of Hawke's baby again. Hell, I may have even agreed to marry her.

Oh, who am I kidding?

That would never happen.

I peer down at my grease-stained jeans before returning my eyes to Jorgie. "Have I got time to shower before Ava arrives?" I'm not trying to impress Ava, but I don't want her looking at me as an unemployed grease monkey. Even if that's what I technically am right now.

Jorgie's eyes flick to the grandfather clock in her small but well-decorated living room before she jerks up her chin. "Oh, yeah, plenty of time. Ava won't be here for at least an hour."

My brows scrunch from the evasiveness in her tone, but I'm so desperate for a shower I act ignorant. "I'll be out in ten."

I've only been in the shower for a matter of minutes, crooning to an old classic, "Footloose" by Kenny Loggins, when a door creaking open resonates into the bathroom.

After twisting off the volume dial on the water-clogged radio shower, I prick my ears. "Jorgie?"

I hear a breathless snicker before, "I have to pop down the street. I'll be back in a few minutes. I forgot the ribs... and the chicken for dinner."

My eyes roll, not surprised by her forgetfulness.

She has a memory like a sieve—full of holes.

"I've thrown your dirty clothes into the wash, so grab some clean ones out of Hawke's closet."

"Alright," I reply as I massage strawberry-scented shampoo into my scalp. "I'm going to smell like strawberry fucking shortcake," I mumble under my breath.

My brow arches when Jorgie's chuckle bellows through the now-closed bathroom door. I didn't think I was loud enough for her to hear my declaration.

Shrugging off my shock, I return my focus to getting clean. Once the smell of sweat and grease is replaced with strawberries, I switch off the faucet and step out of the shower. I am extra attentive not to slip ass-over-tit on the glossy tiles since the bathmat I put down before climbing into the shower has been removed.

My teeth grit when I notice the towel rack I replenished with a fluffy towel is also void of any water-drying apparatus.

"Jorgie!" I yell. "Bring me a goddamn towel."

The last time she pulled this prank, she at least left the bathmat, which covered my junk as I made the ten-second walk from the bathroom to the master suite on the other side of the house.

My naked dash had me strolling straight past Jorgie's co-workers, who were getting ready for a colleague's bachelorette party. When they spotted me sauntering by, saturated and practically naked, they assumed Jorgie hired me for pre-party entertainment.

The humorous gleam in Jorgie's eyes dampened when she learned two valuable lessons that night. One, I'm not ashamed of my body, and two, her co-workers are a bunch of deviant housewives whose husbands lack in the art of seduction.

Within ten minutes, I walked out of the living room two hundred dollars richer and one point higher on Jorgie's and my record-breaking prank tally.

After running my hands over my body to remove the excess droplets of water, I crank open the bathroom door. The house is eerily quiet. The only audible noise heard is the grandfather clock's swinging pendulum.

I strut down the hall, not bothering to cover my junk. My hips are jutted, my cock is swinging, and the biggest, leering grin is stretched across my face.

If Jorgie wants to pull this type of prank, she can suffer the consequences of her actions.

When I detour into the square-shaped kitchen at the end of the hall, I anticipate finding a grinning Jorgie. My steps are eager, excited by the prospect of watching her prank backfire in her face.

My eagerness sails off a cliff when I discover the kitchen is empty.

Perhaps she did need to go to the grocery store?

Deciding to make good use of my detour, I help myself to a bottle of beer in the refrigerator. Thankfully, beer is the one thing that remains unchanged in this house when Hawke is deployed. Strawberry-scented bath products, hand-knitted teapot covers, and hideous floral cushions emerge from the attic within days of his deployment.

When Hawke returns home, he spends a minimum of two weeks returning his house to its pre-Jorgie days. There's no way he'd be caught dead with strawberry shortcake-scented hair.

As I pivot on my heels, the condensation-covered bottle of beer slips from my grasp, plummeting to the floor. I grimace when it clangs against the linoleum flooring, but remarkably, my worry isn't warranted. It stays in one piece.

When it follows the natural flow of the old weatherboard house, the thankfully still-capped bottle rolls away from me. My heart rate kicks up a gear when it stops, thanks to a polished black high heel. It isn't solely the height of the heel, indicating that it doesn't belong to a pregnant Jorgie. It's the fact it is holding up the most stellar pair of luscious legs I've ever seen that's the biggest giveaway.

Legs are my weakness. The longer, the better. This black pump shoe-wearing female has one of the longest, smoothest, and sexiest set of legs I've ever laid my eyes on. That might have something to do with the fact only mere inches of her thighs are covered by a scrap of material some people call a pair of mini shorts. Almost every inch of her legs is on display, and it's the fight of my life to keep my tongue in my mouth while drinking in the enticing visual.

After prying my eyes away from the dick-twitching skin high on the beauty's inner thighs, I peruse the rest of her body. When my eyes drink in a seductive set of hips before they land on the generous swell of a pair of curvy breasts barely contained in a thin skin-colored sweater, I chew on my lower lip. Her outfit is teasing and sexy, a rare combination to find around these parts.

When my eyes finally complete their journey at the captivating stranger's hypnotic face, I choke on my spit. "Ava?" I ask in disbelief, certain I'm dreaming.

For the love of God, someone please tell me this stunner isn't the geeky wannabe dentist, Ava?

One rake of my eyes over her beguiling body and gorgeous face has my dick turning to stone. I could barely suppress the urge to have her beneath me when she had braces on her teeth and a big mess of black ringlet curls sprouting out the top of her head. Now, I don't stand a fucking chance.

"Hey, Hugo," she greets me, confirming my suspicion. Even rattled with nerves, her voice is a husky purr that makes it even harder.

Call an ambulance.

We have a man down.

THREE
AVA

My eyes don't know where to look. I beg for them to move away from the core-clenching visual in front of me, but no matter how loudly my brain begs, they refuse to budge.

Every inch of Hugo's panty-drenching body is on display. And by every inch, I mean every goddamn rock-hard inch. Other than the Air Force squadron tattoo on the lower half of his left arm, the rest of his skin is untouched, wet, and exposed to my overeager eyes.

Ripples of muscles, throbbing veins, and a thin trail of hair flows down the middle of his stomach to join the trimmed patch of dark hair above his...

I gulp as the temperature in the room turns roasting.

My focus shifts from Hugo's impressively large cock to his face when "Ava" sounds from his apprehensive voice.

As his eyes bulge, he tilts his head to the side. He appears utterly surprised to see me.

Did Jorgie not tell him I was coming?

Many times over the past few months, I informed Jorgie my childish crush had matured and moved on, but despite the confidence of my declaration, she continued plotting to get us together. Last week, I succumbed to her hormonal pleas. Although now I wish I didn't. It is clear Hugo had no clue about my impending arrival tonight. If he did, why would he be naked?

When Hugo continues staring at me, wide-eyed and opened-mouth, I stammer out, "H-Hey, Hugo."

The thickness I'm struggling to ignore boosts from my informal greeting. I fight not to squirm at the prospect I'm the cause of Hugo's excitement. I've grown up a lot since the last time my eyes absorbed the hunk of a man in front of me, but his piercing blue eyes and well-carved face still set my pulse racing.

Hugo was my very first crush, but since he was also the epitome of every girl's walking fantasy, it never amounted to anything more than awkward glances, drunken kisses, and the occasional attempts to flirt with the corny one-liners I picked up from the *Cosmo* magazines I read while my mother purchased groceries at our local supermarket.

I often batted my lashes and pursed my lips in that duck-face pose only the Kardashians can make look sexy, but Hugo only ever saw me as a friend—*unless he was drunk.*

But from the thickness standing tall and proud between us and the rugged smirk etched on his handsome face, I'd say he appreciates the handful of changes I've made over the past few years.

It's a pity his craved attention is years too late.

After breathing out to cool my overheated body, I bob down to gather up the beer resting at my feet. The sweat misting my body doubles when the novelty of wearing sky-high stilettos causes me to stumble. I land on my knees directly in front of Hugo's crotch.

One inch closer and I would have lost an eye.

Great position, Ava. Two minutes in his presence and you're already on your knees, begging for a morsel of his attention.

Can anyone say "Loser?"

Once I swallow the meteor my inner monologue lodged firmly into my throat, I slowly raise my horrified eyes to Hugo's face, gasping when I spot his cock twitching in the corner of my eye. His penis is beautiful—thick, long, heavily veined, and cut.

Perfect!

When my eyes finally lock with his face, he smiles down at me. It's only when I return his smile does lucidity finally form. "Shit, sorry," he mumbles as his eyes bounce around the kitchen, looking for something he can use to cover himself.

When his hunt comes up empty, he drops his hands to his crotch, only just concealing the salivating view from my sight. With his hands occupied, I'm left to fight the highness of my stilettos alone. It's an effort to get off the floor without a second tumble, but I get there —eventually.

After blowing a wayward hair out of my eye, I attempt to hand the froth-topped bottle of beer to Hugo. I say 'attempt' because Hugo doesn't try to remove it from my clasp.

My confusion doesn't linger for long. While biting on his bottom lip, Hugo nudges his head to his hands. "Unless you want another visual of my..." he coughs, clearing his throat, "... cock, I can't accept it."

His lips arch higher when I hesitate for the slightest second before I place the beer onto the kitchen counter. My delay is understandable. I've never been quick-witted, but my brain is barely functioning after absorbing the awe-inspiring vision of a naked Hugo.

Just as quickly as the temperature in the room rose, awkward tension suffocates it. We stand across from each other, staring but not speaking for what feels like hours but is barely seconds. It's the quietest we've ever been in each other's presence. During high school, Hugo and I were as opposite as they came in the popularity rankings, but I still classed him as a friend, so this type of awkwardness is extremely unusual for us.

The gaucheness plaguing our gathering gets a moment of reprieve when a car honking wails through the kitchen. It is closely followed by Jorgie's demanding tone. "Hugo, come help me with the bags."

When I glance out the kitchen window, I spot Jorgie waddling to the trunk of her beat-up old Honda. She's huddled under a lopsided umbrella that's miserably failing to keep her dry from the downpour.

After drifting my eyes back to Hugo, I mumble, "I'll go help Jorgie?" My unsure tone makes my statement come out more as a question than a confirmation.

"Alright." His voice is as tempting as his glistening pecs. "While you do that, I'll get dressed."

I shrug. "If you want. You know, whatever suits you," I reply, trying to act unaffected by his nakedness.

His heavy-hooded eyes rake my body before they eventually settle on my face. "Is seeing naked men a regular occurrence for you now, Ava?"

I purse my lips before returning his stare. "I am a doctor."

Sheesh! Here come the stupid one-liners.

I am a dentist. The only thing I'm stripping naked is a tooth cavity, not hot-blooded men.

I have to shelter my face with my hand when a broad grin morphs onto Hugo's face. "Well, in that case..."

He grabs the beer off the counter with one hand before he uses the other to crack it open, leaving himself exposed. My salivary glands work overtime, but even with the urge to drop my eyes—the hardest battle I've ever endured—I manage to maintain his eye contact, somewhat.

When our combat merges onto a battlefield riddled with land-mines, my chin quivers. The beer fizzes over the neck of the bottle, and the droplets dribbling off Hugo's hand drip onto his smooth pectoral muscle. My eyes follow every slither the droplets make when they roll down the impressive ridges of his torso, bumped abs, and formidable V muscle before they're absorbed by a patch of dark hairs above his...

"Oh my god, Hugo! Put on some clothes," Jorgie squeals, stealing me from my inappropriate thoughts. I jump from her thunderous roar echoing around the kitchen before I divert my eyes to the window.

"You're disgusting! We eat in here! Your nephew is going to eat in here!"

My shoulders shake when Jorgie gags. I'm not the only one humored by her horror. Hugo's boisterous laugh activates every one of my hot buttons. This type of jeering is nothing new for these two. They have one of the longest-running prank tallies in the history of sibling rivalry.

Their mom, Edie, said it started before Jorgie even escaped the womb. When Edie was heavily pregnant with Jorgie, any time Hugo climbed onto her lap, begging for attention, Jorgie kicked up a storm. Mrs. Marshall said the aim of Jorgie's monstrous size foot was always firmly rapt on Hugo.

My eyes return front and center when bare feet stomping across the wooden floorboards in the living room resonates through my ears. I'm awarded the quickest visual of a retreating Hugo before he slips into the bedroom at the front of Jorgie's house. A grin tugs on my mouth when I spot Jorgie's narrowed glare. Unlike me, she isn't implanting the visual of Hugo's naked derriere into her memory for future use. She's shooting daggers at his head.

Hugo has always had a spectacular backside, but just like every other muscle in his body, it's improved with age.

Jorgie swings her eyes to me. With scrunched brows, and her skin whiter than usual, she hooks her thumb over her shoulder and asks, "*That* gets you all hot and bothered?"

"*Used* to," I correct. My reply is confident even with my stomach housing so many butterflies, I feel like I'm about to float away.

Jorgie rolls her eyes before delving her hand into the drenched paper bag brimming with groceries. She's never understood my crush on Hugo, and in all honesty, it would be a little weird if she did. Sisters don't see their big brothers in the same light as their friends.

I bump her with my hip before helping her unpack the groceries. My brows furrow when I notice the bag is full of non-perishable supplies most people regularly have stacked in their pantries.

My suspicion piques when I notice the glass canister of cracked pepper is half empty. "Jorgie..." My tone is low and crammed with suspicion.

"What?"

When she moves to the fridge to pull out pre-prepared marinated chicken and ribs, I walk closer to her. "You didn't really go to the grocery store, did you?"

She shrugs but remains quiet. Her silence won't last long. She's sneaky in her endeavors to force Hugo and me together, but she can't lie straight in bed. Even when she tells a little fib to get herself out of trouble, her deceitfulness only lasts a matter of minutes before the truth blurts out of her mouth.

"Okay, fine!" she huffs half a second later. "I didn't go to the store." Overdramatically, she throws her arms into the air. "There, are you happy?"

See? Proof she can't lie.

She puts the chicken in the oven before pivoting around to face me. My first clue that she didn't forget the most vital ingredients for dinner should have been the oven sitting on a preheat setting, but even with the room being heated by the 390-degree setting, it wasn't the oven creating the sweat-forming hotness in the room.

That honor solely belonged to Hugo.

"Didn't your last shower prank teach you that Hugo doesn't fluster about his nakedness being on display?"

My pulse quickens when I refer to his naked body, but I shut it down when Jorgie's face pales. "But you missed out on the fun that night."

"So you thought you'd try again?"

She smiles and nods.

"Jorgie... I told you."

"I know, I know," she interjects, her tone lowering with disappointment. "You no longer have a crush on Hugo."

My heart ceases beating when a smug tone booms into my kitchen. "You had a crush on me?"

I glare at Jorgie before I dart my eyes to Hugo. Although his body is covered with more clothing than it was only minutes ago, I still imagine him naked while trying to claw myself out of the hole Jorgie just pushed me in. "Yeah, *had*, but that was years ago," I respond, acting like it was no big deal that my every thought during my teenage years was about it. "That was way before I knew who you did... umm, what you did... umm, who you really are."

For crying out loud, Ava, shut your mouth!

After propping my hip on the counter, I snag the bottle of beer resting on top. While bouncing my eyes between Jorgie and Hugo, I take a mouth-filling gulp of the lukewarm brew. I don't care how foul it tastes. I'll drink hot sauce if it'll stop the word vomit currently spewing from my mouth.

When Jorgie excuses herself to use the restroom, Hugo helps himself to a beer from the fridge. Once he cracks open the fresh bottle, he hands it to me.

"Thanks," I mumble while placing the half-empty bottle back onto the counter.

When he collects the bottle, I assume he's going to toss it into the trash, so you can picture my surprise when he downs the degassed liquid inside. He isn't the slightest bit concerned that my mouth was pressed against the rim his lips are now sealed over only seconds ago.

I wonder if he can guess the flavor of my lip gloss?

For the next several minutes, nothing but the sound of beer being swallowed echoes between us. I'm too busy fighting to keep the repulsed expression off my face to strike up a conversation, but what's Hugo's excuse?

Beer will never be my drink of choice, but I can admit the coolness of the beverage helps to weaken the intense spasms twinging in my womb.

I smile against the rim of my beer bottle when Hugo props his hip on the kitchen counter, replicating my position. He doesn't speak, but I can feel his gaze on me.

I keep my eyes on anything but him. I don't want to risk the visual of the man fully clothed replacing the more stimulating images of him naked in my mind.

Oh my god! Did I just say that? I meant to say *I don't need to see more of him than I already have.*

Yeah, don't worry, I'm not buying my pathetic excuse either.

As the minutes tick by, the silence becomes unbearable. We were never like this when we were young. We were opposites on paper, but when we were alone, away from prying eyes, we were friends.

Over the silence, I push off the counter to go search for Jorgie. Interrupting a pregnant lady in the bathroom would have to be less daunting than the awkwardness plaguing her eat-in kitchen.

Just as I'm about to exit the room, Hugo questions, "Are you a fully qualified dentist now?"

"Yes," I reply with a little too much flair. Talking about dentistry comes easy for me since it's one of my greatest passions. "Well, kind of... I'm halfway through two years of clinical training. I work at a clinic downtown and assist in the free clinic every Thursday morning at Rochdale Village." I spin back around to face him. "I've already been offered a partnership at the dental office once my practical training is over." Once my hip is back balancing on the counter, I say, "In the main practice, I only work with children, but at the clinic, I also work with adult patients. It's a demanding job, not like a surgeon at a major hospital or anything dramatic like that, but it's still an important industry. I really enjoy it." I stop talking when Hugo's nose scrunches up. "What?"

"Nothing."

"Oh, come on, Hugo, spit it out," I bark, dying to know what has caused the odd expression on his face.

He chuckles before he takes another sip of his beer. When his tongue delves out to gather a droplet of malted liquid glistening on his top lip, my eyes zoom in on his mouth. My needy watch ensures I don't miss a single snicker leaving his mouth when he says, "I just find it amusing that you enjoy torturing little children for a living."

My eyes snap from his mouth to his gleaming blue eyes. "I don't torture kids."

His brow cocks before he bobs his head up and down. "Yeah, you do. You're the equivalent of every child's worst nightmare."

"I am not." I stomp down my foot as if I am five instead of the twenty-four-year-old woman I am. "My patients love me. I even get cute little paintings in the mail and thank you cards."

My pulse quickens when a broad grin stretches across Hugo's face. "They probably say, 'thanks for not drilling my teeth today, Doc.'"

My immature tantrum stops, and a grin tugs at my lips. "That's only every second card," I retort before folding my arms under my chest.

The heat pluming from the oven is even more noticeable when Hugo's hearty chuckle bellows through the kitchen. It was that very laugh that captured my attention well over ten years ago. It's also the laugh that made me realize my feelings for him were more than just a schoolyard crush.

Years ago, Jorgie and I were undertaking a bitch-fest on the queen of bitches herself, Victoria Avenke, oblivious to the fact Hugo was eavesdropping on our private conversation. When he impersonated my mimic of Victoria's pompous hair flick, I sneered at him through my brace-covered teeth before I dove over the sofa to tackle him to the floor.

When I straddled his hips to commence a tickling onslaught on his stomach, an intense tingle dashed through my body before it clustered low in my stomach.

Mortified with embarrassment about the husky moan that spilled from my lips and unable to comprehend why my body was reacting that way, I scrambled off Hugo and bolted out of his house without a backward glance.

I don't know if Hugo sensed my body's reaction to him or if I was paranoid, but things were different between us from that day.

Then, as the years went on, Hugo's presence in my life became less and less. But even with him dating a range of beautiful ladies, attending college parties, and being the cool guy on campus, I still saw him at least five to six times a year. The past six years have been the longest we've gone without physically seeing each other in nearly fifteen years.

When Hugo's laughter dies down, his tear-glistening eyes lock with mine. "What about in your personal life, Ava? Any changes there the past few years?"

It may be my overactive imagination or the fact I feel like I've time-warped back to my teenage years, but I swear there's a heap of sexual innuendo laced in his simple question.

After uncrossing my arms, I pick at the plum polish on my thumbnail. "Yeah, a few changes," I mumble with a shrug.

I hate talking about my private life. My parents are extremely strict and Catholic, and I'm an only child. By the time Jorgie entered my life, I had become so accustomed to keeping my feelings locked away, I've never openly expressed them.

When silence reigns supreme again, I chance a sneaky glance at Hugo. He's watching me with a spark in his eyes I've never witnessed before. It's interesting yet still reserved.

When he catches my curious glance, the unidentifiable glimmer is replaced with the cheeky blaze that regularly fires his vibrant blue eyes.

He smirks against the rim of his beer before taking another mouth-filling gulp, leaving the baton on my half of the court.

I take up his challenge almost immediately. "What about you? How are things with Vicky?"

FOUR

HUGO

It takes all my strength not to spray the beer in my mouth over Ava's beautiful face. She's always been attractive—in a librarian, geeky type of way—but like a bottle of fine wine, she keeps getting better with age.

The last time I saw her, a crazy mess of ringlet curls covered her face, and a hideous pair of baggy jeans and a bulky sweater covered almost every inch of her skin. But today, she's captivatingly beautiful. Not just in her clothes but her skin as well.

Her hair sits just below her shoulders in a wispy design that frames her face with perfection. She's grown into her dark eyes that always seemed too large for her small face, and years of wearing braces finally paid off. Her smile is perfect.

Her allure is so magnetic I completely forgot I was stark naked. If that wasn't bad enough, I also had a raging hard-on like a thirteen-year-old boy who can't control his cock. One rake of her body and I was straight back to that sixteen-year-old boy she tackled to the ground many moons ago.

That was the day I realized Ava was more inexperienced than most girls her age. I'm not saying the girls at my high school were easy, but they had no hesitation hooking up under the bleachers after a football game or at the Mt. Louis lookout, whereas Ava acted as if she'd never kissed a guy before.

When I rubbed my thickened shaft against the warmth her panties failed to conceal, her face paled, and her eyes widened before she bolted out of the house without a backward glance.

It was not the reaction I was aiming for.

It was that night I decided inexperienced girls weren't for me. Virginity snatching is too much of a commitment for any guy to make. It wouldn't matter if you were the worst lay they've ever had, girls remember the guy they gave their virginity to.

That isn't a stigma I want attached to my name.

He was a great lay.

The best sex I've ever had.

He had the largest cock I've ever seen.

They're titles I'll happily accept.

Virgin snatcher? Nope, not happening.

My focus returns to the present when a hand waves in front of my face. Turning my gaze, I catch the amused eyes of Jorgie glaring at me. After absorbing my doe-eyed expression, she huffs before marching to the cupboards under the wall oven. Even with the clanging of the pots and pans rattling through my ears, I hear her murmur, "Probably daydreaming about Vicky's fake double-Ds."

From the grimace that crosses Ava's face, I can assume she also heard Jorgie's quiet ramblings.

"Vicky and I aren't dating," I blurt out, suddenly craving for Ava to know that Vicky and I are not a couple.

"Oh." Ava takes a swig of her beer, hiding her smile behind the bottleneck.

"They aren't a couple," Jorgie confirms, reinforcing my statement.

Ava's smile enlarges.

It doesn't stay large for long, though.

"They just fuck each other." My eyes snap to Jorgie as Ava

chokes on her beer. "What?" She feigns an innocence she'll never be able to pull off. "It's true, isn't it?"

Once Ava regains the ability to breathe through the beer now in her lungs instead of her stomach, she sets the bottle on the counter then moves to stand between Jorgie and me. She wets a dishcloth in the sink then uses it to remove the beer from her top. My hand scraping across the three-day-old stubble on my jaw is the only noise heard when my eyes zoom in on the budded peaks of her nipples. They're straining against her thin shirt, begging to be touched.

My nostrils flare when an oven mitt smacks me upside my head. My teeth grinding together sounds over the doorbell ringing when Jorgie mouths, *"That's what real boobs look like."*

She's acting as if I've never seen a real pair before. Yes, Vicky has a large set of fake breasts, but I've seen plenty of real ones, including Vicky's before she had the augmentation done.

My brow cocks when Ava declares, "I'll get the door." Her appearance has gone from calm to freaked in under a second. She looks like the Grim Reaper is knocking at her door.

After the quickest smirk, she bolts out of the kitchen.

I wait until the clicking of her heels on the tiles in the entryway boom into my ears before I divert my focus to Jorgie. "What the hell did you do to Ava?"

Jorgie cockily winks. "That wasn't me." She arches a dark brow. "That was *all* Ava's doing." I grit my teeth when she smacks me up the head for the second time. "And don't act surprised, Hugo. You've always known what she was hiding under those hideous baggy clothes she wore."

Yeah, I knew, but I preferred being the only guy who did.

When I step closer to Jorgie, my stomach gurgles when the spicy aroma of marinated chicken filters through my nostrils.

Well, that's the excuse I'm going with when I blurt out, "Is Ava still... *innocent?*"

Fuck, that didn't come out how I envisioned.

I know this makes me a chauvinistic ass, but no red-blooded man could run their eyes over Ava's enticing body and not be interested in finding out *exactly* what she looks like under those teeny tiny shorts.

Jorgie's mouth gapes open, and for the first time in her twenty-four years on this planet, she's rendered speechless. The temperature in the room shifts to excruciating when she crosses her arms before squeezing them between the minimal space left between her stomach and her chest. "That's an *extremely* personal question, Hugo."

"I know. That's why I asked you instead of Ava." Jorgie's eyes narrow into tiny slits, unimpressed about my attempt to defuse the insensitivity of my question with humor. "Would you prefer I asked Ava?"

Thankfully, even with all the blood in my body rushing to my cock, I was smart enough not to do that.

"Ask me what?" Ava queries while walking back into the kitchen.

Jorgie's roughish eyes float from me to Ava. "Hugo wants to know if you're a v—"

My hand shoots up to clamp Jorgie's mouth before she can ask her bold question. As a fiery ember ignites her eyes, she waggles her brows, confident she's secured a vault of ammunition in our long-running prank game.

The victorious gleam in her eyes dampens when I mutter, "Do you recall where my hands were earlier?"

As her throat works hard to swallow, her appearance turns gaunt like it was the first three months of her pregnancy. After giving her a second to absorb the enormity of my prank, I wink before lowering my hands from her mouth.

Air whistles between my teeth when she ribs me with her elbow before she knees me in the backside. She sneers at me before she downs sparkling apple cider at a breakneck speed.

"It's alcohol-free, Jorgie. It ain't going to burn away my cooties," I jest, my tone full of cheekiness.

"I can pretend," she garbles between mouthfuls.

My neck cranks back faster than a missile being fired from a jet when a male chuckle fills my ears. My stomach muscles tense when I notice Ava is being held in place by an African American man. As my eyes roam over a face I've seen many times before, my brows scrunch. Even though seven years have passed since I last laid eyes on him, he still has the same clipped close-to-the-scalp afro, prominent nose, dark green eyes, mocha skin, and arrogant grin he's always had.

"Marvin," I greet, only just holding my tongue from calling him his infamous nickname.

Marvin was nicknamed 'Pencil Dick' during our final year of high school. It was because... *Hold on, does a title like that need an explanation? It's pretty self-explanatory.*

Alright, for those of you who are a little slow on the uptake, it means his dick is long and skinny like a pencil.

"Hugo," Marvin greets me before he removes one of his hands from Ava's waist to offer me a handshake.

I suffocate a growl rumbling up my chest before accepting his offer. It isn't that I've staked a claim on Ava, but Marvin is a dawg, and he knows it. Even with his less-than-impressive male appendage, he's one of the biggest bed hoppers in our hometown. It was the reason his nickname spread like an out-of-control wildfire during the summer break before our final year of high school.

It's also the reason he's had so many bed companions.

They never want to return for round two.

Ava was naïve in her younger years, but even if she's been living under a rock for the past six years, she'd have to be aware of Marvin's reputation now.

"Hey, Marvin." Jorgie presses a kiss on his cheek. "Ava said she was bringing a friend to dinner. She just failed to mention it was a man." Jorgie's surprise about Ava's *date* is audible in her voice.

With Ava's caramel skin coloring, it takes a lot to make her blush, but the slightest hue of pink adorns her cheeks from the stern glare Jorgie hits her with. Ava's eyes flick to mine when Marvin hands Jorgie a bottle of Duckhorn Napa Valley Cabernet Sauvignon to gauge my reaction about her arriving with a date.

The concern marring her face fades when I wink at her. In the past, I had some *slight* jealousy issues when it came to men wanting to get close to Ava, but this is different. I have *nothing* to be worried about. The guy has a pencil dick, for crying out loud.

For the next three hours, things go surprisingly well. Marvin and I have a lot of mutual friends, so the conversation flowed as freely as the alcohol in his glass. I gave Marvin updates on the guys he lost contact with, and he rambled incessantly about himself. The only good that came from his long-winded tirade was the discovery as to why a woman like Ava would date a man like him.

His dad owns the dental practice where Ava was offered a position. Marvin is a partner at the same practice, even with him only finalizing his dentist credentials two months ago.

A chuckle vibrates my lips when Jorgie wakes from her latest power nap. As riveting as Marvin believes his conversations are, I swear on at least three occasions, Jorgie has fallen asleep on the sofa. She only wakes when Ava nudges her with her elbow.

While wiping away the drool on her chin, Jorgie's wide eyes bounce between three sets staring at her. She appears utterly confused.

"You might need to cut back on the apple ciders, sis," I playfully quip.

In true Jorgie style, she screws up her nose and sticks out her tongue.

"We should probably get going anyway." Marvin eagerly nods at Ava's suggestion.

"Oh no, don't go," Jorgie pleads when Ava gathers the beer bottles from the table to place them into the trash. "It's only just hitting nine o'clock on a Saturday night."

Ava drifts her eyes between Marvin and Jorgie while she contemplates. Her brows are pulled together tightly, and her lips are pursed, exposing she still takes her time with every deliberation she undertakes.

Marvin glares at Ava, wordlessly reprimanding her for wanting to spend more time with her friends. "I have that paperwork I need to do. Remember?"

"Oh, yeah," she whispers so faintly it's only just audible.

Jorgie's shoulders sag when Ava shifts on her feet to face her. She doesn't need to speak. Jorgie can see her decision marred all over her disappointed face.

"Party pooper," Jorgie mumbles when Marvin squashes his cell phone to his ear to call an Uber.

Her gloomy mood continues when we wait on the front porch for their Uber to arrive. Thankfully, since it's still early, it only takes five minutes for one to pull into the driveway.

Ava propels herself from the wicker chair when she spots the Uber, no doubt eager to get away from the thick stench of awkwardness plaguing our group. Jorgie could never conceal her anger, and for the past five minutes, her annoyance has been firmly rapt on Marvin.

I smile when Ava slings her dark brown eyes at me. "It was good seeing you again, Hugo," she whispers as the twinkle in her eyes relays the truth of her statement.

I band my arms around her shoulders before pulling her into my chest. My nostrils flare when they detect the aroma of the chocolate truffles she ate for dessert. She smells delicious. Almost good enough to eat. Chocolate and strawberries have always been a mouth-watering combination.

Where the fuck did that notion come from?

"Let's not have another six years pass without some sort of contact," she murmurs in my ear before placing a kiss on my cheek.

A smirk curves on my lips when I spot the furious glare Marvin is directing at me. His blatant jealousy ensures my cuddle with Ava lasts longer than what any man would class as acceptable.

My smirk switches to a full-toothed smile when Marvin's face reddens over my playful jibe.

He should be worried. My nickname in high school was…

"Why are there two Ubers?" Jorgie asks, interrupting me from my private thoughts. As her brow is lost in her hairline, her eyes dance between Marvin and Ava.

"Ava lives by Hamilton, and I live in an apartment building on Pinter," Marvin explains.

"Yeah, so?" Jorgie's tone is full of bitchiness. "That's still within a few miles of each other."

"Marvin doesn't see the sense in sharing a fare if you're not going to the same location," Ava explains while slipping out of my embrace. Her tone is pleasant, but her eyes expose her real opinion of Marvin's logic.

She thinks he's as stingy as the rest of us.

"Then why do you have to leave?" Jorgie shifts on her swollen feet to face Ava. "Marvin is the one who has to work. You're not going home together, so why can't you stay and hang with us?"

She hooks her arm around my elbow then tugs me to her side, enticing Ava to join the fun crowd.

It's like we're in high school all over again.

Jorgie's grip on my arm tightens the longer Ava contemplates her suggestion, then a squeal of excitement omits from her lips when Ava asks Marvin, "You wouldn't mind if I hang out with Jorgie a little longer, would you?"

My jaw ticks over the fact she needs to seek permission to stay at her friend's house, and the spasm ramps up when Marvin folds his arms in front of his chest before he glares at her. "I've already requested the Uber. If you refuse their service, they may not come back to collect you later this evening."

"Oh," Ava mumbles, her lips quivering like she's in big trouble.

"I'll drive you home, Ava," I offer, not allowing Marvin to guilt-trip her into going home early when she clearly wants to stay.

Marvin's eyes slit even more, and from the stern glare he directs at me, anyone would swear I was bending down on my knee and proposing to Ava instead of offering her a ride home. "I don't think that would be wise."

"Why not?" Jorgie interrupts.

It's times like this I love that she has no filter.

"Because Hugo has been drinking." Marvin's stern tone makes him sound older than his twenty-five years.

I shake my head. "I've only had two beers. One when Ava first arrived."

When Ava's eyes widen, a grin stretches across my face. Despite her best effort to act unaffected, my naked backside is still in the forefront of her mind even hours after the incident.

"And my second beer was during dinner, so I'm perfectly capable of driving Ava home if she wants me to."

Ava was bullied her entire childhood. It wasn't by who you're thinking. Yes, kids in the schoolyard can be cruel, but Ava wasn't subjected to bullying from them. It was by the man whose idea of a perfect child was one who was seen but never heard.

Ava didn't rebel during her teenage years because she feared the reprimand she'd face if she dared to step out of line. Her father isn't just strict, he's a verbally abusive tyrant of a man who doesn't deserve the right to claim Ava as his daughter.

By the time my parents found out about Ava's family predicament, she was already in her first week of college, so it was too late for them to get her out of his clutches.

Ava's father is the sole reason she shouldn't be with a man who'll give her ultimatums and rules to live by. If she wanted that type of life, she would have stayed living under her father's roof.

"What do you want to do, Ava?" Although I'm close to ripping Marvin's head off from the furious scowl he's directing at Ava, I keep my tone low, ensuring Ava knows the choice is solely hers to make.

Jorgie's breathing ceases to exist when Ava's eyes drift between the three of us. I can hear her silent prayers for Ava to throw caution to the win, Marvin's silent reprimand is the loudest of them all.

"You have work—"

"On Monday," Jorgie interrupts while staring at Marvin with the same intensity he's using to glare at Ava.

My teeth gnawing on the inside of my cheek fail to hide the growl rumbling in my chest when Ava tilts into Jorgie's side and whispers, "I'll call you tomorrow."

The gleam in Jorgie's eyes douses as she nods. I can't hear what Ava whispers in her ear when she bids her farewell, but a vast grin stretches across Jorgie's face two seconds later. She boisterously laughs when she pulls away from Ava so she can run her index finger under her nose.

Weirdos.

After a quick smirk directed my way, Ava dashes to the awaiting Uber. I clench my fists at my sides when a victorious grin stretches across Marvin's face. He waits until Ava's Uber is nothing but a blur in the distance before he enters his Uber, ensuring Ava leaves as instructed. When his Uber reverses out of the driveway, I internally battle not to raise my middle finger into the air in response to the pompous smirk etched on his ugly face.

The instant Marvin's Uber exits Jorgie's street, I turn to face her. "Why is Ava dating Pencil Dick?"

Jorgie doesn't balk at my statement, indicating she's aware of Marvin's nickname and why he has it. "Your guess would be as good as mine," she huffs before throwing her arms into the air. "You know Ava, Hugo. She craves security. Dick Weed can give her that."

I stifle a chuckle. "Dick Weed?"

She smiles and nods. "Our grade called Marvin 'Dick Weed' because his dick is like a weed in a garden. All wilted and shriveled up."

No longer able to hold in my laughter, my loud, hearty chuckle booms through the quiet night air. My laughter is so thunderous, it startles Ms. Mable, who lives next door. She flicks on her security light, blinding Jorgie and me since it faces Jorgie's patio.

"It's just Hugo," Jorgie shouts to ensure Ms. Mable can hear her since she's half-deaf.

I grin when Ms. Mable shrieks back, "Okay, dear."

Once the bright light is switched off, I snap my eyes back to Jorgie. A dancing array of lights obscure my vision for the next several seconds, but they don't hinder my sight long enough to miss the yawn Jorgie fails to suppress. "Aren't you sleeping?"

She grimaces. "You know I can't sleep when Hawke is over there."

I nod. Hawke joined the military two months before he and Jorgie officially became a couple. He's often stated if he knew Jorgie was about to enter his life, he would have never enlisted. It's taken a bit of adjustment for Jorgie to get used to the life of a military wife, but she's handling it better than any of us expected.

"Only two more months and you'll be begging for me to get him out of your hair," I jest.

My heart warms when she giggles. "I can't wait for that day."

I noogie her head because I know how much she hates it. "I'll drop by tomorrow afternoon after my meeting and put a few more hours into Baby."

Her eyes sparkle as a broad grin stretches across her face. She looks like a kid waking up on Christmas morning.

"But until Hawke gives Baby the all-clear, you can't drive her."

Her bottom lip drops into a pout. "Party pooper."

After a final noogie on her head, I make my way to my truck. Once Jorgie is inside and the front door is dead-bolted, I pull my truck away from the curb. I smile when I spot the silhouette of Ms. Mable behind the sheer curtain in her living room. I jerk up my chin in silent thanks for the vigilant eye she keeps on Jorgie.

Rochdale is a large, hard-working lower to middle-class community, but it is and will always be my hometown.

FIVE
AVA

When a tap sounds through my ears, I switch off the water in the shower and slant my head to the side. My ears prick, straining to work out where the banging noise is coming from. This is the only downfall to apartment living. More times than I can count, I swear I hear people knocking on my front door. Only after I begrudgingly scamper to my entryway do I realize the knocks were for my neighbor. Or a handful of times, they've been for the apartment at the end of the hall.

My debate between continuing to shave my legs or going in search to discover the reason for the frequent bangs ramps up when the rumble of a male voice closely follows three brisk taps. My breathing labors when my strained ears recognize the rugged drawl of the masculine voice.

Now there's no doubt the bangs bellowing through my apartment are from someone knocking, or should I say, banging down my door.

After twisting a towel around my drenched locks, I secure another one around my body before racing for the door. My heart thrashes against my ribs, panicked as to what has caused an impromptu visitor to arrive at my apartment at eleven o'clock on a Saturday night.

After ensuring my towel covers my private parts, I swing open my front door. My breath hitches when the delightful view of Hugo in a pair of low-hanging jeans and a short-sleeve shirt swamps my vision.

"Is everything okay?" My words come out shaky, complements to my quickening pulse. His eyes are housing the same unacknowledged spark they had earlier tonight when he offered me a ride home.

Hugo props his shoulder on the doorjamb before he bites on the corner of his lip. "It is now." Breathing is an unnecessary pastime when his eyes scorch my skin as he drags them down my body. "Go out with me, Ava," he blurts out after returning his eyes to mine.

"W-w-what?" I stammer out, certain the words I've wanted to hear him say for years didn't just occur on my doorstep while I'm wearing a skimpy towel, not one ounce of makeup, and with only one leg shaven.

He smirks a panty-wetting grin. "Come out with me. Tonight," he clarifies.

Ouch. A slap to the face would have hurt less than that.

Suddenly, an unwelcoming notion smacks into me. "Are you drunk?"

That would be a plausible reason as to why he's arrived at my door this late at night.

The flutter of my heart increases when Hugo's lips curl higher. "Maybe a little."

A grin stretches across my face. Tonight isn't the first time I've handled an inebriated Hugo. The very first time was at his eighteenth birthday party...

"Sugar," I mumble when my eyes leap around the desolate walls of a coatroom, seeking anything but the visual of a female with cascading blonde hair on her knees in front of a pair of trouser-clad thighs.

Even with the light from the entryway beaming into the compact space, the female's slurping sucks don't falter. She continues with her mission to unravel the man whose pants of ecstasy have my cheeks warming and pulse hastening.

I spin on my heels, preparing to give the couple a moment of privacy in a house overrun by out-of-control, frantic teens, but halfway out, I freeze when "Yeah, Vicky, baby, just like that," sounds from a voice I've heard many times before.

My brain signals for my legs to move, but instead of racing away from the train wreck that will inevitably shred my heart into a million pieces, my head cranks, and my eyes roam over a well-splayed pair of thighs, a half-tucked-in disheveled shirt, and the lust-riddled face of Hugo.

His head is flopped back, his eyes are snapped shut, and his mouth is gaped open.

He is the exact visual I'd conjured of him many times over the past three years.

The twisting of my stomach amplifies when he fists Vicky's hair to increase her pace. When he forces a muffled gag to sound from her throat, I gag too. Mine isn't sexually enticed.

Hugo's eyes snap open when my groan overtakes Vicky's sloppy sucks. His pupils widen when he drinks in the repulsed expression on my face. It has nothing on the shock that rains down on me.

"Sorry," I mumble, scrambling.

Mortified that he busted me ogling him during sexual activity, I dump my coat onto the floor, slam the door shut then dash for the crowd gathered in the sunken living room. Since I had to wait for my parents to go to bed, I've arrived at Hugo's party fashionably late. Blaring music, hot, sweaty bodies, and half of the school population has congregated in the Marshall residence this Friday night.

When Chase, Hugo's older brother, discovered Jorgie and Hugo were going to be left unattended, he decided to throw an early eighteenth birthday party for Hugo. I don't normally attend these types of events, but since it's a significant milestone in Hugo's life, I bent the normally unbreakable rein my father has gripped tightly around my neck. By scaling down the thorn-riddled latticework on the side of my house, I've arrived at Hugo's birthday party a little after eleven o'clock.

Barging my way through a mass of bodies grooving to the latest club beat, I continue with my pursuit of the even more crowded backyard. Even with it being overpopulated with drunken teens, I need fresh air, and I need it pronto.

The brisk night air relieves my overheated skin when I yank open the glass sliding door that leads to the wooden deck, but my heart stops beating when "Ava" is shouted across the room from a deep rumbling voice that invades my dreams every single night.

In the glass's reflection, I spot Hugo standing in the entryway, adjusting his shirt to a more dignified configuration. Once his clothing is back in place, his eyes dart in all directions, seeking me amongst the crowd.

I cowardly hide, but due to Hugo's vast height, he spots me within a matter of seconds. When he commences wading through the sea of partygoers, I dart out the door. My wish to evade him is aided by the numerous party attendees who stop dancing to greet him when they spot Hugo skirting by.

After rushing down a short flight of stairs, I take a sharp left. Just as I reach the edge of the paved fire pit, my elbow is seized. I don't need to look up to know who's grasping me. My body's reaction is all I need to know that Hugo's long strides have caught up with me.

While sucking in a big breath, I neutralize the expression on my face before pivoting on my heels. I smile sweetly, vainly trying to pretend I didn't witness what I just did.

The longer Hugo's glassy eyes roam my face, the more his brows furrow. "Damn, Ava, I'm sorry you had to see that." The repentance in his eyes adds strength to his apology. "Did you not see the scarf wrapped around the door handle?" Due to his closeness, his whiskey-laced breath flutters against my lips.

"The what?"

The tautness on his face firms. "The scarf around the handle."

I return his stare before timidly shaking my head. Blood rushes through my veins, flaming my skin with heat when his eyes bore into mine, calling bullshit on my false statement. I did see the scarf, but I had no clue why it was there. I assumed it was lost property, but from the glimmer in Hugo's eyes and the scowl on his face, I guess my assumption was wrong.

"Happy birthday." I thrust the gift I'm clutching into his chest, praying it will offer a moment of reprieve from the awkwardness suffocating the air surrounding us.

"Ava." His tone lowers as his gaze drops to the black gift box in my hand. "I thought we said no gifts this year."

I push my thick-rimmed glasses up my nose and hunch my shoulders. "It's nothing major."

A boyish grin stretches across his face as he accepts his gift. I inwardly sigh, relieved that the awkwardness has been snuffed.

I fold my arms in front of my chest, hiding my body's reaction to the sexy-as-hell grin etched on Hugo's face when he pries at a piece of Scotch tape on the side seam. For as long as I've known him, he's always taken his time unwrapping presents. He likes to savor the moment, to bask in the glory of being the center of attention.

It's the perfect antidote for the poor, neglected middle child.

Just as the side flap is carefully opened, the swarm of people milling around the pool realize the birthday man has emerged amongst them. Within a matter of seconds, Hugo is inundated by well-wishers wanting to bestow their birthday felicitations.

As the rowdy crowd swarms him, I get elbowed and bumped until I'm once again on the outer circle of the popularity contest that forever launches when Hugo is in the vicinity.

The stabbing pain in my chest lessens when Hugo's gorgeous face pokes out from the heavy crowd. When he spots me standing to the side, he grins a heart-flattering smile. "Thank you," he says, staring straight at me.

"You're welcome," I mouth back, smiling.

When his grinning face becomes nothing but a blur in a crowd of many, I spin on my heels and stalk away. Quietly, I sit in a vacant chair next to Jorgie, not wanting to interrupt her game of tonsil hockey with her on-and-off-again boyfriend, Blake.

While snubbing the sucking-face noises neighboring me, I spend the next several minutes immersed in the world of people-watching. Even though everyone in eyesight knows Hugo in some way, the gathering of people is diverse. School jocks and Barbie doll cheerleaders are gathered near the pool. The dark, moody, artsy crowd is milling around the fire pit, and even though they remain hidden in the shadows, I spot a handful of members from the computer club gathered at the side of the house when I dashed into the backyard.

And then there are the people like me. The awkward anti-social crowd who scatters themselves throughout the groups, hoping one day to work out exactly which faction we belong to.

My people-gawking is interrupted when a plastic cup full to the brim with soda is shoved under my nose. Lifting my eyes, I absorb an older, although not any more mature version of Hugo.

Hugo and Chase are two men cut from the same cloth—their father's. Same dark, thick, shaggy hair hanging loosely on the top of their heads, piercing blue eyes, and well-carved facial features that make my pulse flutter faster.

"Hey, Chase," I greet him before accepting the cup he's holding out for me.

"Ava," he croons in a deep, throaty tone. "Make sure you only accept drinks from Hugo or me tonight."

His inched-high brows lower when I curtly nod. He grins, lessening my confused scowl before he punches Blake in the shoulder with his enclosed fist.

Blake's heavy-lidded eyes snap open, furious that his heavy petting session with Jorgie has been interrupted. His angry gaze switches to panic when he realizes who has disturbed his above PG-rated make-out session.

"Beat it," Chase instructs, glaring at Blake.

"Chase," Blake drawls with a laugh. "Help a brother out."

Any other slurred words preparing to escape Blake's mouth entomb in his throat when an angry growl rumbles through Chase's snapped-shut lips. "You either leave voluntarily, or I'll walk you out myself."

His stern tone causes an ice-cold chill to run down my spine. Even with Chase attending college two towns over, his protective big-brother stance hasn't eased when it comes to men getting close to his baby sister. But I must give credit where credit is due. Even after a vicious caution from Hugo and Chase, Blake continued to pursue Jorgie with as much vigor as he did before he found out she was the Marshall brothers' little sister.

A lesser man would've run for the hills.

Many before him have done exactly that.

"I'll show you out." Jorgie stops glaring at Chase to help a drunk Blake to his feet. Once she has him standing, she squeezes my shoulder. "I'll be back in a minute," she informs with a waggle of her brows.

I smile and nod. That was one of our secret friend codes. Saying she'll be back in a minute while waggling her brows means she'll be no less than thirty minutes.

When I run my index finger under my nose, acknowledging I understand her statement and that I'm fine being left unattended, after a last glare directed at Chase, Jorgie heads for the house with a stumbling Blake shadowing closely behind.

Not long later, a roaring chant drags my attention from the polish on my nails. I smile when six members of the rowing team hoist Hugo off the ground before charging for the vacant pool. Even though Hugo appears to be struggling against their hold, I know him well enough to say he isn't putting in a genuine effort.

On the boisterous count of three, Hugo is thrown into the undoubtedly frigid water. Men hollering resonates over the playful banter when a trio from the cheerleading squad strips out of their clothing and dives into the water squealing, "Pool party!" at the top of their lungs.

A grimace taints my face when the bra and panty-wearing troupe circles Hugo like a pack of sharks in heat. I gag when Victoria Avenke presses her lips to Hugo's, and he doesn't pull away.

I try to act as if I'm not affected, but in all honesty, it hurts.

It hurts like a fucking bitch.

But then I remember, they aren't seeing the real Hugo Marshall.

Tonight, he's the popular school jock who's friends with everyone. By Sunday, he'll be back to the real Hugo. The one only I get to see. The man who lounges around in his pajamas until midday every Sunday morning and hates when I beat him on Mario Kart. That's the real Hugo—the Hugo I have a mad crush on. Not the boy undertaking a course in the art of resuscitation in a pool.

"A pool party and a bonfire. Quite the odd combination."

When I raise my eyes from the dancing embers of the fire, I am met with a knock-your-socks-off smile. My eyes bug when they roam over Rhys Tagget, my childhood crush number two.

Rhys screams bad boy with his clipped dark hair, tattooed arms, and impressive swagger. Even when he was a junior, the senior girls fawned over him. He graduated from high school two summers ago. When he isn't attending college, studying to become a surgeon, he works at the local tattoo parlor. Hence, the vibrant collection of artwork skating up his arms.

"Freeze in the pool, thaw by the fire," I reply while shyly smiling.

Rhys chuckles a hearty laugh. "For some strange reason, that kind of makes sense."

Goosebumps prickle my skin when he nudges my shoulder with a chilled beer. I bounce my eyes between the clear bottle with a wedge of lime crammed in the neck and the bland soda I'm grasping. When my focus drifts to the pool, and I spot Hugo still training to be a lifeguard, I place the soda onto the ground then accept the bottle from Rhys.

I lean back in my chair before taking a generous swig of the frosted beverage. My face grimaces when the bitter flavor engulfs my taste buds. Rhys grins while dragging the chair Jorgie vacated closer to me. When he straddles it backward, his glistening hazel eyes float from Hugo and his posse of female friends to me.

"You're best friends with Hugo's little sister, Jorgie, aren't you?"

I nod before taking another swig of beer. I try to keep the repulsed expression off my face as I swallow the ghastly liquid. It tastes disgusting, but the coolness is lessening the furious rage burning a hole in my heart.

"Then why haven't I seen you at any of Hugo's parties before?"

My eyes snap to Rhys. "Is this a regular occurrence?"

He smiles against the seam of his beer before nodding. "It isn't usually here, though. It's normally held at the lookout or down by the river."

"Oh," I mumble before taking another mouth-filling gulp of beer. "I've never been invited before."

Now, I'm guzzling down my beer so quickly my taste buds don't get the chance to protest the abhorrent taste.

"These parties have an open invitation, sweetheart. You don't need to be invited," Rhys informs me.

My eyes burn as I fight to swallow the beer in my mouth instead of splattering it all over Rhys' face. I've never been called a term of endearment before, let alone one as endearing as sweetheart.

"Ah... now it makes sense."

My eyes snap back to his. "What makes sense?"

His worldly eyes absorb my face before they drop to my baggy boyfriend jeans and one-shoulder knitted sweater. "You're fresh meat."

My cheeks get a rush of blood forming beneath them. "Excuse me?"

I may be naïve, but even I know what that saying means.

"I didn't mean to embarrass you, Ava. It just makes sense as to why I've never seen you at one of these functions before. They're not suitable for..." His eyes say the word his mouth fails to produce.

While striving not to die from embarrassment, I guzzle down the remainder of my beer. When Rhys notices that my beer is empty, he fetches another one from the cooler at his side, cracks it open, squeezes a lime into the neck, then hands it to me.

I throw it down, prompting Rhys to issue me a warning. "Slow your guzzling if you're not used to drinking, Ava. It isn't soda in that bottle."

I smile in thanks before drifting my eyes to the people milling near the pool. With the seam of the bottle pressed against my lips, I freeze when I catch Hugo's murderous glare. His head is angled to the side, and his brow is arched high.

When I lower the beer from my mouth to rest it on my shaking thigh, his stern gaze follows its descent. I sink deeper into the chair, moving away from the fire since Hugo's glare is roasting my skin. When he motions for me to join him in the pool, I timidly shake my head.

His narrowed eyes slit even more before his heated gaze bounces between Rhys and me. Aiming to defuse his anger, I screw up my nose and stick out my tongue.

The furious scowl on his face doesn't lessen from my playful jibe.

If anything, it deepens.

When the muscles in Hugo's arm flex as he lifts himself out of the pool, my heart rate quickens. Even music thumping through the crisp night air, I don't miss the disdained gasps of the cheerleaders devastated by his brisk departure.

I roll my eyes when a flurry of girls swarm Hugo to offer him a towel or a birthday kiss. After inwardly gagging about their desperateness, I revert my focus back to Rhys.

He doesn't say anything, but I know he saw the exchange between Hugo and me. Shockingly, he appears more amused than horrified. "I didn't realize you had an older brother."

"I don't," I reply through clenched teeth.

"Boyfriend?" Rhys probes while staring into my eyes. In the moonlight, the brown flicks in his eyes are more prominent, making them dazzle even brighter.

A heartwarming smirk curls on his lips when I shake my head. While taking a sip of his beer, his eyes return to the pool. His smirk morphs into a grin before he warns, "Prepare yourself, Ava."

I'm so immersed in unearthing what's ignited the spark in his eyes *that I don't notice the prowler sneaking up on me until it's too late. With a yank on my wrist, I'm plucked from my chair and tossed over a broad shoulder. A chill runs through my body when droplets of water are absorbed by my bland red sweater.*

Not having anywhere else to grasp, I secure a firm grip on a pair of wet black cotton boxer shorts jiggling in front of me. When I recognize the smell of the man I'm manhandling, I squeal, "Put me down, Hugo!"

I kick as hard as possible, aiming for the one part of his anatomy I know will slow him down. My squirms come to an immediate halt when he slaps my backside. A sting of both pleasure and pain rushes through to my core, making me ache with desire. "Time for a swim, Ava."

I dig my nails into the rock-hard muscles in his lower back when the marble tiles surrounding the pool come into vision. "Don't you dare throw me in the po—"

Before all my sentence can escape my mouth, my glasses are knocked off my face, my jeans become the weight of concrete, and my nipples turn rigid. They're so firm, they could cut through diamonds.

My screams trap in my throat when the sub-zero water steals my ability to breathe. Even while peering at him through the blur of rippling water, I can't miss the smug look smeared on Hugo's face when he gawks at me under the water.

Fuming mad, I kick him in the shins before swimming to the surface. Numerous curse words escape my lips when I drag myself over the rigid edge. My teeth grit when Hugo exits the pool with ease. My soaked jeans and drenched sweater have doubled my weight, impeding my efforts.

When Hugo holds out his hand in offering, through gritted teeth, I accept his offer. He pulls me out of the pool as if I don't weigh a thing before he tugs me in close to his chest.

Still annoyed, I press my palms onto his drenched pecs then push away from him. The sloshing of water in my boots sounds over the pulse in my ears. "Why did you do that?"

He crosses his arms in front of his chest, strengthening his pose. "You were told not to accept drinks from anyone but Chase or me. You didn't listen."

"It was a bottle of beer!"

He cocks a brow. "I don't care if it was a can of Diet Pepsi, you don't accept drinks from men you don't know."

While tugging off my boots, I glare at him. His lips twitch when he battles to hold in a smile from the contents of my boots creating a puddle around his feet. Even with being overheated with anger, a shiver darts down my spine when a cool breeze hits my chest.

Confident I'm about to catch pneumonia, I thrust my boots into Hugo's chest. Air whizzes out between his teeth from my rueful shove.

"I'll have you know, Rhys isn't a stranger." I yank my limp sweater up my torso and over my head, grunting when the soaked material clings to my arms. "He and I go way back."

The smile curling Hugo's lips vanishes, and a set of hard-edged lips ruefully take its place.

I snarl at him while dumping my drenched sweater on top of my boots.

"Rhys used to tutor me," I enlighten him while undoing the button of my jeans.

"Ava—"

"In French," I add when I notice the conceited smirk on Hugo's face. "All things French. It is the language of love amongst many other things." I overemphasize certain words, loving the quiver they caused Hugo's jaw.

"Ava," Hugo growls again.

"It was the most fun I've ever had studying."

"Ava."

"Who knew being forced to learn a foreign language by my father would be such a riveting experience?" I continue to taunt while shimmying out of the jeans plastered to my thighs.

I nearly lose my footing when the left cuff gets stuck on my ankle, *but after raising my leg high into the air, the rigid material yanks off with one clean swoop.*

After thrusting my jeans into Hugo's heaving chest, I grasp the hem of my white cami.

"Ava!" Hugo rumbles again, louder this time.

"What?" I yell, exasperatingly throwing my arms into the air. Is that the only word he knows today?

His livid eyes glare into mine. "You're stripping in front of half the school population."

"What?" I squeak out before the reality of the situation crashes into me full pelt.

I swallow the rock in my throat before scanning the dead quiet space. The walloping of my heart increases when I spot numerous party attendees staring at me, wide-eyed and open-mouthed. My anger at being dumped in the pool made me lose sight of the bigger picture.

When my eyes shoot from the partygoers to my barely covered body, my horror increases. My drenched cami is too thin to conceal my bra and red striped G-string.

Tears burn my eyes as I return them to Hugo. His expression is no longer laced with amusement. It's full to the brim with remorse and silent apologies.

Yanking my clothes out of his grasp, I rush toward the house. Cat calls, wolf whistles, and sexual propositions thud through my ears as I run through the gauntlet of partygoers gawking at me like I'm the night's free entertainment. I hold my sweater close to my chest, futilely trying to maintain a small shred of modesty as I bolt up the roped-off stairwell.

The first tears splash my cheeks when I slam Jorgie's bedroom door shut and slide down. The clanking of my backside on the blue carpet swamps the sobs tearing from my throat. After dumping my clothes at the side of Jorgie's room, I curl my arms around my legs and burrow my tear-stained face into my knees, hiding from the world.

This is the exact reason I avoid these types of functions. I'm awkward as it is, let alone trying to mingle with strangers.

My head pops up from my knees when, "Ava, let me in," barrels through the door only minutes later. It came from a voice I immediately recognize.

Not wanting Hugo to witness my tears, I attempt to lessen my sobs.

I've barely gotten them down to a sniffle when he begs, "Come on, open up, I know you're in there." His shadow fills the crack beneath the door. "I can hear you crying."

When I snap my mouth shut, trying to mask my tears, the smallest whimper escapes my lips. It sees Hugo rattling the doorknob so firmly, it sounds seconds from snapping. "If you don't open the door, Ava, I'll kick it in," he warns.

"The only thing that needs kicking is my backside for trying to be sexy by wearing a stupid G-string," I mumble.

I snuck the red and white striped scrap of material into the shopping cart last week when my mom and I went to Walmart. I concealed its bland cotton material amongst the red sweater my mom picked out. The cashier's eyes locked with mine when it tumbled out of the rumpled-up sweater, but when she saw my panicked expression, she gathered it up, scanned it, then shoved it into the pocket of my one-size-too-large boyfriend jeans, leaving my mom none the wiser to my sneaky purchase.

I mumbled my silent gratitude to the grinning cashier when I snagged the bags from the carousel and rushed out of the store.

Although I never intended for anyone to see it, it made me feel sexy when I slipped it up my freshly shaved legs tonight.

My head cranks to the left when the door handle stops rattling. Hugo's shadow is no longer beneath the door. I drag my bottom lip between my teeth, shocked he gave up so easily. I shouldn't be surprised. It's not like I'm a princess trapped in a castle waiting for prince charming to rescue me.

My sinking heart suspends halfway to my stomach when, "If you're sitting behind the door, Ava, I need you to move," vibrates through the door.

Hugo wouldn't really kick down the door, would he? Jorgie will never forgive me if she had to live with no privacy until her door was repaired. Knowing how annoying her older brothers are, they'd take their sweet-ass time replacing her busted door. They'd do anything to lessen the chance of her having any 'private' time.

"Have you moved, Ava? Please tell me you've moved. I don't want to hurt you."

My heart clutches from the torment in Hugo's voice, and it sees me scampering off the floor. "Wait."

The darkness shadowing the bottom of the door returns, closely followed by the big pants of Hugo's breath. After sucking in a nerve-cleansing breath, I sweep open the door. A mixture of whiskey and a scent that belongs solely to Hugo filters through my nose when he steps into Jorgie's room. The concern contorting his face amplifies when his eyes zoom in on my tear-stained cheeks.

He smiles a wary smirk before closing the door. Once the lock is latched into place, he spins back around to face me. "Ava, I'm sorr—"

"I'm not leaving this room," *I interrupt while pacing to the middle of the room. Surprisingly, my reply is delivered stronger than I anticipated.* "I'm never leaving this room."

Not just because I don't want to face the taunts of my peers, but also because I'm petrified of what my father's reaction will be if he learns about my strip.

In the sheen of the bedside lamp, my eyes catch sight of a photo frame on Jorgie's nightstand. It holds a picture of Jorgie, Hugo, and me taken during Hugo's thirteenth birthday party. We were so young and carefree back then. Our only concern that day was who got the biggest slice of cake.

Oh, how things have changed in five years.

"You don't have to go out right now, but eventually, you're going to have to leave this room." *Hugo's tone is sincere but with an edge of wittiness to it.*

I pout. "Why? Can't I stay in here forever?"

A smirk tugs Hugo's lips higher as he steps closer to me while shaking his head. "You'd soon grow tired of Jorgie's snoring."

I roll my eyes. Jorgie has a slight wheeze when she's sleeping, but it isn't loud enough to douse my enthusiasm about hiding in her room for the rest of eternity.

"And Jorgie doesn't have cable TV, so how will we spend our Sunday afternoons watching reruns of Friends *if you're locked up in here?"*

As memories of our Sunday afternoon ritual filter in my head, I smile. Jorgie isn't a fan of Friends, *so it's the only time I get Hugo all to myself. It is only an hour out of an entire week, but I cherish every second of our alone time.*

When he senses my determination to be a hermit in Jorgie's room is wavering, Hugo continues chipping at it. "There's also no kitchen in here, and goddammit, girl, knowing your blueberry pancakes are waiting for me every Sunday morning when I wake is the only thing that keeps me going during the week."

No longer able to hide my happiness, a broad grin spreads across my face. I swear I roll over like a dog begging for my tummy to be scratched when it comes to Hugo, but it isn't just his cheeky disposition that keeps me coming back for more. It is the fact he doesn't expect me to change from the dorky girl hiding behind a mask to what society deems acceptable that I love.

Unlike Jorgie, Hugo doesn't care if I wear jeans that are a size too big or sweaters we could both fit in. He greets me with the same amount of excitement no matter what hideous outfit I'm wearing.

Smirking, I lock my eyes with his just as he hands me my black thick-rimmed glasses.

"Thank you, but I don't need them to see," I mumble under my breath.

My heart skips a beat when he confesses, "I know, but they're your protective shield that keeps you hidden from the strangers lurking in the dark."

Placing his hand under my chin, he raises my deflated head. Any leftover tears dry from the kindness radiating out of his eyes. "You're like Clark Kent. You keep your superhero identity hidden from outsiders."

My heart warms as a genuine smile pulls at my lips. I wouldn't say I am a superhero. I'm more like a tortoise. I only emerge from my shell around Jorgie, Hugo, and their family. The instant I'm pushed back into society, the armor I wear to protect myself slips right back into place.

Although I need glasses to stop eye strain when using a computer, they're not a requirement for me to see clearly. My vision is so precise I can see every droplet of water clinging to Hugo's thick lashes as he stares at me in awe.

A stretch of silence spans between us. It isn't awkward. Hugo is just giving me time to calm down from the debacle of my existence.

Once my usual composure is back, his glassy eyes shift between mine as he mutters, "Borrow some of Jorgie's clothes, then when you're ready, come back and enjoy the party. If anyone says anything about what happened, they'll have me to deal with."

I smile to hide the grimace trying to cross my face. The last thing I want is the guy who invades my every thought taking on the role of big brother.

"Thanks for the offer, but I can't borrow Jorgie's clothes," I advise while peering into his concerned eyes.

His face screws up. "Why not?"

Not waiting for me to reply, he strolls to Jorgie's bursting-at-the-seams closet. My brows meet my hairline when he rummages through her vast collection of clothes, but my shock won't stop me from saying, "Because I'm five foot two and Jorgie is as tall as a gir—" I stop talking before my mouth gapes.

Hugo's head cranks back quicker than a bullet being dislodged from a weapon.

"I wasn't going to say it," I squeak out when a huge grin stretches across his face.

"Oh, yeah, you were. You were about to call Jorgie a giraffe."

"I was not!" I retaliate as my eyes dart to the doorway, hoping like hell that Jorgie isn't within earshot. She never forgave Victoria for calling her a giraffe in middle school, and although I'm her best friend, I'm not willing to test her forgiving nature. "I was going to say she's as tall as a gir... gir... a girl!"

Hugo smiles a shit-eating grin. "You're so full of shit."

"Am not!" I respond with a stomp of my feet.

"Oh, yeah, you are," he snaps out with a laugh before he lunges for me.

Squealing, I dash for the door before his tortuous hands can get anywhere near my ribs. Air whooshes from my lips when he wraps his arm around my waist then tackles me to the floor. I giggle like a fifth grader when he straddles my hips before his fingers unleash a torrid of tickles to my stomach.

I squirm and buck my hips, fighting against his cruel tickling onslaught, but within minutes, my face is red, I'm sweating profusely, and I can't breathe through the happy tears seeping from my eyes.

"Okay, okay, I give up!" I squeal, still squirming. "Mercy! Mercy!" I scream at the top of my lungs, knowing it's the only word that will stop his tortuous hands.

Upon hearing my roaring pleas, Hugo un-straddles my hips then flops onto his back beside me. His chest thrusts up and down, matching the rhythm of mine as I endeavor to refill my lungs with air.

I don't know why he's so exhausted. I'm the one who was subjected to torture.

Once I can breathe again, I roll onto my hip, crank my elbow, then rest my saturated mop onto my open palm. Hugo's eyes drift from the ceiling to me. He looks uneased, but when he notices I've caught his odd expression, a roughish grin etches on his sinful mouth.

Oh no. I know that look. It's a look that means he's about to stir up trouble.

"If you tell Jorgie I nearly called her a giraffe, I'll kill you," I warn.

Panic scorches my veins when he waggles his brows before he scampers off the floor. I freeze for all of two seconds before I dive for him. He hits the floor with an almighty roar when I wrap my arms around his ankles and yank back. His thunderous laugh booms through my chest when I hook my legs around his torso to pin him to the floor.

My mouth falls open when he crawls across the carpet, not the slightest bit impeded by my monkey hold. When he stands, taking me with him, I leap off his back and dart for the door. I slam it shut, plaster my back against the wooden material, then lock my eyes on his.

"I'll do anything," I plea breathlessly. "Anything at all."

We're standing so close our thrusting chests connect with each breath we take.

I smile when Hugo loosens his grip on the door handle so he can run his hand along his jaw. That's a sign he's considering my request. It's something he always does when he's contemplating.

His tone drips with innuendo when he asks, "Anything?"

My tongue delves out to replenish my lips before I nod. When he presses his palms on each side of my head then tilts in closer, my heartbeat kicks up. I'm trapped between his imposing body and the thick wooden door.

"Alright," he breathes out heavily. His alcohol-scented breath adds more heat to my already flustered cheeks. "You have to cook me breakfast."

I eagerly nod.

I've done that exact thing every Sunday morning for the past two years, so it'll be a walk in the park.

My eager nod lessens when he says, "I want the works... bacon, eggs, pancakes. If it's associated with breakfast, I want it. And I want it tomorrow morning."

My nose scrunches. "Jeez, what happened to your last slave?"

"Nothing... yet," he replies with a cheeky wink.

My O-formed mouth curves into a grin when he tugs on a curl springing in front of my eye. As my hair starts to dry, super tight curls are beginning to sprout. I was never a fan of my ringlet curls growing up, but they've grown on me the over past two years. I don't know if he realizes he's doing it, but whenever we watch reruns of Friends, Hugo twists my hair around his index finger. It is the meekest gesture, but it sparks a massive surge of excitement every time he does it.

The room turns roasting when Hugo's eyes burn into mine, and he says, "I want my breakfast served in my bed."

I swallow to relieve my parched throat. "Okay."

A bead of sweat rolls down my back when his hooded gaze drops to my lips. "I should warn you if it's edible and in my room, I'm going to taste it."

"Okay," I respond again since my brain has lost the ability to form longer sentences.

Another small bout of silence stretches between us as we undertake an intense, sweat-forming staredown. Hugo breaks contact first. He tilts his head forward, bringing his lips to within a mere inch of mine.

Excitement courses through my body as every fantasy I've ever conjured transpires before my eyes, but just as Hugo's lips brush the edge of my mouth, a knock sounds on the door.

The tap is so hard it vibrates through my heaving chest.

"Ava, it's Jorgie. I just heard what happened. Let me in."

When she pushes the door with her shoulder, my body flattens against Hugo, and our faces smash together. If I were a few inches taller, my lips would have landed on his mouth instead of his chin.

Hugo's heavy-lidded eyes drift between mine for several heart-clenching seconds before he drops his arms then takes a step backward, unpinning me from the door.

After taking a moment to regain control of my senses, I push off the door then move to the middle of the room. The instant I step away, Jorgie charges into the room. Her eyes are wide, her cheeks are flushed, and excitement is beaming out of her.

She looks as flustered as I feel.

"You know how you didn't have a date for the summer fling?" Her words are barely audible in her breathless state.

I nod. My lack of date isn't because I can't find a dance partner for *the night, though. It's the excuse I'm using so I don't have to tell Jorgie I'm not allowed to go to the senior dance. It's the same night my parents are going to Napa Valley for the weekend to celebrate their twentieth wedding anniversary, and my father arranged for me to stay at my grandmother's house two towns over.*

When I requested to stay at Jorgie's that weekend, he said my desire to spend time with my grandmother should outweigh my need for social interaction.

That was the beginning and end of our discussion.

Jorgie grips my arm as her gleaming eyes beam into mine. "You no longer have an excuse not to go. Because not only did I overhear Richie Santo asking Rhys for your digits, but I also saw Chase dragging Robert Parker down the stairwell. Chase didn't say it, but I'm fairly certain Robert was up here looking for you."

Her neck cranks to the side when a thunderous growl booms across her room. Her nose scrunches up when she spots Hugo standing at the side, angry and red-faced.

I don't know how she could miss a man as built as him.

"You're lucky your immature prank backfired, or I would have told Mom what you did to Ava," Jorgie says, her voice snarkier than normal as she shoots daggers at Hugo.

A grin tugs on my lips when a fretful mask slips over Hugo's face. I love Mrs. Marshall. She treats me as if I am her daughter, but I grew even fonder of her when I discovered she's the only person in the world Hugo fears. It isn't a quaking-in-your-boots type of fear. It's the worry he may one day disappoint his number one fan who keeps him on the straight and narrow.

Hugo's tight fists slacken when I mouth, "I'll see you tomorrow?"

He strays his eyes from Jorgie to me before jerking up his chin. After returning my smile, he heads for the door and exits without a backward glance.

We never got our breakfast the following day...

. . .

"So, are you going to get dressed, Ava, or do you want to go out like that?" Hugo asks, interrupting me from my thoughts.

As my eyes dart down to the towel curled around my body, my pupils widen. Although it doesn't match the sleek design of my modern apartment, it was a housewarming gift from Mrs. Marshall, so I couldn't part with it.

I lock my eyes with Hugo's twinkling baby blues. "I guess that depends on where we're going. It's not like half the town hasn't already seen my naked derriere."

SIX
AVA

My sassiness is foiled when a panty-combusting smirk morphs on Hugo's face. Well, they would have combusted if I were wearing any.

My squeal echoes down the hallway of my apartment building when Hugo throws me over his shoulder. As he marches into my apartment, my hands shoot down to the hem of the towel. I don't want my neighbors getting an eyeful of my *lady garden*.

Once again, that is a metaphor. I can't technically call it a garden when it doesn't have any foliage. I've just always found the word pussy a little too risqué if you aren't in the bedroom, and calling it a vagina is a huge no-no in my book.

A rush of excitement pelts my body when Hugo smacks my ass with his open palm. "As riveting as it would be to take you out in only a towel, Jorgie would kill me, so you've got five minutes to get dressed, Ava," he instructs before placing me back onto my feet.

"It's eleven o'clock!" I declare like there could be a possibility he's unaware of the time. "The only place I'm visiting is my bed."

His brow arches high into his thick hair as an unscrupulous grin etches on his sinful mouth.

"Alone," I clarify.

I'm surprised about how confident my statement came out, considering how fast my pulse is racing.

"How old are you, Ava?"

I cross my arms in front of my chest, hoisting my moderately sized bosoms higher into the air. "Exactly six months younger than you, remember?"

"Then stop acting like my mother and get your goddamn ass dressed."

My mouth pop opens over his audacity, but any word vomit preparing to exit my lips traps in my throat when I notice the direction of Hugo's heavy-lidded gaze. It's a well-known fact he has a fascination with legs, and nearly every inch of my legs is on display due to my strengthened stance, but still, his gawking stare is unexpected.

When I uncross my arms, my towel drops back to a more respectable level, and Hugo's heavily dilated eyes return to mine. "If you aren't dressed in five minutes, you're leaving your apartment in a towel. The choice is yours."

With that, he saucily winks before sauntering out of the room. I stand motionless, staring at the door he exited, utterly flabbergasted. I'm not just shocked by his sudden interest in me. I'm also surprised he knew the location of my bedroom.

I'm not bragging, but my apartment is decent in size. I worked hard throughout college and saved every single penny I made so I could afford the down payment. I was called naïve and stupid when I signed on the dotted line after only viewing the blueprint designs for this building. Even living on the other side of the country, I knew one day I'd return to Rochdale. It wasn't a matter of if. It was a matter of when, but the only way I could afford an apartment in this area was by investing my money in the concept of an idea, not a physical building.

It was a risk, but it was one I was willing to take it. The taunts about my so-called stupidity continued when people discovered I was placing my hard-earned cash into the hands of a businessman who was younger than me. Now, almost two years later, I'm the one laughing in their faces.

Purchasing this apartment was the best financial decision I ever made. The value of the apartments in this building skyrocketed the instant the project was completed, meaning I'm now sitting on a very lucrative nest egg.

I dash to my wardrobe like a frantic woman when Hugo declares, "Three minutes."

"Can you at least tell me where we're going?" I yell while rummaging through my closet, trying to find something suitable to wear.

"What does every twenty-five-year-old on the planet do on a Saturday night?"

I twist my lips. "Shave their legs? Or is that just losers like me?"

My cheeky snickers are replaced with a gasp when Hugo strolls into my room unannounced.

"What if I were naked?"

His lengthy strides have him crossing the room in two heart-thrashing seconds. "It wouldn't be anything I haven't seen before."

My brows furrow. "You haven't seen me naked."

My pulse quickens when he stops scrolling through my clothes to stare at me. His eyes are glistening, but there's something more tangible beneath the devious spark that has my interests piqued.

My breathing returns when he says, "Camp Levitt, the lake house, and that time you vomited after we went trick or treating because you ate your candy as it was handed to you instead of putting it into your pink powder-puff collection bag."

My jaw drops. Not just because he's seen me naked on at least three occasions but because he remembered a bag I used for Halloween over fourteen years ago.

Although shocked, I give as good as I'm getting. "Those times don't count. Nothing before puberty counts. And you can't talk. I've seen you naked more times than I can count."

"*Pfft*," Hugo spits out with a chuckle. "Name three times you've seen my junk."

"The morning of spring fling, that time you lost your board shorts surfing after Hurricane Claudette hammered the coastline in 2003, and the night Jorgie and I arrived at a party at your frat house in college," I respond, ticking off each item with my fingers. "Shall I continue? As I'm sure I have at least a dozen more memories I can recall."

That's a lie. Including tonight, I've only seen him naked four times.

"You and Jorgie came to one of my frat parties?"

I roll my eyes before accepting the little black dress he's handing me from my extensive collection of LBDs. I shouldn't be surprised he doesn't remember my admission because, lo and behold, he was drunk.

"Your five minutes are up, Ava," he says while pacing closer with a wicked grin etched on his mouth.

I freeze as my panicked eyes flick between the skimpy towel wrapped around my body and the beast of a man prowling stealthily toward me. "I was waiting for you to turn around," I argue, blurting out the first excuse that pops into my head. "Even though you *may* have already seen me naked, there are no free peep shows happening tonight."

My heart rate soars when his hearty chuckle sounds through my ears. "Party pooper."

"Turn around." I wriggle my finger in a circular pattern to enhance my request.

When he does as requested with a broad grin stretched across his face, I unlatch the side zipper of the black dress and step into the small opening. Within a few tugs, a couple of yanks, and a handful of grunts, I get the skin-tight dress up my body without needing to drop my towel.

I mimic a statue when Hugo asks, "If you weren't going to remove your towel, why did I need to turn around?"

My brow cocks. *How did he know I didn't remove my towel?*

My mouth falls open when I spot his grinning reflection in the full-length mirror in the corner of the room. If I didn't take over-the-top precautions, he would have had a full view of my body.

My naked *post-pubescent* body.

I gulp.

The smirk etched on Hugo's rugged face falters when I throw my drenched towel over his head, concealing his view so I can yank a pair of black panties up my quaking thighs. The hem of my dress only sinks back to a respectable level when he yanks the towel off his head.

I stick out my tongue at the playful wiggle of his brows before sauntering to the vanity mirror to run my fingers through my freshly shampooed hair. After adding a sheen of lip gloss to my naked lips, I place a splattering of mascara onto my already dark lashes.

I'm uncapping a black eyeliner pencil when Hugo wraps his arm around my waist and tugs me backward. Desire clusters low in my womb when the Woods of Windsor aftershave I bought him for his seventeenth birthday filters through my nose.

"Time's up," he declares, breathing heavily into my ear.

My core clenches when my backside brushes against the crotch of his jeans. His nickname in high school announced that his manhood would be impressive, but until I was awarded with a full-frontal visual, I had no idea it was *that* remarkable.

When he carries me to the front door, I remain quiet, silenced with embarrassment. It's not a hard feat for Hugo to cart me around like a child. He's a foot taller than me and a hundred pounds heavier.

"My purse," I beg, pointing to the black clutch hanging on the coat rack near the front door. "I'll need my ID." Even though I'm nearly twenty-five, I get carded every time I order an alcoholic drink.

Hugo's lengthy strides don't falter as he snags my clutch off the rack and a pair of black heels from the entryway cupboard. He strides down the long hallway to the elevator banks located in the middle. The blood pumping through my veins has a fine mist of sweat forming on my freshly cleaned skin. The night air is already suffocated with humidity from the downpour earlier today, but Hugo's clutch makes the heat even more pulverizing.

When the elevator doors snap shut with us on the inside, I wiggle, wordlessly demanding to be placed down.

"You can put me down now," I say when my squirming comes up fruitless.

As Hugo's grunt bounces around the elevator, he shrugs.

I grit my teeth then suck in a big breath. "I'm not a child," I reprimand him, even though I'm being carried as if I am.

You'd think not aging the past seven years would be an invigorating experience I'd shout from the rooftops.

It isn't.

My colleagues don't take me seriously because they think I'm the female equivalent of Dr. Howser. Grown men assume I'm jailbait, so they won't touch me with a ten-foot pole, and for the past three years, my professor has called me one of the most ridiculous nicknames I've ever heard.

Babyface.

That hideous nickname was the sole reason for my latest makeover. I worked hard throughout college. My nose rarely left the inside of a book. So now it's time for my dedication to pay up, but if I can't get my colleagues to take me seriously, I'll never obtain the reputation I need to remain viable in the thriving dental conglomerate. So, with a hefty increase in my credit card limit and nothing but my pride at stake, I went a little crazy.

My dark brown afro was chemically straightened to wispy waves that now sit an inch past my shoulders. My wardrobe that was once filled with baggy boyfriend jeans, sweatshirts, yoga pants, and soccer-mom outfits were gifted to Goodwill, and my natural plain-Jane makeup was switched for a more daring color palette.

Although I've been sporting this new look for six months, this is the first time Hugo has seen the spit-polished version of Ava, but with him once again wearing his infamous beer-googles, he probably still sees me as the braces-wearing and baggy jeans, pimpled-faced teenager he recalls from our youth.

To be honest, until I ran into the hot-blooded male version of Hugo this afternoon, I was still imagining him as the teenage boy who both tilted my axis and shattered it...

Unless you have battled the wrath of a Jorgie Marshall storm, you'll never understand the next part of my story. An hour after I was planning on borrowing a dress and toodle home to hide my embarrassment under a pair of gaudy pink sheets, I'm walking into the converted den in the attic of the Marshall residence, preparing to team up with Jorgie in a game of pool against two graduating seniors who were, I quote, "dying for the chance to meet me," unquote.

Hugo's eyes, along with numerous others, stalk Jorgie and me when we enter the den. This is nothing out of the ordinary for Jorgie. She has remarkable beauty that draws the attention of every male in the room. Her big blue eyes are prominent against her pale skin, and her dark hair makes them blaze, giving her an alluring mix of seduction and uniqueness.

Needing to gauge Hugo's reaction about my decision not to go home, I smile warily at him. His lips crimp before they're hidden behind a glass when he takes a generous gulp of the liquid inside.

Even though I can't see his smile, I feel his eyes on me as I continue shadowing Jorgie into the den.

Panic sets in when my attempts to conceal my face with my thick curly hair come up fruitless. Before we left her room, Jorgie pulled my unruly hair into a tight ballet-style bun, fully exposing my face. My invisibility glasses have been dumped on the vanity of her shared bathroom with Hugo, and the lightest splattering of makeup has been applied to my face.

I feel out of place like I'm in the midst of an out-of-body experience, but my dash for the door is thwarted when Jorgie strengthens her grip on my wrist. "They're not looking at you because you look weird," she affirms as her eyes drift around the room. "That spark you see in their eyes is the spark of interest and intrigue. Trust me, Ava, you want to see that spark."

After inhaling a big breath, I endure with my shaky steps toward the blue felt billiard table. Jorgie scribbles our names onto a chalkboard, advising we're the next set of players for a game of pool before she pivots to face the group of partygoers crammed into the space.

A clap of her hands gains her the devotion of nearly every man in the room. My attention only diverts from her when the trio of cheerleaders from the earlier pool party stalk Hugo's way. Head cheerleader and number one bitch of our school, Victoria, leads the pack of scantily clad women vying for his attention.

Victoria is dressed in a curve-hugging designer dress. Every hair on her head has been straightened and brushed to perfection, falling to her shoulders in a gloss of blonde waves. Her face, although made-up, isn't overly done.

My heart flips when Hugo angles his head to the side, brushing off Victoria's attempt to re-acquaint their lips. The pulse in my neck thrums when his heavy-hooded eyes lock with mine. Even with Victoria jabbering in his ear while intimately touching his chest, his eyes remain steadfast on mine. His alluring gaze spears me in place and has my pulse quickening.

I clutch the hem of my dress, inwardly battling not to squirm from his piercing blue stare. I lose the ability to control my fidgeting when his glassy gaze lowers to absorb the dress Jorgie selected for me to wear. The length of this skirt would be best described as indecent, but by adding a pair of heels, it became downright corrupt.

An idiotic smile forms on my face from Hugo's lengthened stare. Feeling brazen, I grasp the flare of my skirt and do a princess curtsy. I giggle when Hugo waves his hand in the air like the paupers in fairytale movies do when the princess saunters by.

Our fire-sparking staredown is interrupted when a pool cue is waved in front of my face. When I shift my focus back to the present, I am met with the charming smile of Rhys Tagget. "We're going to play *a game of doubles. Did you want to pair up with me or Jorgie?" His tone is friendly with a dash of sexiness.*

"Umm..."

My eyes seek Jorgie. She grins before nodding, encouraging me to accept Rhys' offer, but before I can, a deep voice at my side says, "You pair up with Jorgie. I'll play with Ava."

My heart beats double-time when I recognize the rugged drawl. It's Hugo.

Jorgie's expression morphs to repulsed. "I don't want to play against you. Pool is about flirting and seduction, not embarrassing your brother in front of his little buddies."

Hugo's chuckle rumbles through my chest. "I'll be sure to let Blake know that the next time I see him."

Jorgie's eyes bug out of her head. "You wouldn't dare."

"Bring it on," Hugo mocks before waving for Jorgie to bring it. "You're just afraid I'm going to remind you whose name is written on the leader board." He points to the Marshall Pool Champion Leader Board hanging proudly on a side wall. "Either bring it or wipe your name off the board and let another player take your spot."

"Oh, I'll bring it. Then, I'll bring it some more." Jorgie whips her head side to side in a matching pattern to her hips. "So be prepared, brother." She overemphasizes the word 'brother.' "Because you're about to go down."

Their playful jibe gains the attention of the twenty-plus people still sober enough to focus on something other than the drink in their hand.

Rhys smiles at me before making his way to the other side of the table with Jorgie.

"I'm not very good at this game," I warn Hugo when he hands me a pool cue that has a new dusting of blue chalk on the tip. Any time I've played, my skills were best described as woeful.

My jaw drops when Hugo says with a chuckle, "I know. You suck." He grins at my annoyed expression. "But that's okay. I'll teach you a few tricks." His words come out with a thick slur, making me wonder how many drinks he downed the past few hours.

"Ava breaks," says Jorgie, fully knowing I can't hit the colored balls when they're an inch in front of the white ball, let alone across the table.

When I sneer at her, she playfully puckers her lips. Sensing my apprehension, Hugo smashes down the last of the beverage, dumps the glass onto a table, then moves to stand in front of me. My brows furrow when he adds a sprinkling of white powder to the edge of my palm. A smile curves on my mouth when the freshness of baby powder filters in the air.

"It will stop the friction and make everything nice and smooth so the stick can glide through your hand with ease." He demonstrates what he means by gliding the pool cue between my hand.

After blocking out the curious stare of the spectators surrounding me, I arch over the table and prepare to take my shot.

"Lean your torso over the table more, then raise your ass higher in the air," Hugo instructs while placing his hand on the middle of my back and pushing down.

Air rustles out of my mouth when his spare hand smacks my backside. "Higher, Ava."

If I were still wearing my glasses, his playful tease would have had them steaming up, but it isn't just his frisky tease that has me sweating like I'm sitting on a furnace. It's the burning glare from Hugo's posse of female friends. They're snarling at me, making me feel like a pig roasting on the spit. Victoria's thin-slitted eyes shoot daggers at me as she prances to the chalkboard to rub out my name and replace it with her own. My throat becomes scratchy from the particles of chalk dust filtering into the air from her overdramatic dusting.

Ignoring the odd tension plaguing the den, I adjust my position according to Hugo's advice. Several male eyes drop to the front of my dress when it tips dangerously low, but I lean over the table and thrust my backside into the air as instructed. A ghost-like smile tugs on my lips when I realize one of the handful of cleavage spectators is Rhys.

Snubbing the dropped eyes from across the table, I squint one eye and line up my shot, pretending I know what I'm doing. My eyes pop back open when Hugo's hand grazes the skin high on my inner thigh as he leans over my shoulder. "Don't aim for the middle of the ball. Target slightly to one side. It will give it a curve effect."

Unable to breathe, much less speak, I nod. My pulse thrums in my neck from Hugo's closeness as I glide the pool stick through the skin between my thumb and index finger. Once I have everything lined up, I give it a crack.

Just before the tip of the cue hits the white ball, I close my eyes and exhale a big breath. Time slows to a snail's pace, and the room plunges into such deathly quietness, the sound of the white ball rolling across the felt is the only noise resonating through my ears.

My eyes pop open when a loud crack booms around the room. Colored balls roll in every direction from my powerful hit. I jump into the air as an excited squeal ripples from my mouth. Anyone would swear I'd just won the lotto.

My party for one halts when Victoria spits out, "Why are you excited? You just lost the game, you idiot."

My disbelieving eyes dart up to Hugo. He doesn't need to confirm Victoria's testimony. The truth is written all over his face.

"How?"

He stares at me with amused eyes. "You sunk the black ball." His peers past my shoulder. "Rack them up again, Rhys," he requests before lowering his eyes back to mine. "Give it another shot. Just don't use so much power this time," he suggests with a cheeky wink.

I smile at the playfulness in his tone before nodding.

"No... she had her shot. She lost. Now, we move on to the next person on the list," wails Victoria.

I roll my eyes before turning them to Vicky.

"Oh, look." She acts surprised while pointing her long index finger to the chalkboard. "That person is me."

Her obnoxious tone fuels my annoyance, not to mention her smile as she lurks toward Hugo. I grit my teeth when she snatches the cue stick out of my hand before she cozies up to Hugo's side. Jorgie's mouth twitches in preparation to reply to Victoria's cattiness, but I stop any words spilling from her lips with a brief shake of my head.

"It's okay. I was thirsty anyway." I smile to reassure Jorgie and Hugo that it wasn't a quiver they heard in my voice.

I hear Hugo whispering something to Victoria when I head for the bar, but I can't make out any words he speaks. A genuine smile curls on my mouth when Chase says, "I'm glad you decided to stay, Ava, but no more accepting drinks from anyone but Hugo and me." He props his elbows onto the bar, exposing the dancing gypsy tattoo on his arm when his shirt rides up high on his thick biceps. "We wouldn't want Hugo's feathers getting ruffled again," he adds with a brash wink.

When my brows hit my hairline, Chase mumbles incoherently under his breath before he pours orange juice into a champagne flute and hands it to me. I plop my backside onto the barstool then take a swig of my drink. My nose screws up when its weird flavor hits my tastebuds.

"I think your orange juice is out of date," I say, repressing a gag.

Chase chuckles and shakes his head. "So innocent."

"It's a mimosa," informs a cavernous voice to my side.

I twist my torso to face Hugo. "A what?"

"Mimosa. It's champagne and orange juice. The perfect drink to accompany the hearty breakfast you're making me tomorrow." He removes the glass from my grasp then downs the generous serving in one gulp. Lucky I was only using my thirst as an excuse to evade an awkward situation.

When Hugo's tongue delves out to lick a smidgen of orange pulp from his top lip, my thirst turns dire. "Can I grab another?" I ask Chase.

His eyes shoot down to the bar refrigerator under the counter. "Looks like you're shit out of luck," he replies after returning his eyes to me. "If you don't mind running to the kitchen, there's some orange juice in the fridge upstairs."

"Alright." I jump off the barstool. "I'll be back in a minute."

Chase drifts his eyes to Hugo. "Go give her a hand, Hugo." He throws a dishcloth at Hugo's head before nudging him to the stairs.

"It's okay. I know where to find everything," I inform him, my tone confident. "And Hugo is partnered in a game of pool with Vicky." I surprise myself by keeping my tone friendly while saying Victoria's name because my thoughts are anything but.

I inhale a sharp breath when my pivot has me stumbling onto two new opponents versing the current tournament leaders, Jorgie and Rhys. Jorgie's lips are pressed together, and her head occasionally bobs at whatever strategy Rhys is whispering in her ear.

Jorgie is highly competitive. It doesn't matter if it's a game of pool or if you're climbing Mount Everest. If there's a possibility of her winning, she gives it her all.

My skin prickles with bumps when Hugo mutters, "I guess you're not the only one colorblind," into my ear.

My jaw falls open. "Did you sink the black ball?"

I giggle when he nods his head. "It wasn't as impressive as your stellar performance, though. I had two turns before the black ball found a home in the right corner pocket," he jests while following me into the hallway.

"Don't worry, you'll eventually get there. Being this perfect takes practice," I respond, smiling brightly.

A moment of silence stretches between us before he mutters, "That it does. That it does."

He remains quiet as we walk through the Marshall residence. Numerous partygoers stop dancing to greet Hugo when he strides by. The boys pat him on the back, and girls kiss him on the cheek, so by the time we reach the kitchen, jealousy is hitting me fairly in the gut, and Hugo's cheek is covered with lipstick smears.

Ignoring the twisted pain in my heart, I move to the refrigerator while Hugo swigs out of a bottle of beer I didn't realize he was holding until now. Cool air blasts my face when I pull open the double-door appliance to hunt for the orange juice. Mrs. Marshall's refrigerator is well-stocked with two young adults and two teens under one roof, and today is no exception, except there's no OJ.

I tilt my torso out of the refrigerator. "Does your mom keep the orange juice in the fridge or the pantry?"

He doesn't reply. His gaze remains arrested on something lower than my face. When his hand scrapes his jaw, my pulse quickens. I dart my eyes to his mouth when his tongue delves out to replenish the dryness impinging his top lip.

Once it's moistened and his tongue is returned to his mouth, my eyes shoot down, eager to discover what's got him all hot and bothered. A thin sheet of sweat mists my body when I spot the budded peaks of my nipples. They're standing erect through my thin cotton dress and have me curious if that is what has attracted his attention.

When Jorgie handed me this dress, years of dictatorship saw me placing a cropped jacket over the skimpy material. Jorgie, forever on the ball with my prudish ways, promptly removed it before assuring me that we weren't going outside, so a jacket wasn't necessary. I was panicked, but now I'm delighted I didn't stick to my guns.

Hugo's eyes track mine when I float them back to his face. The streak of desire blazing his baby blues spears me in place and instigates a warm slickness between my legs.

After a beat, he mutters, "She keeps it in the fridge."

I stare at him, utterly confused. My mind is nothing but mush from his avid gaze. When he pushes off the counter and stealthily prowls my way, my grip on the refrigerator handle firms. Even swamped by its coolness, sweat still slicks my skin with every step he takes.

He towers over me when he tilts into the refrigerator to grab the carton of orange juice at the very back of the top shelf. The heat radiating off his body warms my already inflamed skin and don't get me started on his scent. When his woodsy smell invades my senses, I close my eyes and inhale deeply through my nose, drinking in his delicious scent.

When my eyes flutter back open, I balk and take a step back. The amusement warming Hugo's eyes proves he noticed my vigorous sniff of his tempting smell.

"Sor—" I attempt to say before his warm, beer-flavored lips press against mine, stealing my words.

My mouth opens to accept his kiss, but the rest of my body freezes, unsure of how to react. I've never been kissed before, but within minutes, I melt into his embrace.

Hugo is a very convincing teacher.

With his hand gripping my bun, his tongue slips between my lips to sample and taste every inch of my mouth. A low groan simpers from his mouth when I return his kiss by mimicking the slow sweeps of his tongue and the soft caresses of his lips.

When he crowds in close until my back is splayed against the open refrigerator door, the coolness of the pickles and spreads stored in the door refreshes my overheated skin. Our kiss builds in intensity when he wraps his spare hand around my waist to pull me in close so he can ravish my neck.

Needy desire courses through my body when I feel the thickness straining against his trousers. I can understand the red-hot needs of his body. Our kiss is warm and wonderful. Mind-stealing.

I've only just finished raking my fingers through Hugo's long, shaggy hair when someone coughing clatters through my ears. I whimper when Hugo yanks away from our embrace to glare at the intruder interrupting our private time.

When I follow his gaze, I find Chase's smirking face. "I take it you found something more appealing to drink than orange juice, Ava?"

Grinning, he peers down at the dumped carton of juice on the floor. I was so entranced by Hugo's kiss, I didn't notice the cool, sticky contents is puddled around my borrowed shoes.

My eyes lock with Hugo's when he runs his thumb along my kiss-swollen top lip. He stares into my eyes for what feels like hours but is only mere seconds before he stalks out of the room without a backward glance...

. . .

My focus returns to the present when Hugo sniffs my hair. The wrinkles in my forehead extend to my nose when I catch the scent of his exhale.

"Liar, liar, pants on fire," I squeal when I fail to detect the smallest smidgen of alcohol on his breath.

When my overly girly pitch bounces off the woodgrain walls of the elevator, I grimace. Unfortunately, no amount of makeup, fancy clothes, or pretty hairstyles can alter my immature voice.

My squeals shift to laughter when Hugo replies, "I don't care, I don't care, I can buy another pair."

Once my laughter dies down, I ask, "How'd you remember that?"

He chuckles a full-hearted laugh. "How could I forget it? You and Jorgie said it a million times a day."

Any refute I attempt to give is cut off when Hugo cocks a brow, daring me to deny his statement. I remain quiet, unable to negate his accusation since it is one hundred percent accurate. Jorgie used that statement numerous times a day from the age of ten until... last week. She breaks it out whenever she accuses me of denying my attraction to Hugo.

"You can run with a lie, but you can't hide from the truth. It will *always* catch up with you," Hugo says before setting me back onto my feet.

I smile at his statement, but my heart isn't into it. Hugo has never been one to hide anything—not his feelings, his mistakes, nor his body —so his comment is somewhat surprising for a man who's always been so forthright.

While peering at his downcast face, I wonder if it was just my life that altered the past six years. Perhaps Hugo's has as well.

A grin furls my lips when a second after the elevator door dings open, Hugo clutches my hand in his to guide me outside. I nod in thanks to the doorman when he pulls open the glass door for Hugo and me. Warm air hits my face when we merge onto the sidewalk. Even being late April, the conditions are warm since the heat from the day is trapped by the clouds still darkening the sky.

I crank my head to the left before shifting it to the right, seeking Hugo's truck. A decent number of people are still loitering on the sidewalks at this time of night, but Hugo's truck is nowhere in sight.

When I stray my eyes to his in silent questioning, his lips tug high, but he remains as quiet as a graveyard at midnight. A smile stretches across my face when a limousine pulls to the curb in front of us not even five seconds later. Excitement races through me, closely followed by confusion.

Why would he hire a limo?

"Come on," he says, dashing toward the idling stretched BMW.

We hustle through a throng of people, wanting to avoid the rain drizzling from the sky. I can't contain my childish giggle when I have to jog to keep up with Hugo's long strides. His lazy steps are the equivalent of me undertaking a marathon stride.

My eyes shoot in every direction when we enter the cab of the limousine, eager to absorb the dark, moody interior. You'd think the dark varnished wood, black leather seats, and the heaviness of the tint would give it a morose appearance, but it doesn't. It has the ambiance of seduction with intrigue deeply engrained in it.

"When did you win the lotto?"

Hugo's chuckle booms around the limousine. "It's one of the perks of my soon-to-be new job."

"Are they still hiring?"

He laughs even louder. "You don't seem to be doing bad for yourself, Ava," he says, motioning his head to my building shrinking into the background as the limo merges into traffic.

I smile while glancing at the place I call home. It's a beautiful building designed to withstand the test of time. It is at the forefront of architectural design, both elegant and masculine.

Other than the dream of one day owning my own dental practice, having a place to call home has always been one of my greatest wishes, so passing that goal before I turned twenty-five was a remarkable accomplishment I'll happily praise myself for achieving.

I turn my gaze back to Hugo. He appears to be watching the dense flow of traffic outside, but I'm not buying it. I can feel his scorching eyes on me.

"What really brought you to my apartment tonight?" I query, no longer able to assuage my curiosity about his spontaneous visit.

Before Hugo can reply, the driver advises that we've reached our destination.

"Wait here. I'll come around and get you."

I smile and nod at Hugo's request. As he darts around the car, my eyes absorb a long line of men and women wrapping halfway down the block and around the corner. Hundreds of well-dressed patrons are huddled together under the shopfront awnings, vainly trying to keep dry from the sprinkling of rain falling from the sky.

A middle-aged gentleman with a thick silver mustache rushes out of a set of double doors. The umbrella in his hand shelters Hugo from the rain when he opens the limousine door and offers me his hand. I press my thighs together before slithering out of the car, futilely attempting to maintain my modesty in the super short skirt Hugo chose for me to wear.

"Good evening, ma'am," greets the gentleman with the mustache.

"Hello," I reply shyly.

The crowd roars in protest when the large Māori bouncer at the club's door unlatches the red velvet rope and gestures for us to enter. My pulse increases with every step we take. Brushed metals, rich, dark woodgrain material, and hot, sweaty bodies writhing together to the latest club hits make a stimulating visual.

As the heat in the room elevates, so does Hugo's grip on my hand. When we reach the edge of the dance floor, he stands on the balls of his feet, extending to his full height. His head cranks to the right before switching it to the left, exposing he's seeking someone amongst the sweat-drenched clubgoers.

When his hunt fails to locate his target, he strides to the bar. Since he's still clutching my hand, I shadow closely behind. A broad smile stretches across my face the closer we get to the polished wood bar. It's like the cast from *Coyote Ugly* and *Cocktail* danced beneath the sheets and had a baby. Beautiful, scantily clad women perform a provocative dance routine on the bar top while equally attractive male bartenders flip and twist bottles of liquor into the air behind them.

Even though the scene could be construed as overly seductive, the beaming smiles on the bar staff's faces give it more a fun, playful vibe. Just the happiness projecting out of them forces a smile onto my face.

When the performance is over, Hugo seeks the attention of a female bartender serving customers halfway down the bar. "Tammy, is he still here?"

The beautiful blonde tilts her head to the side. "No, sorry. You missed him by ten minutes."

Hugo lifts his chin in thanks before he runs his fingers through his glorious, thick mane. My fingers twitch with jealousy. The music blaring from the speakers hanging from the ceiling cannot drown out the swear word that seeps from Hugo's lips when he drinks in someone at the end of the bar. My breathing halts when I spot who he's glaring at. *Rhys Tagget.*

Smiling, Rhys saunters our way. Just like Hugo, age has been gracious to him. His body is lean with a splattering of muscles in all the right places. Just from the way he walks, you can tell he'd be extraordinary in bed—and he knows it. He brazenly winks before leaning over the counter so his eyes can rake in my body. He studies me with as much attention as I bestow to him. Every inch of my skin flushes with heat from his vivid perusal.

When his eyes return to my face, he croons. "*C'est un plaisir de vous revoir*, Ava." His voice is rich, like Marvin Gaye whispering sweet serenades in my ear.

Masking my surprise that he remembers me, I accept the hand he offers in greeting. "Nice to see you again, too, Rhys." I try to make my voice sultry and mature, but it still comes out a little girly.

I flick my eyes to Hugo when his grip on my hand tightens. His jaw flexes as he watches the exchange between Rhys and me. "You remember Rhys, don't you, Hugo?"

A dangerous smirk etches on Hugo's mouth. "How could I forget your French tutor."

My heart gallops when a streak of possession forms in his vibrant blue eyes. I have no trouble recognizing that streak as I've worn it many times in the past when dealing with the troupe of women who always flounder around Hugo when he blesses them with his presence.

Even now, with Hugo's hand curled around mine, women circle him like a kettle of vultures, waiting for the opportunity to attack and devour their prey. Hugo's rugged looks attract a broad caliber of women from prima-donna Barbie dolls to a geeky professor.

My eyes revert from the skimpily dressed carcass-eaters when my name is spoken by a voice that still invades my dreams even after years of absence.

"Sorry, what did you say?"

Hugo flashes his photogenic smile that has the vultures hovering in closer. "I've got to run a quick errand. Any drinks you want are on the house."

"Okay, thanks," I say with a shy smile.

After placing my clutch onto the countertop, I accept the cocktail menu from a smiling Rhys.

Hugo paces one step away before he spins back around. "Do I need to remind you of the non-fraternization policy of this club?" he asks Rhys.

A smug grin morphs on Rhys's face before he raises his eyes to the clock hanging above the glass shelving behind the bar, which displays 11:50 p.m. "Nah, it's all good. In ten minutes, my shift is over, so that won't be a problem anymore."

Hugo's fists ball as his face lines with anger. "I'll be back in five."

His eyes drift to mine for the briefest second before he pivots on his heels and struts through the crowd. Yes, I said strut as Hugo Marshall has the perfect man-strut. The right amount of swagger, a little bit of attitude, and a glimmer in his eyes that tells you he brings the kind of trouble your mother warns you about, but you can't help but want.

And I want it bad.

EIGHT
HUGO

Irrational jealousy weighs down my chest as I make my way through the horde of people grinding together on the dance floor. It is irrational as I have no reason to be jealous.

Ava isn't mine.

She's never been mine.

She'll most likely never be mine.

But watching her go gaga over Rhys had the green monster on my shoulder rearing his ugly head. It was primed and ready to yank Rhys over the bar and pummel some sense into him. Maybe a good beat-down will remind him that Primal, the first stop on my club-hopping adventure for the night, has a very strict non-fraternization policy between staff and patrons. Isaac, the club's owner, doesn't believe in the concept of mixing business with pleasure.

Until tonight, I never paid much attention to Clause 23.1 in the employment contract I've been perusing the past two weeks. Although it's there printed in thick black ink, I never considered it set in stone. Now, I'll happily remind Rhys that any break in the terms of the contract he signed will make his employment with Holt Enterprises null and void.

I'll use any tactics I can to keep his hazel eyes off Ava.

Don't get me wrong, Rhys is a great guy. He's only working at Primal to occupy his time until he commences his internship as a surgeon at a local hospital in two weeks. He has the rare combination of both brains and good looks. If I were forced to pick a man for Ava to date, he'd be the first on my list, but even knowing that my illogical jealousy is building faster than Usain Bolt running the one-hundred-meter sprint.

What does that mean? You tell me, as I don't have a fucking clue.

By the time I make it through the mass of energetic partygoers grinding to the dub beats blaring out the speakers, the back of my shirt is drenched in sweat, and the five-minute timeframe I gave Rhys is already up. After racking my knuckles on the wooden door marked 'private' at the back of the club, I push down on the handle and sweep open the door. Isaac's head lifts from the paperwork scattered on his desk. He motions for me to enter as he continues with his conversation on an old, outdated phone.

Isaac is a young entrepreneur who would rival the likes of well-respected nightclub owners, Jeff Soffer and Noah Tepperberg. After our impromptu interview six weeks ago, I did a little snooping on Mr. Trust Fund. Even though Isaac is only twenty-two, he already owns a handful of nightclubs in the lower New York region.

His amassed fortune is rumored to be somewhere in the millions, but just like his personality, he keeps the actual value of his wealth well hidden. He's loaded and has looks that would make David Beckham pale in comparison, but what does Isaac lack that the others named above have? Some would say a heart.

Lucky for Isaac, I have a stellar knack for reading people. I can tell under his layers of darkness there's a good guy just waiting to be exposed. Since I've never been one to shy away from a challenge, I've made it my mission to unravel the mystery sitting in front of me.

Once Isaac finishes his phone call, he slides his ancient cell in his suit jacket's breast pocket and gestures for me to take a seat.

"You should consider updating your phone. Wearing a thousand-dollar suit looks tacky when you're carrying a brick in your pocket."

He tries to hide it, but I see his lips tug a little higher from my playful jibe. "Did you find Ava?"

Although Isaac is only twenty-two, his demeanor makes him appear a lot older than he is. He's well-respected amongst his peers and feared by his rivals.

I nod. "Yeah, but Tammy said Pencil Dick left ten minutes before we arrived."

This time, there's no doubt a smirk etches onto Isaac's mouth.

After leaving Jorgie's house, I headed out for a night on the town. Drinking and escaping in the music were the only plans I had for the night. Isaac sweetened the pot in our ongoing negotiations by offering me the use of a chauffeured limousine from his private collection and unlimited drinks in any of his clubs.

The first thing my eyes zoomed in on when I stepped out of the limo was the long line of patrons vying to be admitted into Isaac's latest club. The second thing I spotted was the guy who drove the first half of my night into the abyss of boredom.

Marvin failed to notice my furious glare burning a hole in the back of his head as his nose was buried deep into the neck of a girl who isn't even half the woman Ava is.

I initially considered interrupting Marvin and his date, but like all good books, the whole show-not-tell notion popped into my head. It was then I decided I was better off showing Ava that Marvin is a dawg rather than telling her.

After a quick word to Isaac, requesting him to grant Marvin and his date access to his capacity-filled club, I headed back to Rochdale. All my best-laid intentions flew out the window when Ava opened her front door in nothing but a tiny and completely hideous-looking bath towel. I didn't even attempt to put up a fight when my brain signaled for my eyes to run her barely covered body not once but twice.

It was a battle I would never win, so why fight it? Ava was wet, exposed, and had a doe-eyed look of innocence that forced X-rated thoughts into my head quicker than I could process them.

After a stern reprimand to myself that Ava wasn't some tail I was chasing for the night, my initial game plan kicked back into gear. I may have selected the shortest dress Ava had in her wardrobe for her to wear, but that wasn't just for my benefit. It was to show Marvin what he lost by fooling around.

I tried to keep my eyes off Ava's legs for the five-mile trip from her apartment to Primal, but they incessantly peered down at her smooth caramel thighs. I couldn't help it. I am a man, and Ava has a stellar pair of legs that would only look better if they were wrapped around my head.

I plop into the leather chair across from Isaac and rest my ankle on my opposite knee. "What's your surveillance like in this club?"

Isaac sinks back in his chair. "Lacking. That's why I'm knee-deep in negotiations to secure a manager of operations. Once I get him to stop pussyfooting around and sign on the dotted line, I'll have him organize new state-of-the-art surveillance to be installed in all six of my clubs."

My chuckle bounces off the walls of his office. That manager of operations he's referring to is me. The only reason I haven't 'signed on the dotted line' is because the final negotiation of my salary has yet to be discussed.

Although Isaac has advised on numerous occasions that I'll be well-compensated if I become a member of his empire, until I see a dollar amount written down, my signature will remain void on the one-hundred-plus page employee contract my advisor, aka Jorgie, is still combing through.

Isaac arches his brow. "Why, what were you after on the security tapes?"

"I figured since Ava missed the opportunity to see Marvin as the dawg he is in person, showing her on tape might be just as effective."

Isaac shakes his head. "I disagree. Seeing it for herself is one thing, but you forcing her to see it, that will just cause you trouble."

My brows meet my hairline. "I'm not the one who pretended I had to work then went out to sharpen my pencil with another lady's sharpener. How could this cause me any trouble?"

My brows become lost in my hair when Isaac's chuckle bellows through my ears. This is the first time I've heard his genuine laugh. "There are two people in the world, Hugo," Isaac says once his laughter dies down. "Healers and hurters. You, my friend, are a healer." He runs his index finger across his brow when he spots the odd expression on my face. "When Ava discovers what Marvin is up to, you'll help her get back on her feet. Until then, you have to wait."

"What if she never finds out?"

Isaac's brow arches high into the air. "Give her some credit. She's a woman, and they're very perceptive. For all you know, she could already be aware of his indiscretions." My eyes follow him when he stands. "Now, unless you're planning on signing on the dotted line, get the fuck out of my office. Some of us actually have to work for a living."

From the neutral expression on his face, I can't tell if he's being serious or not. Not wanting to push the boundaries of our newly developed bro-bond, I stand and make my way to the door. Just before I exit, I crank my neck to peer at Isaac. When he senses my presence, he stops riffling through the papers on his desk and lifts his dark gray eyes to mine. "Write a figure on a piece of paper... any figure. I don't care how much it is. Just write it down, and I'll sign the contract."

When someone hands you a golden ticket, grasp it with both hands. Don't make the ticket manufacturer jump through hoops to prove its authenticity.

Music blasts my eardrums when I exit Isaac's soundproof office. When I lift my gaze, the first thing I see is Ava's bright smile. My lips curl when her head flies back, and laughter spills out of her pouty lips.

Although I can't hear her laugh over the thumping music pumping out of the speakers, I can recall how angelic it sounds. Ava has a beautiful laugh, the type that shreds your soul. When I was younger, anytime I'd hear it, my good intentions would waver.

Tonight is no different.

I pop my head back into Isaac's office. "Can we change our meeting tomorrow morning to the afternoon?"

His brow arches high.

"She's just a friend," I say, my tone as unconvincing as the grin twitching my lips.

His gray eyes bore into mine. "Friends don't want to shred off other friend's panties."

"Who said I'd shred them? I'm more a pull-them-to-the-side type of guy," I reply with a saucy wink.

I just set a new record. I've made Isaac smirk more in the past ten minutes than I have the entire time I've known him.

"Although no official documents have been signed, I'm happy to accept your verbal confirmation on joining my empire, but with me returning to Ravenshoe tomorrow morning, the finer details of our agreement will need to wait until I return."

Noting a slight pang of hesitation in his voice, I ask. "Everything alright?"

He nods. "Everything is fine."

Never the talkative type, his attention returns to the documents on his desk. After jerking up my chin in farewell, I spin on my heels then leave his office.

The battle to keep myself in check ramps up the closer I amble to Ava. All my good intentions are misplaced when my eyes zoom in on the strappy heels on her tiny feet. When she crosses her legs, the scant hem of her dress edges closer to the pair of lace panties she sneakily slid on earlier. Dirty images of seeing her in *nothing* but those sexy heels and panties run rampant through my head.

After shaking off my improper thoughts, I prop my hip on the counter next to Ava. She flashes me a quick smile before continuing with her conversation. "So for nearly an hour, you watched two guys on stage perform *genitalia* origami?" She squeaks during the genitalia part of her sentence, and my brows shoot up into the air.

Rhys laughs a candid chuckle. "Yep. Seriously, it was the most hilarious thing I've ever seen." Ava's pupils widen when he adds, "I also learned a few new party tricks that night too." Although his tone alludes to cheekiness, an absurd rush of jealousy blackens my veins.

"Tucking your dick between your legs and pretending you have a vagina isn't a new party trick, Rhys. You've been pulling that move for years." That's my half-assed attempt at keeping the conversation lighthearted and out of jealous territory. It is a futile attempt, but it's all I've got.

Rhys's chuckle gains him the attention of a handful of women milling around the bar. "Hey, no breaking the locker room code. What happens in the locker room, stays in the—"

"Locker room," I fill in with a laugh as my eyes drift to Ava.

I can't help but smile at her flushed expression. For a woman whose off-the-Richter-scale sexiness has instigated a stream of improper thoughts to flood my mind nonstop for years, it astounds me that she can also pull off the virtue of a saint at the same time.

"Let me get washed up, then we'll get this show on the road," Rhys says with his gleaming eyes staring at Ava.

When Ava timidly nods, Rhys heads to the staff room at the back of the bar.

"Are you going somewhere?" I ask Ava once Rhys is out of earshot.

My eyes shoot up to Jazzy, the bartender, when she places an ice-cold bottle of beer in front of me. After smiling a thank you for her service, I return my eyes to Ava.

Her tongue delves out to lick her top lip before she mumbles, "Umm... I kind of agreed to participate in a dare." Her face grimaces as sweat beads on her forehead.

I arch my brow but remain quiet, waiting for her to elaborate. When we were younger, I never backed away from a dare, no matter how crude it was, but Ava wouldn't lick a droplet of rain off a leaf, so

I'm somewhat surprised she's decided to undertake a dare in the middle of a bustling nightclub.

Perhaps it isn't just Ava's shell that's altered the past few years.

Maybe her insides got revamped as well?

Ava stares into my eyes while smiling a furtive grin. "If I win, I'll be living on easy street. Ten freshly printed one-dollar bills will be lining my pockets."

I smirk and shake my head. "What happens if you lose?"

"Not a possibility," she blurts out.

Unable to maintain my eye contact, her eyes drift around our surroundings. I swig on my beer with the hope of simmering the heat coursing through my body from watching her sexy-as-fuck lips wrap around the straw of her drink. Her lips are why fantasies were created. And I've fantasied about them in more ways than what could be classed as acceptable the past ten years. In case you're wondering, my thoughts have been anything but pure.

When Ava lowers her cocktail, I thrust my gigantic head into her peripheral vision. "If you lose?" I ask again.

She mumbles something under her breath, but she's so quiet, I can't hear a word she's speaking.

I arch my brow. "What?"

"I have to go on a date with Rhys," she mumbles weakly.

"What?"

I heard what she said, but the green-eyed monster missed it, and he's demanding for her to repeat it.

Her shoulders square as her chin jerks up. "I have to go on a date with Rhys," she says more forcefully. As her brow arches, her eyes lock with mine. "Do you have a problem with that?"

Loving the whip of feistiness in her voice, my lips twitch as I struggle to repress a smile. "Nope, no problem."

Her chin dips, then her shoulders sag.

I angle my head to the side and peer into her downcast eyes. "Why would there be a problem? You said there's no possibility of you losing, so unless you're going to recant your statement, I've got nothing to worry about."

She tries to hide her smile, but the whites of her teeth peek out the sides of her cocktail glass. Cringing, she downs the rest of her drink in quick succession. When I follow her fretful gaze, I spot Rhys sauntering toward us. His focus remains steadfast on Ava as he moves through a group of women vying for his attention. Jealousy places a stranglehold on my throat when I drink in the eagerness of his strides. He looks like a kid in a toy store who's been told he can pick any toy he wants.

His choice is a pretty little doll named Ava.

"You ready?" he questions while waggling his overly manicured brows at Ava.

After expelling a deep breath, Ava stands to her feet then runs her sweaty palms down her dress. The frown on her face remains firm as she thrusts her clutch into my chest. "Can you save my seat?"

Nodding, I sit on her barstool and swivel to face the crowd. My back molars grind together when Rhys and Ava walk toward the dance floor hand in hand. When they reach the edge of the wood-lined space, Rhys releases Ava's hand and heads for the DJ's booth at the side.

Maverick, the DJ, smiles a beaming grin when Rhys points to Ava nervously fidgeting on the edge of the dance floor. When "Scream and Shout" by Will.i.am and Britney Spears mellows, a new, very familiar beat beams out of the speakers.

My eyes snap to Ava, shocked. Her appearance is just as fretful, and her face pales. After releasing a big breath, she rolls her shoulders and loosens her toughened stance.

No way, the old Ava would never be brave enough to do this.

When Rhys moves toward her, bopping along to the beat of the music, a cock-twitching smile stretches across Ava's face. As the song progresses, the color on her face returns, and confidence beams in her eyes.

I spit out my beer when the song hits the chorus, and Ava starts ponying on the spot.

Oh, yeah, she's going there.

I slap my hand over my mouth, fighting in vain to conceal my chuckle when Ava lassos her arm in the air. The crowd surrounding the dance floor congregates closer to Ava when her Gangnam-style dance moves rapidly gain her the attention of everyone under the age of twenty-one.

I stand from my chair then stretch to my full height when the crowd circling Ava blocks my view of her hideous yet somehow arousing dance moves. Side-splitting laughter tears from my lips when she places her hand on her cocked hip and impersonates PSY's famous side-step to perfection. Mine and numerous other male eyes dart down to the globes of her ass when she bends over to flick her knee.

By the time her dance solo is finished, I have tears streaming down my face and a hard-on my trousers cannot contain. I've also smiled more the past three minutes than I have the previous two years. And I swear to God, I've never been so fucking hard.

If Ava has enough gall to get up in front of hundreds of people and dance like nobody is watching, imagine what she'd be like beneath the sheets? Bedding a woman who's not only confident in her skin but also willing to try new things would be a riveting experience.

Just the thought of taking Ava out of her comfort zone has my cock twitching.

After curtsying to the wolf-whistling crowd, Ava gathers her ten one-dollar bills from Rhys and saunters back my way. Her face is flushed, her nape is dripping with sweat, and she has a knock-your-socks-off smile plastered across her face.

"I seriously didn't think you'd do it," says Rhys, jogging to catch up with her.

My teeth grit when he wraps his arm around her shoulders and pulls her into his side.

"I told you I knew all the moves."

Even though she's talking to Rhys, her eyes remain steadfast on mine.

"Yeah, but most girls are all talk. You followed through. That's a rare find these days."

Nearly as rare as your teeth still being in your mouth, I gabble to myself.

Rhys signals for a bartender. "Tammy, another piña colada for Ava, and I'll have a double of vodka."

Ava plops into the vacant barstool next to me. "I'm loaded." She fans the one-dollar bills in the air like they have extra zeroes written on them.

"Tuck them into your pocket because you'll need them when I show you how real people dance."

She props her elbows on the bar and tilts to my side. "Is that a challenge I hear seeping from your lips, Mr. Marshall?"

Losing the ability to keep myself in check, I lean in intimately close to her side. I'm so close, her sugary sweet smell engulfs my senses, making my cock even stiffer. "That's not a challenge, baby. That's a sure-fire promise."

The sweat slicking my body thickens when the deep richness of Hugo's voice taunts me. Normally, I'd never get up and shake my tushy in front of strangers, but the two piña coladas I downed while waiting for Hugo to run his errand made me a little bolder than normal.

In all honesty, when Rhys configured the bet, stating if I lost, I had to go on a date with him, I had every intention of driving that bet straight off the bridge and into a freezing cold lake. Many women before me have invented far worse ruses to secure a date with him, but my best-laid plans went to poop when Hugo sauntered back to join us at the bar.

Just like the past ten years of my life, every time I get a grasp on my childish crush, Hugo comes crashing back into my life with an almighty bang and throws a wrench into the works. Flirty one-liners, drunken kisses, and the hope that one day he'd see me as more than just his little sister's best friend kept me dangling on the line, waiting patiently for an opportunity to prove my worth.

Rhys's eyes drift between Hugo and me as he accepts the freshly prepared piña colada from Tammy. When his face becomes washed with confusion, I realize how intimately close Hugo and I are sitting.

I scoot to the edge of my chair before accepting the cocktail glass from Rhys. "Thank you," I praise with a smile.

My heart stops beating when Hugo adjusts his position so the space between us is even more minuscule than it was before. The hairs on the nape of my neck spike when the blast of his hot breath flutters my neckline.

Curtly nodding, Rhys's lips quirk as his eyes dart to the watch on his wrist. "Oh, shit, look at the time. I forgot I had a... umm... appointment tonight." He downs his double vodka before placing his glass on the countertop then shifts on his feet to face me. "I'm sorry I have to dare and run, Ava, but I completely forgot about the... appointment."

"That's okay. It was great seeing you again." I press a quick kiss on his cheek. "If you're ever after a dance-off partner, look me up."

Smiling, he gives me a quick hug. "If things here cool down, I'll be sure to take you up on that offer," he whispers into my ear. Turning his attention to Hugo, he says, "I guess I'll be seeing you around?" He seems hesitant, making me unsure if his statement is a question or an observation.

Hugo's eyes snap to mine when Rhys mutters something in his ear. After nodding, Hugo pats Rhys on the back and gives him a brief man hug.

The fake smile burning my cheeks sags the instant Rhys scurries out the double doors of the club as quickly as his lean legs can take him. I flop into an empty barstool and chew on the straw in my drink.

"It was probably your Gangnam dance moves that scared him away," I grumble to myself.

My suspicions are confirmed when a broad grin stretches across Hugo's face. I huff before pulling the straw out of my drink to throw it at his mocking face. I smile when it hits its mark on his left cheek.

"Alright, let's just get this done and dusted, then we can move on. I'm an idiot. I made a fool out of myself to ensure I wasn't forced to go on a date with a man most women would give their left lung for." *All so I could continue my non-date with a man who never gives me the time of day unless he's drunk.*

This, ladies and gentlemen, is a prime example of why I'm still single.

Hugo's brows scrunch. "Why did you give up the opportunity for a date with a guy most women would give their left lung for?"

Because he's not the one I want. He isn't the one who dangles a carrot in front of my face and dares me not to touch it. He's not the one who makes me strive to make my fantasies a reality. And he's also not the one who sets my pulse racing just from hearing his laugh.

Those honors have always solely belonged to Hugo.

Instead of saying what I really feel, I shrug. "I'm not really looking for any companions right now," I fib.

Hugo's lips set into a hard line. "Because of Marvin?"

I try to hide the cringe crossing my face, but Hugo is incredibly perceptive. He notices it before I get the chance to suffocate it.

"Marvin and I aren't dating," I blurt out, mimicking his denial of dating Victoria earlier.

Hugo's lips twist, and he eyes me with curiosity but remains quiet. Marvin and I have been on a handful of *dates.* I use the term *dates* lightly as they were *nothing* to call home about. It was like two work acquaintances decided to hold an informal meeting in a restaurant instead of a boardroom.

Our conversation never veered away from work, and one peck on the cheek is the closest contact we've had the past two weeks. He only came to Jorgie's house for dinner tonight because I accidentally let slip that Hugo was going to be there.

On that revelation, Marvin invited himself, rationalizing that he and Hugo were friends in high school, and it would be a great opportunity for them to catch up. It was only after witnessing the testosterone-riddled staredown between Marvin and Hugo on Jorgie's porch did I realize three things.

Marvin and Hugo have *never* been friends.

Marvin wants to push our *friendship* to a level I'm not comfortable with.

And, last but not at all least...

Marvin has *way* too many similarities to my father.

Seeing the warning signs flash in front of my eyes, I leaned into Jorgie's ear and whispered that I was going to 'weed the garden' the instant I got home. When she slid her index finger under her nose, signaling she understood my coded statement, I fled for my Uber without a backward glance.

I was still in the process of working out how to inform Marvin of my decision when Hugo arrived on my doorstep. As much as Marvin demanding that I leave Jorgie's house irked me, I must tread carefully when it comes to him. I'm already struggling to pay my mortgage as it is without adding exorbitant tuition fees into the mix.

When I agreed to become a partner at Gardner and Sons, part of my contract was that they were to pay for the last two years of my college fees. If that contract slips from my grasp before I officially take my position in a year, I'll be required to pay back any installments they paid on my behalf. Since that is a debt I cannot incur, I will tread cautiously when it comes to Marvin.

After a few moments of uncomfortable silence, I raise my eyes to Hugo. His lips twist as his panty-combusting eyes scorch my skin. His heavy-hooded gaze has desire surging through my veins and flooding my nether regions.

"Now that we have that out of the way, can we continue with our night?" I squeak out, fighting the urge to squirm.

I lift my cocktail glass to my mouth to hide my flushed cheeks. My eyes widen when Hugo places his hand on the base of the glass and tilts it higher. My nose hairs tingle when the freezing cold liquid slides down my throat to settle in my flipping stomach. Once all the scrumptious but bitterly cold goodness is consumed, Hugo removes the glass from my grasp and places it on the countertop.

After a quiet word with a female bartender, he grips my hand in his and stalks toward the people cavorting on the wooden dance floor. Halfway there, a sharp pain twinges through my brain. I dig my heels into the plush carpet and shoot my spare hand to my temple.

Hugo angles his head to the side and eyes me curiously.

"Brain freeze," I cringe.

"Blow hot air on your nose," he instructs, his words muffled by a breathless chuckle.

Opening one of my squinted eyes, I glare at him. "What?"

Apparently, my ability to think straight around him doesn't just hamper my astuteness.

It also affects my hearing.

He smirks a heart-fluttering smile. "Blow hot air onto your nose."

A smile tugs on my lips when he demonstrates his instruction by puckering out his plump lips and fanning his nose with his breaths. Deciding I can't look any more ludicrous than I already have tonight, I blow hot air onto the tip of my nose.

The more I blow, the more my brows lower.

"I can't believe that actually works," I say once the pain of a knife digging into my skull vanishes. "How did you know that?"

Hugo grins. "You're not the only one with cool party tricks," he says with a bold wink.

"You thought my dancing was cool?"

"Not at all," he replies, his tone unapologetic.

My bottom lip drops into a pout. Heat blemishes my body from the tips of my toes to the top of my head when his index finger twangs my protruding lip.

As I draw my lip back in, he says, "It was a little dorky and *totally* uncool, but every person in this club under the age of twenty-one is looking at you like Beyoncé just graced them with her presence."

My nervous eyes peer around the space. Not quite everyone, but many young adults with an 'Under-21' illuminated band secured on their wrists are gawking at me. A few are smiling, a handful are laughing, and a group of males is winking while suggestively gyrating their hips.

Their cheeky flirting halts the instant they cop the wrath of Hugo's firm glare.

My brain freeze turns into a rush of giddiness when Hugo yanks me in close to his body so my chest is flush with his. "Are you ready to learn one of my party tricks?"

Not giving me a chance to reply, he dips the top half of my body then rolls his hips. I stumble, unsteady on my feet, when he flips me back up and swings his hips in rhythm to the music thumping around us. Unlike many men before him, Hugo's dance moves aren't robotic and stiff but uninhibited and fluid. *Captivating.* He moves in a way that shows how well in tune he is with his own body.

Although we hung out a lot when we were younger, we've never danced like this. The vibe at a club has never failed to excite me. Tonight is no different, but it is even more energetic dancing with Hugo. I've dreamed of nights like this, so I am tempted to pinch myself to make sure I'm not dreaming.

When Hugo pulls me in closer, I grip his shoulders before getting lost in the magic of dancing with a guy whose moves could rival the likes of Channing Tatum. In a haze of pussy tingles and shaky steps, we're quickly swamped by a mass of writhing bodies on the dance floor. The crowd mingling around us thumps with bountiful energy, spurring the excitement trickling through my veins. The intoxicating smell of sweat on heated skins filters through my nose.

When I lift my eyes, the music fades to a hushed buzz. With the seductive scent mingling in the air and Hugo's heavy-lidded eyes locked on mine, my libido hits a previously unventured level. Hugo bands his arms around my waist, then we spend the next three songs dancing as if there are no clothes between us. The tension is static, like a storm brewing on the horizon, full of electric energy just waiting to combust.

When the music switches to a higher tempo beat, Hugo releases me from his grasp and takes a step back. My body screams in protest about the loss of his contact, but my attention remains focused on him.

He dances like he's auditioning for the *Magic Mike* sequel. If it weren't for the smell of sweat in the air from the mass of bodies dancing in the one space, I would have sworn I had ordered a personal strip-a-gram. Except, unfortunately, this stripper keeps his clothes on.

Upon catching my lust-filled gaze, Hugo's eyes roam my face before they scan my body. When his gaze returns to mine, my breath hitches. His pupils are wide, his eyes have darkened, and the undeniable glimmer of lust is beaming from them.

Like they could get any more seductive his dance moves become more provocative and entrancing. Pussy-thumping good. Fighting the urge to dig the dollar bills out of my pocket and tuck them into the waistband of his jeans, I close my eyes, raise my arms into the air, and let the music overtake me.

Over time, the air grows thick with humidity as the mass of bodies intermingles. Sweat glistens my skin, and my lips are parched even with downing fruity cocktails like they're cans of soda. For the past hour, the bar staff kept Hugo's and my supply of alcohol flowing like water from a tap.

Before my body could announce its thirst, a waitress arrived with a thirst-quenching drink. I feel like a celebrity attending a ritzy after-party. My every whim is being taken care of without a single word seeping from my lips. Blood teems through my veins at a rapid pace, and my head is fuzzy with both the infusion of alcohol and adrenaline. Even with a horde of people bumping into me, I can't wipe the smile off my face. I'm loving every single moment of my newfound freedom.

My grin doubles when my eyes lock with Hugo. His hair is messy and wet from the dampness suffocating the air. His eyes are snapped shut, and his plump lips are parted. It's a sexually gratifying visual that causes a cool slickness to form between my legs. As bolts of electricity spark in my womb, I'm unexpectedly grasped from behind and yanked deeper into the dense crowd.

A body enveloping my back and the roll of a man's hips have my eyes widening. Panic about being mauled by a stranger, my body stiffens, and my pupils dilate. I snap my eyes down when my dance partner's hands slither across my stomach before inching toward my erratically beating chest.

I clutch his wrists, securing them onto my hips before he can grope my breasts. His alcohol-laced breath hammers my senses when he slurs, "You're so fucking beautiful."

"Th-th-thank you," I stutter while attempting to maneuver myself out of his firm clutch.

Bile scorches the back of my throat when his fingers dig into my right hip as he strengthens his hold. Dizziness plagues me when his erection pokes my backside, and his hands recommence their wander back to my chest. My stomach swirls from the excessive sways as he grinds against me.

I stab my nails into his hands, clawing to get away from him. When my attack fails to stop his unwanted groping, my unnerved gaze seeks assistance. My breathing labors when I spot Hugo sidestepping numerous clubgoers as he rushes my way. His fists are clenched, his face is taut with anger, and his steps are urgent.

Relief engulfs me when he pulls me into his chest with one hand while the other peels the unnamed dance partner off my back. His stealth moves have my feet leaving the floor and my assailant landing on his ass with an almighty thump.

The ear-splitting music blaring out of the speakers is unable to drown out the mad beat of Hugo's heart when he lays a boot into my aggressor. The blood roaring through his body is so thick, the veins in his neck bulge as he steps over the man lying on the floor, cradling his stomach.

His fast and furious steps don't falter until we reach a hidden nook between a mirrored wall and an office door at the side of the club.

When I peel my head off his chest, wanting to express my gratitude for his assistance, my words entomb in my throat. His gaze is predatory and full to the brim with silent rage.

My eyes rocket to the side when a manly voice asks, "Is she okay?"

My brows stitch as my eyes scan the face of a man I swear I've seen before. Although he's not as built as Hugo, his impressive frame fills his tailored suit. His hair is dark and well-kept, his face is clean-shaven, and he has charmingly handsome good looks that would set most girls' hearts racing, but his angry scowl and unapproachable demeanor have my insides quaking more with fear than sexual interest.

"She will be." Hugo places me onto my feet. The strobing lights of the club flicker in his eyes as his narrowed gaze dances between mine. "Stay here. I'll be back in a minute."

Air whips the hair off my neck when he abruptly spins on his heels. Suddenly, the suit-clad gentleman's hand darts out to seize Hugo's elbow. Knuckles popping resonate in the eerie quiet of the alcove when Hugo clenches his fists. The veins on his exposed biceps throb when he glares at the unnamed man.

"Look after her. I'll take out the trash." The suit-clad man's tone is stern and authoritative.

Not waiting for Hugo to reply, he relinquishes Hugo's elbow and heads in the direction we just left. Sensing his unnerving composure, the crowd parts like the Red Sea. The last thing I see before my vision is filled with Hugo's fury-riddled face is the suit-wearing gentleman yanking my assailant off the floor by the scruff of his rumpled shirt.

While tucking a stray tress of my hair behind my ear, Hugo's eyes run over my face and body, vigorously assessing every inch of my sweat-slicked skin. "Are you okay?" he asks after finishing his assessment.

I nod. "Yes, thank you." My words come out breathless. My breathlessness isn't caused by my near attack. It's from how close he is standing to me. We're standing so close my breaths rebound off his mouth before blasting my lips with a fruity cocktail scent.

"Did he hurt you? Are you injured?"

I shake my head. "No. You got there before he had the chance."

"I should have gotten there faster."

My heart pains from the guilt clouding his eyes. The muscle in his jaw quivers when I run my thumb over the heavy groove in the middle of his eyes, trying to smooth the regret dampening the mischievous spark that typically fires in his vibrant eyes.

"I'm fine, Hugo. Truly, I am." I keep my tone spirited, desperately endeavoring to lighten the mood. I fist his long-sleeve shirt in my hand. "I've never been better."

I stare into his eyes so he can see the openness being relayed by mine. Tonight is the first time I've ever truly let go. The awkward teenage girl who sat in the corner and watched everyone else have fun would have never gotten up and shook her tuchus in front of hundreds of people.

I've never danced like there would be no repercussion in the morning because normally there would have been. Not from my peers but from my father. It wouldn't matter if I forgot to say "thank you" after already saying "please," he would have heard about it, and I would have been reprimanded for it. Everything I did, no matter how minute, was monitored and reported back to him, but tonight— tonight I was free. I could finally extend my wings.

Upon noticing Hugo's demeanor slipping back onto common ground, I continue with my ploy of easing his uncalled-for guilt. "I guess these are the consequences of impersonating your stripper moves."

His lips curve into an unsure grin. It isn't his usual impish smile, but I'll take anything I can get. "Stripper moves?"

"Yes," I say with a laugh. "I was waiting for hidden cameras to jump out from behind the curtains and say 'surprise, you're on hidden stripper cam.'"

As my eyes drift over Hugo's fetching face, the concern marring it changes to a more relaxed expression. My lips pucker as I eye him with fake curiosity. "Have you been harboring secrets from me?"

His brows furrow, and he swallows harshly.

"Because no white man should have moves like that."

Energy surges through my body when his chuckle booms through my ears. I smile, loving that I can still switch his mood from infuriating to playful in under thirty seconds. Once his laughter dies down, he takes a step closer, entrapping me in the tiny alcove with his impressive body. A whimper ripples from my lips when the coolness of the mirrored wall refreshes my inflamed skin.

All playfulness stops, and a new type of friskiness impinges the air when his hankering eyes lock with mine. "If I were a stripper, wouldn't that mean I should have been removing my clothes?"

My eyes remain locked with his, but I don't speak. *I can't.* I can barely breathe, much less articulate a response.

"Is that what you want, Ava?" He stares at me with wild eyes, his chest rising and falling with every breath he takes. "Do you want me to dance for you... *naked?*"

I stare into his lusty eyes. "I have the dollar bills for it."

My pupils widen as my mouth gapes, shocked by my audacity. Any apologies for my inappropriate remark are crammed back into my throat when the suit-wearing gentleman returns to stand next to us. My dropped jaw gains leverage when the mysterious stranger pulls a handkerchief from the breast pocket of his jacket so he can remove smears of blood from his swollen, red knuckles.

Once the evidence of a fight has been removed from his hands, his eyes lock with mine. "I hope the puerile actions of one doesn't deter you from visiting my clubs in the future. I can assure you that that type of foolhardiness will never be acceptable in any of my clubs."

I shrug. "I guess it's part and parcel of spending your night out drinking and dancing."

He shakes his head. "Not in my establishments, it isn't." Even though his tone is stern, his eyes relay his genuine concern. After shifting his dark eyes to Hugo, he asks, "Are we good?"

Hugo nods. "We're good."

"Good." He stuffs his hands into the pockets of his trousers before sauntering through a wooden door at the side of the mirrored wall.

When he enters the office, I divert my focus to Hugo. "Who was that?"

He grins a full-toothed smile. "That's my new boss."

My head ricochets to the office door. "That's your *boss*?"

If I had to guess, I'd say the suit-clad gentleman would be my age, if not a little younger. Although he looks impressive in his expensive designer threads, and his allure presents as a fierce man, his eyes give away his true self. Even guarded, they show that beyond his tough exterior is a young man trying to find his place in the world.

How do I know this? Because Hugo's eyes have the exact same appearance.

My attention returns to Hugo when his finger brushes my cheekbone. Feverish heat follows his index finger as it trails down my neck and along my collarbone before stopping at the swell of my breasts peeking out of my strapless dress. The tempo of my breaths quickens when his eyes lift and lock with mine. Even though he's been drinking, his gaze is vivid and clear. Almost readable.

I pull in a slow, shaky breath when he asks, "Do you want to get out of here?" The provocative tone in his words has butterflies fluttering in my stomach.

Stuck in the trance he forever instigates, I nod.

TEN

AVA

Smiling at my agreeing gesture, Hugo entwines his fingers with mine.

"C-can I use the bathroom first?" I catch my eye roll halfway through from the dimness of my voice. All the work I've done the past six months transforming myself into an independent, strong woman becomes null and void after one glance into Hugo's eyes.

Although I'm certain the throb between my legs is more associated with the gleam in Hugo's eyes than the fact I've downed half a dozen cocktails in quick succession, it was engrained in me from a young age to use the restroom before traveling in any mode of transportation. It wouldn't matter if we were driving to the corner store or halfway across the country, my father demanded I use the washroom before we left. He even went as far as to check the vanity sink was wet before I could exit the bathroom.

Remaining quiet, Hugo guides me out of the safety of the alcove with his hand on the curve of my lower back. The earlier feeling of celebrity-ism catapults to a new level when his eyes dart in all directions. He looks like a bodyguard protecting his target from potential threats. His protective stance is so convincing, numerous cell phones capture the 'celebrity' amongst them.

The blinding lights of camera flashes impede my vision as we make our way through the writhing bodies mingling around the vast space. The energy bouncing off the crowd is amazing, but it has nothing on the buzz of energy dashing through me from Hugo's mildest touch. It is intense and electrifying.

My face scrunches when I notice the long line waiting to use the women's restroom. It's nearly as long as the queue outside of the club. My curiosity piques when Hugo walks past the line and turns down a corridor on our left.

While opening a door to reveal a ladies' restroom, he mutters, "Employee perks."

Snubbing the curious glare of two ladies washing their hands in the vanity, I hurry into a vacant stall, lift the seat, then sit down. I've only just finished my business when a rowdy group of women enter the washroom via the regular entrance.

"I can't believe her damsel-in-distress ploy actually worked. Some women are so desperate."

A volley of giggles bounces off the elegantly designed washroom walls.

"Help me! Help me! A naughty man wants to touch me."

Curious as to whom they're talking about, I peer through the crack of the stall door. From this angle, I can only see the back of three women standing in front of a dark-framed mirror shackled to the wall—two blondes and one brunette.

"Did you see the hideous shoes she was wearing?" the blonde in the middle asks, suppressing a gag.

The blonde on the left applies lipstick to her already heavily coated mouth. "The shoes have nothing on that revolting dress. She looks like she's going to a funeral. Blah and bland," she says before kissing the edge of the mirror.

When she pulls away from the mirror now bearing her big red lipstick stain, I catch sight of her reflection in the mirror. Although

I'm certain I've seen her before, I have misplaced her name. "You can't buy style," she snickers.

"I thought she looked cute," squeaks out the brunette on the right.

My breath catches in my throat when the head of the blonde in the middle snaps to the side. I recognize that sneering profile. It is the Queen of Bitches herself—Victoria Avenke.

"Cute? You thought she looked cute?" Victoria sneers.

The brunette runs her hands down her light blue pleated skirt before timidly nodding. "I don't think she's a threat to you, Vicky. They're most likely just here as friends."

"Of course, they're here as friends! What else would they be here as?" Victoria's angry snarl reverberates off the walls.

The brunette swallows harshly when Victoria steps closer to her. "Are you trying to say there's a possibility they could be more than friends?"

The brunette shakes her head as the scent of fear permeates the air. "N-n-no. Of course, they're only friends. J-j-just friends. She's his sister's best friend."

Victoria's manicured brow arches high into the air. "Exactly. Tonight was nothing but a pity date to keep in his sister's good graces." My heart plummets into my stomach when she adds, "It wouldn't matter how many drinks he's had. A man like Hugo would never be interested in a woman like Ava Westcott." Her lips form a snarl when she strangles out my name.

My eyes shoot down to my strappy heeled shoes. Although not as expensive as some pairs I've seen in fancy boutique stores, these shoes still cost me eighty dollars. That's a lot of money for one pair of shoes. Even with eating ramen noodles for a week, they were worth the sacrifice. They're my favorite pair. With their wide heel and cushioned insoles, I can dance for hours and never get a blister.

As for my bland dress, you can't go wrong with a classic LBD. Sophisticated, yet classy. Comfortable, yet sexy.

Well, I thought that was the case.

My attention is pulled to the trio of women when a dark shadow fills the gap in the door. A vein in my neck thrums when a pair of apologetic eyes peer at me through the crack. The only brunette in the trio offers me a contrite smile before following Victoria and the other blonde out of the washroom.

Did she know I was here all along?

After ensuring the coast is clear, I flush the toilet and head for the vanity to wash my hands. When I pick up a paper towel from the countertop, I wince when I look in the mirror. My hair is a damp, frizzy mess clinging to my sweat-drenched neck, my eyes are wide, and the small splattering of mascara I put on before leaving my apartment has oozed off my lashes and is now smeared under my eyes.

Proof that what Victoria said is true reflects back at me.

After wetting the paper towel, I run it under my eyes while muttering personal insecurities to myself. Most follow the same tune —there's no possibility a man with panty-wetting looks like Hugo would ever be interested in someone like me. Although I could have sworn earlier, there was a spark of attraction between us. The flirty banter, the suggestive dance moves, the streak of possession in his eyes. What was that all about if it was just a pity date?

After throwing the crumpled paper towel into the waste receptacle and ignoring the pain in my heart, I make my way out of the bathroom. When the door snaps shut behind me, I find Hugo standing at the side, clutching my purse in his hand. His shoulder is propped against the wall, and he appears deep in thought.

When he notices me approaching, his expression changes from overwrought to easygoing. His eyes track my body as he pushes off the wall and strides toward me. When he stops in front of me, he stares at me, wide-eyed and confused. The anxiousness in his eyes somehow calms me. The type of concern they're reflecting isn't something that can be manufactured on a whim. It is genuine and honest, making me realize even if Hugo only ever classes me as a friend, it will be enough.

"Are you ready?" The smooth rasp of his question smothers any leftover unease jittering my stomach.

"Yes," I reply, nodding.

When he laces his fingers with mine, a jolt of energy surges up my arm. There's no way my brain is making this stuff up. That was electrifying!

The wind whips my hair off my neck when we exit the club's double doors. While gathering my hair, I spot the limousine from earlier idling at the curb. The gentleman with the thick silver mustache greets me with a smile as he opens the back passenger door for me to enter.

"Thank you," I say graciously.

The skin on my thighs clings to the coolness of the leather material as I slide across the bench seat. On the drive back to my apartment, I catch sight of Hugo's impassive face in the tinted windows, but for most of the drive, his thoughts remain elsewhere.

"I could have taken an Uber if you wanted to stay," I say, no longer able to stand the frustrating silence between us.

His eyes turn from the darkened night to me. "It's fine, Ava. I want to make sure you get home safely."

"You can drop me off and head straight back out," I say with a shrug. "If you want."

When my suggestion is greeted with silence, I cross my arms and sink deeper into the leather seat. With Hugo's grim mood, anyone would swear it was his ego that copped a beating in the washroom, not mine.

Unable to comprehend the tension suffocating the air, I mumble, "Or you could just sit there and continue sulking like a five-year-old."

The flash of a smirk freezes my heart. "Really? I'm sulking like a five-year-old?"

"Uh-huh," I huff out with a nod. "You have the same pouty-face look you had when the waiter wouldn't let you order blueberry pancakes as your main course at Jorgie's sixteenth birthday celebration."

He scoffs. "Name one restaurant that stops serving breakfast at eleven in the morning!"

"That one," I retort with a roll of my eyes.

My lips twitch as I try to hold in my smile from his shocked expression. Hugo has a fascination with breakfast foods. His love is so strong he tried to order pancakes for dinner when we went to a fancy restaurant for Jorgie's sixteenth birthday.

He threw a tantrum like a kindergarten student when the male waiter told him the breakfast menu closed at eleven. The only thing that stopped his immature gripe was my suggestion that I could make him a double batch the following Sunday. When he agreed, I did exactly that for the next two years.

During my high school years, every Sunday morning, my father begrudgingly dropped me off at the Marshall residence on our way home from church. Because we attended the dawn service, most of the Marshall family members were still sleeping when I arrived at eight. Everyone except Mrs. Marshall.

For the first few weeks, our talks were based on school and what happened at church that morning, but as the weeks went on, our conversations grew to a wide variety of topics, including Hugo's fascination with anything relating to breakfast.

It was Mrs. Marshall who taught me how to make blueberry pancakes, homemade hash browns, and eggs Benedict. Although I've never told her this, Sunday mornings were the highlight of my week.

I sling my eyes to Hugo. The surly mood fettering his face has vanished, and sparks of the beloved old Hugo have fired in his eyes. "How long has it been since you've gone home for Sunday brunch?"

He runs his hand down his face. "Not since my first tour in Afghanistan."

"If you're not busy, you should come next weekend," I suggest. "Then you can test out Helen's rendition of scrambled eggs."

A chuckle escapes my lips when Hugo grimaces. Helen, Hugo's older sister, is brilliant at anything she does, except cooking. She's the spitting image of Hugo's mother with cascading blonde hair and vibrant green eyes, but that's as far as the similarities go. She didn't get Mrs. Marshall's cooking skills or nurturing nature.

"Are you going to be there?" Hugo questions.

Smiling, I nod. "Yes. I wouldn't miss it for the world."

My heart flips when he says, "Alright. If you promise to make me a double batch of your famous blueberry pancakes, I'll be there bright and early next Sunday."

Nodding, I bite the inside of my cheek, battling to keep my excitement from bursting out the seams. My eagerness intensifies when the limo pulls up in front of my building, and Hugo rushes around the hood to open my door for me. I can't wipe the excitement off my face when he intertwines our fingers again so he can walk me into my apartment building.

Patty, the seventy-three-year-old part-time night watchman, greets me with a dip of his hat and a broad grin. "Good morning, Ms. Westcott. No goodies today?"

I smile. "Morning, Patty. I think three in the morning is a little early for biscuits and gravy."

My cheeks inflame with heat when he replies, "It's never too early for a little bit of sweetness," as his glistening eyes dance between Hugo and me.

After entering the elevator, I spin on my heels and peer into Patty's worldly eyes. "I'll be here for our date at eleven like I always am."

"Yes, ma'am," he replies with a smile just as the elevator doors snap shut.

When quiet snickering echoes in the elevator, I glance over to Hugo. His brow is arched high in a sarcastic, jeering way.

"Hey, don't let that wrinkled skin fool you. In that seventy-three-year-old shell is a twenty-five-year-old man dying to recapture his youth. Wasn't it you who said dating someone with experience comes with its advantages?"

Ignoring the bitter taste in the back of my throat, I relish Hugo's hearty chuckle for the second time tonight. His laughter is so bois- terous it drowns out the ping of the elevator when it announces its arrival at my floor. I become lightheaded when he entangles his fingers with mine, and we stroll toward my apartment. Every step we take has my heart rate increasing and my palms sweating.

When we reach my front door, I place the key into the lock before turning to face Hugo. "Did you want to come in?"

The most panty-drenching visual I've ever seen transpires when he rubs the nape of his neck while biting on his lower lip. *There's nothing sexier in the world than a grown man biting his lip.* He shoves his hands into his jeans pocket as his eyes scan my face for several heart-clutching seconds. "I really should go. It's late and... I've got a thing in the morning... and you've got your *date* with Patty..." His ramblings simmer as he runs out of excuses to leave.

"Okay," I mumble. Putting the feeling of rejection to the side, I say, "Thanks for everything. I had a lot of fun tonight."

Even though I still have no clue why he suddenly decided to hang out, I enjoyed our time together. It is like the past six years never happened. I'm once again a teenage girl fawning over the college quarterback.

Ignoring the tremor shaking my hands, I balance them on his chest and place a quick peck on the edge of his mouth. Dizziness clusters my head when his delicious woodsy scent engulfs my nostrils. "Bye," I whisper faintly.

A grin tugs on his lips. "You don't say goodbye. You say, 'I'll see you later.'"

My heart squeezes. That was exactly what he said to me when I said goodbye to him at the airport six years ago. His words were the only thing that stopped a flood of tears from streaming down my face. I truly didn't believe so much time would pass between us until I saw him again.

I hope I never have to experience that extent of absence again.

"I'll see you next week?"

"Without a doubt," I whisper, smiling.

After flashing a quick smirk, Hugo heads for the elevator banks. Halfway there, his hesitant steps stop. He stands frozen in the middle of the blue-carpeted corridor. My heart pounds fitfully when he suddenly pivots to face me. The streak of possession in his eyes has returned full pelt, and it sends my pulse skyrocketing.

My mind fritzes with confusion when he mutters, "Fuck it," under his breath before he strides back my way, his steps agile and long. Air whistles between my teeth when his lips brutally crash into mine. He kisses me with a sense of urgency like a man worried I'm about to vanish.

The brutal roughness of his kiss sparks a carnal desire in me. I grip his hair, pulling him closer, strengthening our kiss even more. My lips feel bruised, but it doesn't dull my eagerness. I've been dying for years to taste his cinnamon-flavored mouth again.

He cups the back of my thighs, encouraging my legs to wrap around his waist. Desire surges through me when the thick crown of his cock brushes the throbbing wetness between my legs. My breasts are aching to be touched, and my inner muscles are clenching, begging for attention. A growl rumbles through Hugo's lips when I grind against him. I need friction to lessen the intense, tingling throb between my legs.

My pleasurable moans turn into a groan of frustration when he pulls back before he sets me back onto my feet. He rests his sweaty forehead against mine, but he keeps his eyes shut tight. Mine drift over his beautiful face, categorizing every perfect feature into my memory. He looks so peaceful, like the teenage boy who stole my heart at the tender age of sixteen.

After opening his eyes, his alarmed gaze flicks between mine. "Tell me to leave." His throat is hoarse and dry, making his words husky. "Please, Ava, ask me to leave."

I peer at him in shock, surprised he'd ever think those words could leave my mouth. His breaths flurry against my swollen lips when I shake my head, denying his plea, but he doesn't voice any further objections.

Every fiber in my body sparks as I precariously step over the fine line that separates friends from bed partners. I fist his shirt with one hand while pushing down on the door handle with the other. The rise and fall of his chest amplify when my apartment door opens with a slight creak. My heart hammers against my ribs as he shadows me into the entryway of my apartment.

My attention is sidetracked from staring into his lusty eyes when plastic crunches beneath my feet.

In sync, Hugo and my eyes dart down to the floor. When I discover what caused the noise, my eyes snap back to Hugo. A spasm plagues his jaw when he bends down to collect the clear cellophane-wrapped red rose resting against the doorjamb. I eye him quietly when he reads the card attached. The tension shifts from playful to uneasy when his hooded eyes lift to mine.

He stares at me, his mouth tugging into a phony smirk. "I've got to go," he says, handing me the rose.

Not waiting for me to respond, he pivots on his heels and makes a beeline for the elevators. I remain speechless, staring at his impressively large frame as he stalks away. I must still be dazed by his beguiling kiss.

The muscles in his back flex when he stabs the call button. When the dashboard announces the elevator is still in the lobby, a curse word emits from his mouth. With a sense of urgency, he shoves open the fire door of the stairwell and exits my apartment building without a backward glance.

After blowing out a hot breath of frustration, I enter my apartment. On the way to my bedroom, I detour into the kitchen to dump the red rose into the trash.

While rambling under my breath, I kick off my heels and peel out of my skintight dress. After diving beneath the crisp pink sheets on my bed, I bury my head into the pillow and scream obscenities at the top of my lungs.

Anger pummels through me. I'm not just mad at Marvin and his stupidly timed rose. I'm frustrated. And do you know what makes matters ten times worse? It's sexual frustration.

There's no worse frustration in the world than sexual frustration.

That kiss... my God!

That kiss was... panty-drenching... core-clenching... mind-blowingly good!

But do you know what makes it worse? Hugo won't remember it in the morning.

He hasn't previously, so why would today be any different?

ELEVEN
HUGO

I push open the fire exit door and sprint down the stairwell as if I have fire ants in my pants. Putting it bluntly, if I don't leave, I'll hunt Marvin down and shove his ass-kissing rose in a place where the sun doesn't shine, thorns and all.

Some may say it's part of the game, and I should hate the game, not the player, but that's fucking bullshit. Yes, if it tickles your fancy, play the game, but play it fairly. Be open and honest. Surprisingly, most women appreciate when you're forthright and upfront. You may even get extra brownie points for the effort, but it's guys like Marvin who ruin it for the rest of us.

Even if it isn't written in the handbook, every guy knows you don't go out clubbing with one girl while sending another one a rose telling her how much you're missing her and can't wait to see her again. It's a dawg act, and it proves Marvin's tactics haven't changed since we left high school.

But in all honesty, even if I hadn't seen Marvin with his nose burrowed in the neck of another lady, I would have still reacted the same way. Even after years of absence, nothing has changed. Just one flash of Ava's killer smile, and I'm ready to drop to the ground and kiss her fucking feet.

I always thought Ava's pull was because I was young and hadn't experienced life yet, but it isn't that. I've been through more the past two years than most men endure in a lifetime, aging and maturing me well beyond my twenty-five years, but Ava's pull is just as magnetizing now as it was when we were kids.

All the proof I needed was staring me in the face earlier tonight. I didn't feel the slightest ping of jealousy when I spotted Victoria dancing with James Moreno, but when Ava vanished into the crowd, my first reaction was jealousy.

That quickly changed to fury when I saw the terror on her face when her dance partner's filthy hands slithered over her body. Blinded by rage, I charged for Ava and her attacker. A barrage of memories pelted my brain when I yanked Ava into my chest before I laid my boot into the asshole's ribs. It took all my restraint to walk away from her attacker, writhing on the floor, holding his stomach, but my wish to ensure Ava was unharmed was more vital than my need to pummel her attacker into the next century.

Even once Ava was safe and protected, standing directly in front of me, I couldn't stop the thoughts running through my head about what could have happened if I didn't get to her in time. *If I failed again.*

Those dreary deliberations had my mood souring quicker than the excitement of waking up Sunday morning and realizing it is Monday. Normally, it takes a good dose of whiskey and a few hundred sit-ups to drag me out of my woeful mood, but just like during our childhood, Ava pulled me out of my glum mood with nothing but wit and a cheeky smile.

But even my morose mood couldn't dampen my desire to taste Ava's lips again. I fought the urge. I gave it my very best shot. I stepped away from her when we were dancing. I battled the yearning when we were in the hidden nook at the club, and she was looking up at me, wide-eyed and eager. I even made it halfway down her hallway before the devil on my shoulder whispered wicked thoughts into my ear. No matter what I did, nothing worked.

I am drawn to Ava like a magnet. I'm attracted to her, and I don't just mean her stellar looks. She's the entire package—sweet, kind-hearted, and off-the-Richter-scale sexy.

That kiss.... *my fucking god.* It had my cock breaking the zipper on my jeans, wrangling to get out and plunge into her ravenous pussy. Even through my jeans, I could feel how wet she was. She was the combination I like best—drenched and begging.

There are kisses, and then there are *kisses.* Ava's are the latter.

I've never been interested in a lengthy game of tonsil hockey, preferring to focus on the more needy regions of the female body. But kissing Ava forces an exception to that rule. I could kiss her for hours and never get enough.

Snubbing the erection I'm still sporting, I step onto the sidewalk outside of Ava's apartment building. I'm out of breath, wheezing for air and sweating like a pig.

Karma's way of biting me on the ass for my impatience.

While sucking in a big breath, I curl into the back seat of the limousine waiting at the curb. My heart hammers my ribs when a mannish voice asks, "Is she as innocent as she seems?"

After gathering my heart off the limousine's floor, I'm met with the complacent smirk of Isaac.

While returning his smug stare, I reply, "A gentleman never kisses and tells."

"Lucky for me, you're not a gentleman."

Lewdly smirking, he places an empty crystal decanter into a concealed stainless-steel minibar in the middle console between our seats I didn't even know existed until now. Once the leather is returned to its original position, his dark gray eyes drift to mine. "Since my *business* dealings in Ravenshoe will take a little longer than originally planned, I brought our meeting forward."

My brows scrunch about the unease in his voice, but I nod, acknowledging I've heard him.

After smirking at my agreeing gesture, his hand digs into the breast pocket of his suit jacket. "After seeing you defend Ava tonight, I know you'll be a valuable asset for my empire. You think quickly even when you're under pressure, and you didn't let prior events in your life influence your decisions. So, with that in mind, I increased your initially devised salary."

He hands me the folded-up piece of paper he removed from his pocket. My eyes bounce between him and the cream-colored document as I unfold it. A tickle scratches my throat when my eyes roam over the figure written in the payee amount of the bank check I'm now clutching for dear life.

Unable to grasp the reality of the situation, I lift my disbelieving eyes to Isaac's. "Are you pranking me? Because this shit can't be real."

He downs the overgenerous serving of whiskey in one hit. After running the back of his hand across his mouth, his dark eyes bore into mine. "The figure written down is correct." The inside of the cabin becomes rife with muggy heat as my blood boils with excitement. "On one condition…"

My eyes rocket to his. I'll do anything to cash this check into my dwindling bank account.

Nothing is beneath me for this amount of money.

"You need to talk to someone about what happened in Afghanistan."

Except that.

My brows lower quicker than my heart plummets into my stomach. "How do you know about that? Those files are meant to be sealed."

"With a bit of money, even the stickiest glue comes unstuck." He stares at me, not the slightest bit concerned about what my reaction will be that he invaded my privacy.

"I didn't do what the file says I did," I sneer through gritted teeth.

"You don't think I know that? I would have *never* offered for you to join my empire if I believed a single thing in that file."

"Then what the fuck is wrong with you?" I interrupt breathlessly.

"Only a lunatic would take the word of a stranger over an official government document."

Isaac shakes his head. "I'm not taking anyone's word. I'm trusting my intuition. My intuition is telling me you're not the man your file says you are. Until you prove me wrong, I'll continue to trust my intuition... and you." After securing the middle button of his jacket, he slides out of the stationary vehicle. My eyes lock with his when he pops his head back in. "You start two weeks from Monday. The details of your employment are contained in the white envelope in the back of the seat."

I wait all of two seconds for him to leave before delving my hand into the back pocket of the seat in front of me. Although I am excited about securing employment, I'm also anxious about the stipulations he may have included in our agreement now that he's aware he is dealing with a criminal.

When I empty the contents of the envelope into my lap, the first thing my eyes zoom in on is a set of keys. The fake gold bullion key chain has four house keys and one black vehicle key dangling from it.

After dumping the keys back into the envelope, I collect a folded-up piece of paper with a four-digit code scribbled on it. There are no indications as to what the code belongs to, just four digits. 3156. From the neatness of the handwriting, I'd say Mr. Trust Fund himself wrote the note.

After storing the number in my memory, I place the piece of paper back into the envelope and gather a gold-embossed business card.

"Avery Clarke," I read off the card.

Air puffs from my nostrils when I read she specializes in psychology and the interpretation of dreams in real-life settings. I scrunch the card into a ball before dumping it onto the limo floor. The fourth and final content of the envelope is a small, typed note on official business letterhead. It reads:

Your apartment:

No. 32

River Vista Luxury Apartments

1324 Hamilton Way

Rochdale

I double-read the address to make sure I'm seeing it right. Once I've assured all the numbers are in the right order, my eyes float between the building on my right and the address on the piece of paper.

You've got to be kidding me. This can't be right.

Unexpectedly, the back passenger door opens, and the still unnamed gentleman with a thick silver mustache enters the frame. My brows meet my hairline when he says, "Welcome home, Hugo," while gesturing his hand to Ava's apartment building.

TWELVE
AVA

"**A**re you okay, dear? You don't look very well." Mrs. Marshall's eyes scan my face with concern. "You don't have that dreaded flu going around, do you?"

Jorgie's mouth twitches when her mom places the back of her hand on my forehead to check for a temperature.

"I'm fine. I just had a few late nights." *Fantasizing about your son.*

When Mrs. Marshall turns her back, I throw the dishcloth into Jorgie's grinning face. I bite the inside of my cheek, fighting hard to keep my laughter at bay when the drenched dishcloth slaps Jorgie's face before it droops down her cheek and plops into her half-full mug of coffee.

"Still, you don't look very well. Perhaps you should go sit down and let me finish up here," Mrs. Marshall suggests before she spins back around to face me and removes the spatula out of my hand.

"No, it's fine." I snatch the spatula back. "I've got this."

A smile stretches across my face when I flip the blueberry pancake on the skillet, and a perfect golden coloring emerges. I've spent the last two hours making the perfect batch of pancake batter. I kept the eggs at room temperature and floured each blueberry to ensure they didn't sink to the bottom of the batter. Now, I only have the last few remaining pancakes to fry, and the double batch I promised Hugo last week will be ready for him when he arrives...

If he arrives.

Mrs. Marshall's brows furrow, and her vibrant green eyes stare at me with uncertainty. "Okay, dear, but if you change your mind—"

"I'll let you know," I interrupt, smiling.

When Mrs. Marshall moves to the sink to peel potatoes, Jorgie props her hip onto the counter next to me. "I haven't seen you this eager to make blueberry pancakes since the day after my sixteenth birthday." While picking at an invisible piece of lint on her shirt, she adds, "Hugo hasn't been to Sunday brunch in years, Ava, not since he went to Afghanistan. I don't see that changing anytime soon."

Ignoring the twisting pain in my stomach, I say, "I know, but today might be different."

"Because you went out with him last week?" My confused eyes snap to hers, confused as to how she knows about our impromptu 'date.' "He had to get your address from someone," she explains to my bemused expression. "Did anything... *happen?*" Her tone is low and crammed with unease.

My pupils widen, and my throat dries. "Umm... no. We just went out... umm... dancing," I stammer out before turning my attention back to the pancakes.

No longer able to ignore Jorgie's entreating gaze burning a hole in my head, I sweep my eyes to her. The expression on her face has switched from anxious to playful in under two point five seconds. "Dancing, hey?" she questions with a waggle of her brows. "What type of *dancing?*"

Blood rushes to the surface of my skin from the sexual innuendo laced in her voice.

Spotting my blemished cheeks, she squeals. "Ava Westcott, you dirty little hussy!"

"Shh," I request, panicked.

My eyes dart around the eat-in kitchen of the Marshall residence.

Once I'm satisfied no one is paying any attention to Jorgie and me, I devote all my focus to Jorgie. "Not that type of *dancing*," I inform her softly. "Dancing, *dancing*. Clothes-left-*on* dancing."

She cocks her brow. "What else happened?" she questions over-dramatically. "You can act innocent until you're blue in the face, Ava, but I know something more happened. I can see it in your eyes. So come on, spill it. I want all the *raunchy* details."

Is it just me, or does that seem wrong coming out of the mouth of Hugo's baby sister?

Seeing my repulsed expression, Jorgie says, "Hugo may be my brother, but you're my best friend. What kind of friend would I be if I didn't help my bestie wade her way through the slimy frogs until she finds her prince sitting on the edge of the pond?"

My brows furrow. Jorgie has never been a fairy tale and Prince Charming romance type of girl. Her idea of a true romance story is *Romeo and Juliet*. The pregnancy hormones running through her body must have made her a little whacky.

"Pregnancy and wedding planning are making your insides soft and squidgy," I joke, poking her rounded stomach.

Her mouth gapes open. "They are not!"

"Yeah, they are. You're turning into a marshmallow!"

"Whatever." She rests her arm on her stomach, trying to fake annoyance, but the smile tugging on her lips displays her deceit. "You betta watch yourself. I get to choose who I am friends with, but I'm stuck with Hugo. He's family."

I bump her with my hip. "Yet, you still love him."

She smiles. "Yes, I do, but I love you too, and I know this is something you've wanted for a long time."

Now it's my turn to huff and roll my eyes.

"Deny it all you want, Ava, you can't—"

"Fight fate," I interrupt.

"Exactly! Now spill the beans. This knocked-up, soon-to-be-married marshmallow needs to live vicariously through you."

Grinning, I exhale a deep breath before my panic eyes nervously glide around the room. Once I am happy no one is watching, I mumble, "We kissed."

My hand shoots up to cover Jorgie's mouth when her squeal gains us the attention of every Marshall in the kitchen and every dog within a five-mile radius. Her eyes are huge and unapologetic as she stares at me with nothing but glee.

Her excitement intensifies when the screen door at the side of the kitchen squeaks open, and the intoxicating physique of Hugo enters the room. My heart beats double-time as my eyes drift over the man who kept me awake until the wee hours every night this week reminiscing about our kiss.

I've scrutinized every detail of our night, every word he spoke, every look that crossed his face, and every time he touched me in great depth, but even after an investigation Sherlock Holmes would have been proud of, I still went to bed just as confused as I was hours earlier.

When I notice the eerie quietness encroaching the kitchen, my hands lower from Jorgie's mouth as my eyes sweep the room. Helen and Chase are staring at Hugo like a stranger has entered their house uninvited. Mr. Marshall's eyes are twinkling with happiness, and Mrs. Marshall's hand is covering her mouth as her eyes well with tears. Their joy about the return of their beloved son is etched on their faces.

As a tear escapes Mrs. Marshall's eye, she rushes to her youngest son to throw her arms around his broad shoulders. Warmth blooms across my chest when Hugo soothing his mother breaks through the silence plaguing the small gathering.

After being greeted by Helen, Chase, and Mr. Marshall, Mrs. Marshall guides Hugo through the kitchen to the makeshift dining room on the outside deck. When Hugo ambles past Jorgie and me, his hand darts out to rub Jorgie's rounded belly, and I'm greeted with a cheeky wink and a smile.

Once it is just Jorgie and me left in the kitchen, her glistening cornflower blue eyes stray to mine. "That must have been one hell of a kiss, Ava. Because you got him to do something I've been begging him to do for years." My nose tingles as fresh tears form in my eyes when Jorgie places her ruined coffee onto the counter then wraps her arms around my neck. "Imagine all the things you could get him to do when you dive beneath the sheets?"

My pupils widen as my throat dries. Just the thought of having nothing but sheets between Hugo and me has my lady garden throbbing.

Spotting my flushed expression, Jorgie giggles before leaving the kitchen. While pouring the final batch of pancakes onto the skillet, my mind wanders—images of Hugo and me dancing last week flash before my eyes. My visual isn't entirely accurate. It's a little more X-rated since clothing is an optional requirement.

The sweat-producing image only leaves my head when smoke filters through the air, closely followed by alerting scream of the smoke alarm.

Oh, shit! The pancakes!

A whimper vibrates my lips when the skillet burns my hand from me stupidly pushing it off the flame without using any protection. Peering down, I cringe when I notice a blister forming on the edge of my palm. The sting becomes non-existent when my back is engulfed by a delicious-smelling man.

My breathing turns erratic when Hugo's woodsy scent invades my senses. He leans over my shoulder, and with an oven mitt, he removes the skillet from the open-flamed cooktop. The thick, black smoke choking the room of oxygen fades when he dumps the skillet into the sink before he switches on the tap full pelt, dousing the now charcoal-black pancakes with water.

The heat intensifies when portions of his formidable V muscle peeks out beneath his shirt when he fans the smoke alarm with a kitchen towel. Once it stops announcing my failure to the world, Hugo's amused gaze drops to me. "I thought my kitchen fire days were over once Helen realized she couldn't boil water."

The deep rasp of his voice makes the blemish on my cheeks

switch from embarrassed to excited. As his eyes drop to my wounded hand cradled by my uninjured one, he moves to stand in front of me. "Let me see," he requests, his tone low and full of concern.

"It's fine. It's nothing." I drop my hands to the side of my body. My insides tense, but I give no outward appearance to the pain felt when the blister rubs the hem of my skirt.

Hugo's eyes bore into mine as he gently clasps my hand so he can inspect it. The hairs on my nape prickle when he runs his finger over the wound, being extra cautious not to touch the blister forming on the red welt.

I can't control my breathing from his meekest touch. My heavy pants echo in the silence of the kitchen. Upon hearing my shameful response to his touch, Hugo's eyes lift to mine. Even with his eyes sparked with the same trepidation they had when he begged me to ask him to leave, the intensity of his blue eyes spears me in place.

My brain turns to mush when he raises my wounded hand to his mouth so he can blow on the scalded skin. His breath makes my burn a forgotten memory. From the sparks of sexual energy surging through my veins, anyone would swear he was blowing on another region of my body.

Shamefully, a breathless moan whooshes out of my parted lips, then the heat in the room jumps to roasting. Cringing with embarrassment, my eyes snap shut when, "If she has a blister, you better go get the iodine out of the bathroom cupboard," sounds through my ears.

When Hugo's hand is replaced with a cooler one, I hesitantly flutter my eyes back open. Mrs. Marshall's translucent-skinned hand cups mine as she thoughtfully inspects the blister. The heat on my cheeks increases when I stray my eyes to the side of the kitchen, and I spot Chase, Helen, Jorgie, and Mr. Marshall staring at me with a hint of intrigue in their eyes.

After locking her eyes with Hugo, Mrs. Marshall says, "Grab the alcohol wipes and the needles from my sewing kit while you're getting the iodine."

My eyes bug at the mention of a needle. I hate needles. It isn't a small dislike. I hate *hate* them.

After shooing Hugo and the rest of the Marshall gang out of the kitchen, Mrs. Marshall pulls over a stool from underneath the counter in the corner of the room then gestures for me to sit. When I do as asked, the feeling of being sent to the principal's office for reprimand overwhelms me.

"Umm... that wasn't what it looked like," I stammer out, mortified she busted me panting like a dog in heat in the middle of her kitchen.

Mrs. Marshall runs her hand down her frilled apron before her green eyes lock with mine. "Do I look like I was born last century?"

Through a gaped mouth, I shake my head. Although she is in her mid-fifties, she has cascading blonde hair, eyes that show she hasn't hit her prime yet, and one of the most rocking bodies I've ever seen on a lady of her age.

I'll be more than happy to look like her in my mid-thirties let alone fifties.

"Even being married for thirty years, I can recognize the sparks of attraction as well as the next person." She clasps my uninjured hand in hers. "This is something you've wanted for a long time, Ava."

My pupils widen. *Am I the only idiot who thought I did a good job of hiding my crush on Hugo?*

Mrs. Marshall's brow curves. "You wear your heart on your sleeve as clear as day for all to see, just like Hugo. But in saying that, Hugo is *not* the boy you remember from high school. He's changed. The war changed him."

Pain inflicts my chest when I spot the tears pricking her eyes. "What happened over there?"

Rumors ran rife through our hometown when Hugo was discharged from his position earlier than the rest of his squadron. Speculations ranged from him being insubordinate to his superiors to a botched mission that caused casualties during friendly fire.

Never being one to believe rumors, I politely excused myself from the conversation whenever the topic of his dismissal came up.

Over time, the rumors fizzled, and the town gossips found something new to bitch about.

Mrs. Marshall's face scrunches. "Nobody knows exactly what happened because Hugo won't talk to anyone about it. But I know my boy. I can see in his eyes that he's suffering."

I blink several times in a row, hammering my eyes with flutters of air, praying it will stop my tears from falling. There's no greater love in the world than a mother's love for her child. That is exactly what projects out of Mrs. Marshall's eyes when she talks about Hugo.

After running her index finger under her eyes to ensure her tears haven't spilled, she says, "Because you're like a daughter to me, Ava, I feel it is my responsibility to ensure you're not walking into this blindfolded."

My breath hitches from her calling me her daughter. "Thank you, but I can assure you I'm not. My eyes are the most open they've ever been," I say, smiling.

While peering into my eyes, the concern in hers vanishes, and a smile curls on her lips. "I'm glad to hear that," she murmurs as Hugo strolls into the kitchen with a bottle of iodine in one hand and a sewing kit in the other. She squeezes my hand before her eyes drift to Hugo. "You look like you have this under control. Once you have Ava cleaned up, come and join everyone for brunch."

After a quick smile, she taps her hand on Hugo's forearm then bolts out of the kitchen like it was her backside set on fire instead of the pancakes.

THIRTEEN
HUGO

Ava's big doe eyes track me when I grab a stool from under the breakfast bar and drag it to sit in front of her. Even with her eyes plagued with dark circles and her skin a little gaunter than it was last week, she looks beautiful.

She always looks beautiful.

When I entered the kitchen, I nearly spun on my heels and exited straight back out, knowing there was no way I could trust myself around Ava when I saw her clothing selection. She's wearing one of the shortest white pleated miniskirts I've ever seen. If that isn't bad enough, she teamed it up with a pair of heels that make her legs go for days and days.

My attention was only diverted from her spellbinding legs when my mom threw her arms around my shoulders and wept into my neck. For as long as I can remember, the Marshall family has held a family brunch on the first Sunday of the month.

Our get-togethers aren't exclusively for members of the Marshall clan, though. They're an open invitation, available to anyone who doesn't mind rolling up their sleeves and getting their hands dirty to prepare the food. Or, in Helen's case, wash the dishes.

During high school, Sunday was my favorite day of the week. Not just because every breakfast food you could possibly imagine was displayed across the dining room table ready to be devoured once a month, but because every Sunday morning, Ava would greet me with a big braces-covered grin and the largest stack of blueberry pancakes I'd ever seen.

So much has changed since then.

My mom's reaction when I walked in the door is one of the reasons I haven't been to brunch in nearly three years. After I returned from my first tour, any time she peered into my eyes, hers would well with tears. She's always had a knack for knowing when her children are hurting, so she saw right through the ruse I dangled in front of her.

She's so in tune with me that when I was younger, she knew I'd skinned my knee before I even fell off my bike. Although I still visit my parents regularly, I prefer my mom's tears to be shed in private. The only way I could achieve that was by avoiding brunch, but last week, I told Ava I'd be here. Being a man who always keeps his promises, here I am.

This is hard for me to admit, but my mom has a legitimate reason for her tears. I've changed a lot in the past few years. I'm no longer the little boy who begged her for an extra cookie with my glass of milk before I went to bed or the one who agreed to any dare Chase conjured up, no matter how crude it was.

Many people say my change was part of the crazy rollercoaster ride from adolescent teen to mature adult, but for me, that wasn't the case. I changed because I joined an industry I should have never been a part of, an industry that nearly tore my life apart.

Afghanistan was nothing like I was expecting. Like every teen, I played *Medal of Honor* and *Call of Duty* from sun-up to sun-down every weekend. I held the number one spot in the rankings for over three months, completed every mission to the precise detail, and collected every medal there was to achieve.

But it wasn't until I was over there, killing on demand, did I realize it was *nothing* like the video games portray. You can't smell the scent of death through a television monitor. You don't hear the cries of mothers when their babies are killed or the sounds of fathers on their knees begging for their sons to be returned home, safe and in one piece.

Here, once you've finished your mission, you switch off the television, gallop down the stairs, and eat blueberry pancakes until you need to vomit. There, it never switches off. The game never ends, but even more concerning than that was finding out the men I was playing with, my brothers who were supposed to have my back, were the biggest enemies of them all.

When I was in the field, I was always on alert, seeking out potential threats. I should have been looking in my own backyard because that is where the real danger laid.

My attention is pulled back to the present when a warm hand curls over my clenched fist. Lifting my gaze, I'm met with Ava's wide, concerned eyes.

"Are you okay?" She stares into my eyes. "You're shivering. Are you cold?"

Not waiting for me to reply, she gathers my dad's wool-lined raincoat from the rack at the side of the kitchen. A smile curls on my lips when she drapes it over my shoulders before retaking her seat across from me. I'm not smiling because of her thoughtfulness. I'm grinning because after Ava's little fire incident, the temperature in the kitchen went well above one hundred degrees Fahrenheit.

It's so hot, Ava's forehead has a layer of sweat beading on it, so you can be assured the shivers wracking my body have nothing to do with being cold and everything to do with the hell I'm still trying to forget.

I shrug off Dad's jacket then place it on the island counter beside the items I gathered from the bathroom. Ava watches my every move, but she remains as quiet as a church mouse.

After soaking a cotton ball with iodine, I remove a needle from Mom's sewing kit. Ava's tongue darts out to replenish her lips when I run the alcohol wipe over the needle to sterilize it. The fretful scowl marring her face amplifies when I throw the alcohol wipe into a bin full of eggshells and empty blueberry containers.

Once I have everything ready, I grasp Ava's hand in mine. "Are you ready?"

My smile turns genuine when the hairs on her arms bristle from my meekest touch. When she nods, I move the needle toward the nasty-looking blister on her palm.

Just as the needle is about to pierce her skin, she screams, "Wait!"

When her eyes zoom in on the needle, her pupils widen.

"It won't hurt," I assure her.

"Says the guy who's about to jab me with a pointy object." The fret marring her beautiful face fades when she hears my quiet snickering. "Don't be rude. We're in your mother's kitchen," she reprimands while gazing over her shoulder to make sure our earlier spectators have left. She tries to keep her face serious, but the smile inching her lips high gives away her deceit.

"Trust me. The counter is the perfect height for fucking."

The smile on her face weakens, and her earlier gaunt appearance returns from my inaccurate tease. I may have been a little mischievous in my younger days, but our house was rarely empty, and I was too busy keeping the guys in my grade away from Ava that I've never had the opportunity to test out the theory.

"Here, I'll show you." Ava's breathing quickens, and her eyes widen. Her chest rises and falls with every breath she takes. "Not the counter height," I say with a chuckle. *Although if she keeps looking at me like that, I may not have the strength to fight her alluring pull any longer.* "That the needle won't hurt."

Before she can protest, I lift her uninjured hand and prick her pinkie finger with the needle. "Ouch," she whimpers as her eyes dart down to the bead of blood sitting on the tip of her finger.

Her sobs are muffled with a moan when I soothe the sting of the needle with the lash of my tongue. Heat scorches through my veins when she squirms on her seat.

Once the tangy taste of blood is gone, I drag her finger out of my mouth. A loud pop sounds from my mouth when her finger twangs my lip on the way by. Ava's pupils dilate, and her lips part, revealing she's aroused by my flirty tease.

Deciding to make good use of her distraction and needing to distract myself before I seal my mouth over her pouty lips to steal every whimper escaping them, I pop the blister before she can process what is happening. Once all the mucky ooze has seeped out of the small hole, I run the iodine-drenched cotton ball over the wound before covering it with a Band-Aid.

"There you go, just like new."

She remains stunned like a deer trapped in headlights.

"It's not how a trauma surgeon at a major hospital would have done it, but it gets the job done," I say, quoting some of the words she said last week.

Her bright white teeth are exposed in a full smile. "I guess I'm not the only one who enjoys torturing people for a living?"

"There's a *very* fine line between pleasure and pain." I try to keep sexual overtones out of my reply, but my words are drenched in them.

While smirking at Ava's wide-eyed expression, I lace my fingers with her uninjured hand and guide her out of the kitchen. Unsurprisingly, the large wooden deck in the backyard is packed with over three dozen people. More than half are strangers to me.

When I spot two empty chairs across from Jorgie and Chase, I place my hand on the small of Ava's back and direct her toward the makeshift dining table. Ignoring the snicker of Chase across the table, I pull out Ava's chair and gesture for her to sit.

For the first hour of brunch, the only audible noise is me shoveling Ava's blueberry pancakes into my mouth. I've never tasted anything more delicious—except Ava's lips. They taste even sweeter than her world-famous pancakes.

Like she can hear my private thoughts, Ava's focus shifts from Chase to me. Her eyes float over my face before she flashes me her killer smile. My cheek muscles twitch when she licks the tip of her thumb and runs it along the right-hand corner of my mouth. "You had syrup on your lip."

Everything blurs when she pops her thumb into her mouth to suck off the syrup with a little groan. Thoughts of her lips circling another part of my body rush to the forefront of my mind, turning my dick to steel. It's only when I catch sight of Ava's lips twitching as she tries to repress a smile do I realize what she's doing. She's returning my earlier tease with one of her own.

Who would have thought innocent little Ava would grow up to be a cock-tease?

Deciding I need to put some distance between us before I drag her onto the table and taste the syrup directly off her skin, I excuse myself before making my way inside. When I spot Jorgie washing dishes, I snag a kitchen towel off the bench and commence drying the mountain-load of crockery stacked in the drying rack.

Jorgie's lips tug into a thankful smirk, but she remains quiet, which is very unlike her.

Once all the dishes are clean and packed away, her cornflower blue eyes glare at me. "If you hurt Ava, I'll kill you."

I scoff. "I thought this was what you wanted." My reply relays my genuine confusion. She nagged relentlessly for months for me to go out with Ava, but now things get a little interesting, she pulls out a yellow flag.

"No, this isn't what I wanted," Jorgie replies. "I wanted you to fall in love, have two point five children, and live in a house with a white picket fence. Not look at Ava like you want to devour her on the kitchen counter."

I grin and waggle my brows. There's no use denying the accuracy of her statement. Even if I did, Jorgie knows me well enough to see straight through it.

Upon spotting my contemptuous face, Jorgie huffs before throwing a damp kitchen towel at my head. "You're disgusting."

"Who are you, and what happened to the real Jorgie Marshall? The one who would take Baby up to the Mt. Louis Lookout every weekend just to *look* at the *scenery*? The same Jorgie Marshall who danced on the tabletops at senior prom and went skinny-dipping in the Hudson River because it was a full moon? The shackles aren't even locked on your ankles yet, and you're already acting like a middle-aged citizen."

Her nose screws up as she stomps her feet. "What is it with everyone giving me crap today? First, Ava said I'm getting squidgy, and now you're saying I'm turning into our mother."

My wholehearted chuckle booms around the kitchen. Jorgie loves our mom, but no self-respecting twenty-four-year-old wants to be compared to their mother.

My laughter dissipates when I see tears welling in her eyes. Jorgie's hormones have been all over the place the past few months, but this is the first time I've seen tears well in her eyes in years.

I pull her into my chest. "What's going on, Jorgie?" The trembling of my heart is heard in my question.

"I'm scared."

My brows furrow. "Of what? What have you got to be scared about?"

She takes her time deliberating a response before she faintly answers, "That everything will change between Hawke and me when we become parents."

I'm taken aback by her statement. I'm not kidding when I say Jorgie and Hawke are the strongest couple I've ever known. Even when she's up to mischief, nothing but love beams out of Hawke's eyes when he looks at his soon-to-be-wife.

Her head pops off my chest, then her glistening eyes lock with mine. "What if he doesn't find me attractive anymore?"

Like the sun rising over the horizon, clarity forms. Hawke was deployed when Jorgie was only a few months pregnant. She wasn't showing at that time. Tomorrow afternoon will be the first time he will see her with a rounded stomach.

"He loves you, Jorgie," I assure her. The smallest grin tugs on the corners of her mouth. "Watermelon belly and all."

Her smile sags, and a frown ruefully takes its place. I peel her off my chest and noogie the top of her head. She tries to fight me off, but she isn't putting in a real effort. As much as she acts like she hates being the baby of the family, on the inside, she loves every goddamn minute of it.

A short time later, her grunts of annoyance shift to faint giggles. Her laughter eases the heaviness weighing down my chest.

"Trust me, by tomorrow night, you'll be wondering what all the fuss was about. He never shuts up about you and the baby. You're his every want and desire. That won't change because you shoved a basketball under your shirt."

I grit my teeth when she uses my shirt as if it is a tissue before nodding.

After lifting her head, she takes a step back. "Pregnancy hormones suck."

"Tell me about it," I playfully jibe. "That's why I'm *never* having kids."

She snarls at me before moving to the back entrance of the kitchen to check her face in the mirror. Once she's happy her makeup is in its rightful place, she gathers a stack of Tupperware containers off the entryway table. Over the next several minutes, I assist her in placing the leftover food from brunch into the containers.

"Are you heading straight home after this?"

She nods. "I have a few things to do before your housewarming party."

I cringe from the way she says *housewarming party*. To me, this afternoon's get-together is a few mates cracking open some cold beers in celebration of my new apartment. Calling it a housewarming party sounds like a bunch of old ladies drinking tea out of china teacups.

"Have you asked Ava?" Jorgie questions.

"To the party?"

I place an overstuffed Tupperware container into a heated bag. Jorgie snickers and shakes her head. I arch my brow and stare into her amused eyes, soundlessly advising I have no clue what she's referring to.

"Asked her out... *out*," she overemphasizes her last word.

I inwardly gag. "Am I twelve? That's not how things work these days."

Jorgie scoffs and rolls her eyes. "How is she supposed to know you like her if you don't ask her out?"

"Who said I liked her?"

Her brows hit her hairline. "Do I look like I was born last century?"

"No, but you do sound like our mother."

Air leaves my mouth in a huff when she punches me in the arm. "Deny it all you want, Hugo. You can't fight fate."

I chuckle and rub my arm, feigning injury.

Jorgie places her hand on her cocked hip. "Don't think I haven't noticed the new look you're sporting. You've got that loved-up puppy-dog look you had on your face years ago when I interrupted you in my room with Ava."

I roll my eyes but don't negate her statement. Any time I'm around Ava, I turn into the teenage boy who pinned her against the door, dying to taste her lips. If Jorgie hadn't interrupted us that night, I wouldn't have been able to fight Ava's alluring pull for a second longer.

Jorgie peers up at me while placing the final Tupperware container into a heat warming bag. "If you don't hurry up and snag her, someone else will."

My teeth grit as an absurd rush of heat surges through my veins. Before I can configure a reason for my insane reaction, Ava and my mom enter the kitchen, juggling stacks of dirty dishes. An intangible string of emotions pummels me when Ava smiles. It's hard to believe, but it feels like the past six years vanished with a snap of my fingers. I'm once again a teenage boy chasing after a beautiful girl.

When Ava bends over to collect a kitchen towel from the floor, exposing inches of her smooth thighs, my desire to taste every inch of her turns rampant.

It's a pity for me we're in a room with my nosey sister. "Hey, Ava, did you need a ride home?" Jorgie's tone is super high, exposing her excitement.

Ava places a stack of white crockery plates onto the sink before shifting on her feet to face Jorgie. "Yeah, sure, that will be great. When are you leaving?"

"Now," Jorgie replies before loading me up with the Tupperware containers we just finished filling.

An adorable smile stretches across Ava's face. "Great. Let me grab my stuff."

Jorgie nods. "Hugo will meet you in his truck out front."

My eyes snap to Jorgie. She has a vast grin stretched across her face and is rocking on her heels, pleased at giving Ava and me one final push.

My eyes float to Ava when she asks, "Do you mind, Hugo?"

A ghost-like grin stretches across my face before I shake my head, advising I have no objection to driving her home.

When Ava leaves the kitchen to gather her belongings, Jorgie snaps her eyes to mine. "Grab her, Hugo, and don't let go."

The beaming smile on her face intensifies when I nod.

FOURTEEN
HUGO

"Did you want to play a game?"

I sling my eyes from the road to Ava, who's sitting quietly in the passenger seat of my truck. "What type of game?"

Her grin stretches wider when she adjusts her position to face me. "Twenty questions."

I cringe. I've never had a problem stringing sentences together. I'll happily admit I'm a communicator, preferring to talk things out rather than let them sit and stew, but if I want to know something, I'll ask. If I want you to know something, I'll tell you. Being forced to share information makes me uncomfortable.

Ava's shoulders slump as she picks at the polish on her nail.

"You go first," I suggest. I'll be subjected to any torture she wants to dish out if it swipes the frown off her beautiful face.

My grip on the steering wheel tightens when a dimpled smile creeps across her face. Her lips twist as she considers a question. "Sweet or sour?" she asks a short time later.

"Drrr, sweet." *Although I don't think I'll ever find anything sweeter than her lips.*

"You can't have one without the other." Ava snags her handbag from the floor of my truck and throws a packet of sour Skittles at my chest. After tucking her legs under her bottom, she twists her torso to me while popping a handful of skittles into her mouth. "Your turn."

I arch my brow and stare into her eyes, pretending I'm stumped for an appropriate question. When she cocks her brow, mimicking my expression, I snicker. I love that she can read me so easily. She's the only woman who's ever seen through my bullshit.

"Do you know how many fights I got into the night of my eighteenth birthday party after I threw you into the pool?"

Ava coughs, splattering the cream leather dash of my truck with rainbow spit. As her hand clutches her throat, it works hard to swallow the leftover Skittle juice in her mouth.

"Are you alright?"

The faintest flush of color sneaks across her cheeks before she nods. Once she's recovered from a mini coughing fit, she asks, "How many?"

"Three," I inform her.

Her eyes pop open. "Who?"

"Richie Santo, Robert Parker, and Bryson Trapper."

She slants her head then glances into my eyes. "Because you were protecting me like you always did with Jorgie?"

I shake my head. "No," I reply, truthfully. "I just hated the idea of any guy touching you." She inhales a sharp breath but remains as quiet as a monk on a vow of silence. "I never meant to hurt you that night, Ava. I just had an irrepressible need to get you away from Rhys."

An adorable glint brightens her eyes. "I know."

"And while I'm being totally forthright, I fucking hate the *Friends* sitcom."

Ava's beautiful laugh resonates over the quiet. "So do I!" Her words are barely audible through the laughter bellowing from her lips. "I only watched it because I thought you loved it."

My brow arches high. "What? You knew all the characters' names, job titles, even what their pets were called."

She laughs uncontrollably. "That's only because I studied their bios, wanting to impress you."

I grimace. "God, how many hours did we waste watching a show we both hated?"

She laughs so hard tears stream down her cheeks. "Too many to count," she says breathlessly between giggles.

She clutches at her stomach, easing the cramps from her thunderous laugh. Once her laughter settles down, she lifts her tear-stained face to me. The flutter in her neck quickens when I brush the back of my fingers across her heated cheeks, removing her tears.

A smile curves on my lips when she leans into my hand instead of pulling away as I should be begging her to.

The smile Ava wore the three-mile trip widens when we make our way into the foyer of our apartment building. The man at the reception desk greets Ava with a smile before granting her access to a hidden office behind the impressive black and gray marbled reception area.

A security guard sporting a crisp black suit and a military haircut lifts his head when Ava saunters into the space. When he notices me shadowing Ava, his hand sweeps into his jacket, no doubt to brace the concealed gun holstered on his hip. He stares at me with both alarm and annoyance in his fiery eyes.

His focus only returns to the bank of security monitors in front of him when Ava nudges her head to the Tupperware containers in my hand. Although his attention appears to revert to monitoring the live feed, I feel his eyes tracking me as I follow Ava into the manager's office at the back of the room.

After placing two Tupperware containers on the edge of the desk, Ava removes four still-warm containers from my grasp.

My eyes absorb the space when she heads for a floor-to-ceiling cupboard at our side. Compared to other offices I've seen, this one is the size of a closet. The minimal floor space is taken up by a glass and chrome desk. There's a faded, cracked leather chair behind it and a safe bolted to the floor on my left.

Just as Ava places cutlery and plates onto the desk, the office door swings open. A waft of Old Spice drifts into the room, closely followed by Patty. From the potent strength of his aftershave, I'd say he only put it on mere minutes ago.

"You're half an hour early today." Although his gruff tone could be construed as annoyed, his face does not give that illusion.

Ava smiles a beaming grin while she greets Patty with a kiss on his cheek. A smile curls on my lips when Patty's stark white cheeks turn a shade of red. I can't blame him. Just the thought of Ava's lips on *any* part of my body sets my pulse racing.

"I'm a little early because Hugo was kind enough to offer me a ride," Ava informs Patty while gesturing to me.

Patty's head cranks to the side as he eyes me with caution. His stance is strong. He's primed and ready to shred me to pieces if needed.

"Patty, this is a... *friend* of mine, Hugo," Ava introduces. "Hugo, this is my dear friend, Patty."

The smile on my face broadens from the stumble she made introducing me.

"Nice to meet you," I say, accepting the handshake Patty offers.

My brow arches, surprised by his firm grip. Maybe what Ava said last week is true. Perhaps there is a twenty-five-year-old hiding in his body, dying to break free?

Patty's grip on my hand tightens as his worldly eyes stare into mine, assessing my soul from the outside. As I return his stare, my initial opinion of him alters. He isn't a man wanting to recapture his youth by parading around with a young trophy wife on his arm. He displays the qualities of a man trying to protect one of his most valued possessions. He cares for Ava. Not in a weird, dirty-old-man type of way. He truly cares for her like she is his family. Like she is his daughter.

God, if I can read that just from looking into his eyes, what is he reading from mine?

After a beat, he says, "I like you, Hugo."

Nothing more.

Nothing less.

Ava's excitement at his approval washes over her face. Seeing her excitement eases the tight knot in my stomach. Gushing, Ava directs Patty to the leather chair on the other side of the desk. While giving him an update on everything that transpired at the Marshall family brunch, she layers his plate with a selection of scrumptious goodies.

The twinkle in Patty's eyes illuminates when Ava opens the last container holding her blueberry pancakes. Even though I devoured enough pancakes to sustain me from needing to eat for a year, my stomach still grumbles when their delicious smell filters through the air.

Patty's eyes snap up from his overflowing plate. "Were those fighting words I heard?"

My brows meet my hairline, utterly confused by his statement. *I didn't say anything.*

When I see the possessive streak plaguing his eyes I was expecting earlier, I realize what his statement is referring to.

I rub my stomach. "It's all good. I'm stuffed."

Patty drags his plate across the table and guards it possessively. "Good, 'cause your mitts are not to go anywhere near *my* pancakes. All their sweetness belongs to me."

I need to get fucking laid.

Even though Patty's statement is referring to food, my mind went straight to the gutter. Every improper thought that ran through my mind included Ava in some form of sexual activity—on her knees, in the shower, bent over the very desk Patty is eating his breakfast on.

My thoughts turn even more perverted when Ava pops her backside onto the desk and gestures for me to join her by patting the desk with her hand. Trying to act like a man, instead of the teenage boy Ava forces out of me every time I'm near her, I accept her offer.

Over the next forty-five minutes, Patty eats his breakfast while updating me on his life history. He met his wife, Calista, when he was sixteen. They married six days after her eighteenth birthday. They had three children—two sons and one daughter. His wife passed away eight months ago, and since he was lonely, he decided to rejoin the workforce after being retired for over five years.

He was ecstatic when he secured this position as a night watchman in Ava's apartment building six months ago but disappointed when he discovered his employer won't let him carry a gun like the rest of the security personnel.

"I've never failed an eye exam," he exclaims, shouting to emphasize his point.

When Ava leans over the desk to tap Patty's spot-blemished arm, I try to keep my eyes away from the delectable skin on her thighs. I fail miserably. "They don't let you carry a gun to keep the staff morale up."

Patty stares at Ava with just as much confusion as I'm bestowing on her.

"They don't want you bruising the ego of the younger guards when you show them how a real man operates."

Patty's chest puffs high, proud of Ava's compliment.

"Besides, what's that saying you quote all the time?" she questions while tapping her index finger on her lips. "A real man doesn't need to carry a weapon. His body is his weapon."

"Damn straight." Patty stands from his chair, his chin higher than it was earlier and his shoulders more square. "Thank you for breakfast, Ava, but it's time for me to get back to showing these boys how it's really done." He places a kiss on Ava's cheek before marching out of the room with a newfound spring in his step.

Ava's brows scrunch. "I think my little pep talk backfired."

"Why?" I query. "Patty walked out of here with his head held high. Isn't that the purpose of a pep talk?"

"But Patty works the graveyard shift. He's supposed to be going home to sleep, not showing the boys how it's done," she says with a little laugh.

I chuckle with her before helping her clear away the Tupperware containers.

By the time we walk out of the office, the worry fettering Ava's face fades. Patty is slouched in a grandpa rocking chair in the corner of the room, fast asleep. With a broad grin across her face, she bids farewell to the security officer still watching me cautiously with a wave of her hand before she walks through the heavy-weighted door.

When the elevator pings, announcing its arrival to the lobby, I guide Ava inside by placing my hand on the curve of her back. After pushing the button for her floor on the elevator panel, I shift on my feet to face her. "Do you have plans this afternoon?"

Smiling, she shakes her head.

"Did you want to come and christen my new pad?"

Her body blooms with heat.

I shake my head, trying to conceal the smile furling my lips. *I thought I was the only one in this elevator with the mind of a thirteen-year-old boy.* "I meant to say a housewarming party." I cringe at the thought of old ladies sitting in my sunken living area with china teacups in their hands.

All my good intentions for treating Ava like the woman she is crash into oblivion when she peers up at me, wide-eyed and eager. The hardness of my cock hasn't eased any since her little tease earlier this morning, and if she keeps looking at me how she is, it will never quit.

My morals are left for dust when Ava says, "I'd love to come *christen* your new apartment."

FIFTEEN
AVA

Even with my insides dancing like they're performing on *America's Got Talent,* I maintain a calm, rational façade. Although I tried to keep my tone laced with cheekiness, there was no denying the sexual undertone in my voice when I told Hugo I'd love to christen his apartment. The instant I issued my bold statement, the air in the elevator turned roasting, and the energy crackling between Hugo and me had my skin prickling with goosebumps.

In all honesty, half of me is jittering in excitement, but the other half is shivering in terror. Although Hugo and I kissed last week, I have no clue what that means. Do friends kiss? Is this crazy connection we have just the lust required for two people to be fuck buddies? And before I get ahead of myself, does he even want to be more than friends?

I guess that's something I should have sought clarity on before I brazenly accepted his invitation.

While I'm being totally forthright, even though I've never found the idea of casual relationships appealing, I'd consider entering one with Hugo if it means years of fantasies will have a chance to transpire. I'd be willing to give up anything just to be with him for one night.

When the elevator arrives at my floor, Hugo laces his fingers with mine before he heads for my apartment door. My struggle to fill my lungs with oxygen ramps up more the further we stroll down the hallway.

The air between us shifts when he releases my hand to grasp the gold-engraved door handle. My nipples bud when my eyes meet his rapacious gaze. After running his heated eyes over my body, he licks his lips before returning his gaze front and center.

After pushing the key into the lock, I ask, "What time does your party start?"

Hugo's eyes stray from the door he had me pinned against last week to me. "Most people are arriving in around an hour, but whenever you're ready is fine."

"Okay. I'll be there in an hour," I say with a smile.

He smiles an uneasy grin. "Alright, I'll see you then."

"Bye," I say, placing a kiss on the corner of his mouth.

He arches his brow. "You don't say goodbye—"

"You say, I'll see you later," I interrupt. "And I will."

After placing a second peck on my mouth, Hugo saunters down the hall. While unlocking my front door, clarity forms in my mind, which forever muddles when Hugo is in my vicinity.

I spin on my heels while I shout, "I don't know your address!"

"Jorgie will pick you up."

My mouth gapes when the aloofness of his reply dawns on me. "What if I had plans?"

He spins on his heels before walking backward. My heart flips when I see the boyish grin stretched across his face. "I would've rocked up to your door, thrown you over my shoulder, and dragged your ass there myself."

Feeling cheeky, I shout, "I have plans!"

He graces me with a heart-fluttering grin before he pivots then increases his brisk stride.

Once his frame retreats into the elevator, I enter my apartment. I have a ridiculous grin on my face and am feeling the most carefree I've ever felt. While smiling like the cat who swallowed the canary, I throw my keys onto the entryway table. My feet pad along the cork-wood floors, eager for a quick shower to remove the stickiness from our sweat-producing showdown in the elevator.

The sparks firing between Hugo and me were like watching a meteor shower in a dark sky. It was nerve-wracking and awe-inspiring. We've always had a weird, unexplainable connection, but now it feels different. It's stronger and uncontrollable.

After a quick shower, a spray of perfume, and a splattering of makeup, I rush to my apartment door. My plan to arrive at Hugo's party within an hour is foiled the instant Jorgie drinks in my denim jeans and long-sleeve printed top. With her brow cocked, she demands I return to my room like she did every time we attended a party during our high school years.

While stomping my feet like a child, I drop my bottom lip before doing as instructed.

Like always, our twenty-minute mini-makeover sees two hours ticking by on the clock. Once I'm dressed in a curve-hugging pale blue strapless dress and high-altitude stilettos, I snag my purse off the nightstand and strut to the door. I feel like a cast member of *Sex and the City*.

"What did Hugo say when you told him we were going to be late?"

I use the mirrored elevator doors to dab a tissue on my over-sheened lips. After placing the tissue back into my clutch purse, I secure my grip on the bottle of wine I'm gifting Hugo and turn to face Jorgie.

Her eyes are riddled with guilt, and she has a crass smile etched on her face.

"You texted him to tell him we were going to be late, didn't you?"

She doesn't need to answer me. The guilt in her eyes is the only answer I need.

"Jorgie!" I reprimand as we walk into the elevator.

"It's a housewarming party, Ava. You won't get a tardy slip for being a few minutes late."

I gawk at her. "Two hours is more than a few minutes."

Shrugging off my reply, she moves to the dashboard of the elevator. My bewildered eyes shoot to hers when she presses the P button at the top before she enters a four-digit code into a security panel.

After swallowing to clear the tumbleweeds lodged in my throat, I ask, "Where is Hugo's apartment located?"

A broad grin stretches across her face, and she rocks on her heels, but she remains as quiet as a church mouse. My heart pounds furiously against my chest with every floor the elevator glides past.

When it reaches the top level, Jorgie grasps my free hand and strides out of the elevator.

The wild beat of my heart kicks up when we walk to a door at the end of the hallway. My jaw drops when my vision is swamped by sharp steel, crisp lines of gray linen, and a large gathering of people mingling in the vast space.

My ridiculously high stilettos clicking on the marbled floors overtake the ringing of my pulse in my ears. "Hugo lives in *my* apartment building. In the penthouse?"

Giddiness clusters in my head when Jorgie waggles her brows. Her grip on my hand firms when we step into the sunken living area. Plush, body-hugging sofas with massive scattered cushions line the edges of a gigantic space, a colossal television hangs above the open fireplace, and a glass bar full to the brim with bottles sits in the corner.

"Did you want a drink?" Jorgie asks when she notices the direction of my gaze.

My throat is parched, but I shake my head. "Maybe later?" I

stumble out, my voice riddled with nerves. Even though I'm seeing it with my own eyes, my brain can't comprehend that Hugo lives in my building. *This could be both an ingenious and foolhardy move.*

My eyes shoot in all directions, absorbing the space when Jorgie moves us through the extravagantly impressive apartment. *Calling this place an apartment seems a little understated.*

When we enter a well-decorated hallway, I notice three full-size guest bedrooms painted in pastel colors on the right and a set of black wooden doors halfway down the hall on the left.

I stumble in my stilettos when Jorgie's fast pace has us reaching the doors in two heart-fluttering seconds. After resecuring my grip on the wine bottle, I scan the impressive-size den. A sleek, black, full-size slate billiard table sits in the middle of the room. It is surrounded by round, black bar tables. An air hockey table is on my left, and a pinball machine is on the right. My brows scrunch when I notice five full-size plasma televisions lining the back wall. *Why in the world would one room need five televisions?*

Although the first kiss I shared with Hugo was over seven years ago, the vibrancy in the room makes it feel like I've stepped back in time. That night was full of playful teases and sneaky feather-like touches before the night hit a climax with a once-in-a-lifetime kiss.

I can only hope tonight follows a similar path.

My heart launches into an excited rhythm when Hugo enters the den from a second entrance on my left. He looks delicious in a dark t-shirt and a pair of snug jeans. His shaggy hair is wet and pulled back, exposing his breathtaking face.

He's smokin' hot!

My neck prickles in excitement when he spots me standing at the side, gawking at him. The smile that morphs onto his face doesn't indicate he's annoyed about my tardiness. His eyes glide over my face before they drift down my body.

When his eyes return to mine, I jingle the chilled bottle of wine. *"Fridge?"* I mouth.

He holds up his index finger, requesting a minute. When I nod, he turns to speak to a blond gent at his side. Once they've finished their brief conversation, he nudges his head to a door on the far right of the room.

"I'll be back in a minute," I say to Jorgie.

A giggle parts my lips when she drags her index finger under her nose. After bumping her with my hip, I weave my way through the intimate crowd huddled in the den. Just like the last Marshall party I attended, the gathering of people is diverse.

A shy grin twists on my lips when, from the corner of my eye, I spot Hugo making his way through the room. His long, efficient strides have him reaching the swinging door before me.

"Thank you," I say when he holds the door open for me. My mouth falls open when I take in the grandeur of his kitchen. "This is ten times bigger than the one in my apartment."

Hugo chuckles at my reaction while pacing to a bank of cabinets in the middle of the ginormous space. My lips quirk when he opens a cherry oak door, revealing a built-in refrigerator. Cool air blasts my overheated face when I place my wine inside. I smile for the hundredth time today when I take in the well-stocked refrigerator. Mrs. Marshall's is always packed to the brim with food. It seems Hugo is following in his mother's footsteps.

My heart rate revs up when I notice most of the items in the refrigerator are breakfast foods. "Are you expecting early-morning guests?"

A grin etches on my mouth when Hugo replies, "No harm in being prepared. One day you might decide to fulfill your debt."

My heart leaps when he presses his lips to my neck. I inhale deeply, dying to secure a full breath when he peppers my skin with feather-like kisses. I'm practically panting, the anticipation of his next move too much for me to bear.

When I slant my head to the side, giving him full access to my neck, he ravishes my skin. He bites and sucks it during his arousing kiss. The scratchiness of his five o'clock shadow intensifies the sensitivity of his kiss.

I close my eyes, riveted beyond comprehension from his devotion when his hand slithers around my body. A husky moan parts my mouth when he pulls me backward, and I feel the enormity of his excitement. It proves I'm not the only one captivated and in a trance. He's just as spellbound as me.

I spin on my heel, the desire to taste his lips again spurring my boldness. A knee-buckling groan rumbles in his chest when I seal my mouth over his. I moan while running my tongue over his lips, absorbing his delicious cinnamon flavor swamping them before I plunge it into his mouth.

I stroke my tongue along his, coaxing him to return my embrace. My heart flips again when he fists my hair before he tilts my head back, demanding control of my mouth.

I give it to him.

Giddiness overwhelms me from the demanding control of his kiss.

I'm in complete awe.

My lips tingle when he pulls his mouth away. "You taste just as good as you did the first time I kissed you in a fridge."

When I glance into his eyes, unlike our kiss last week, they're free of any encumbrance.

"You remember our first kiss?" My tone is high as a wave of emotions surges through me.

Hugo looks down at me. Shock is evident in his hooded gaze. "You thought I'd forgotten?"

I nod, a little overeager. "You were drunk. *Very* drunk."

An adolescent grin stretches across his face. "It wouldn't matter how many drinks I had had. I'd never forget kissing you." Hunger clenches my core with anticipation when he runs his index finger along my collarbone, sending goosebumps racing to the surface of my skin. "Is that why you didn't show up for breakfast the following morning? You thought I'd forgotten?"

My brows lower as quickly as my heart rate. I stare into his entrancing eyes before shaking my head. His eyes bounce between mine, his concern building by the minute.

"What happened?" he asks after a short length of time.

I swallow the lump in my throat. "My dad saw my neck."

Hugo's brows scrunch, but he remains quiet.

"He saw the mark *you* left on my skin."

He sucks in a quick, sharp breath. "I gave you a hickey?"

I bite my lip before nodding.

"And your dad saw it?" Utter shock highlights his high tone.

My rapid head nod increases.

"Fuck! I'm so sorry, Ava."

"That's why I went to college on the other side of the country," I disclose as emotions strangle my vocal cords. "My dad sent off an application that very morning."

Hugo's frame stiffens, his pupils widening as the reality of the situation dawns on him. My eyes prick with tears as memories of that day I left Rochdale filter through my brain. The Marshall family was the closest family members I'd had. Leaving them was the hardest thing I've ever endured.

Hugo cups my jaw. "I'm so sorry, Ava. If I'd known—"

"I know," I interrupt, peering into his repentant eyes. "But there was nothing anyone could have done."

As much as moving to the other side of the country devastated me, it also saved me from the clutches of my father, so it was both a godsend and a tragedy.

Hugo's eyes dance between mine. "The past cannot be changed, forgotten, edited, or erased. It can only be accepted."

I smile and nod. "Accept the past, embrace the present, and believe in the future."

A mesmerizing stretch of time passes between us as we stand across from each other, staring but not speaking. Like always, the connection is intense and fired with lust, but there's something more potent in his eyes than a fiery connection. It's so strong, I feel his yearning in the core of my heart.

It is truly beautiful. If I could stay in this moment forever, I would.

Our emotion-packed staredown ends when an ear-piercing squeal screeches through the room. The scream is so loud, the windows rattle, and my heart leaves my chest.

Our eyes meet at the exact moment we realize the howl of pain came from Jorgie. Panic scorches my veins as I bolt for the den, shadowing Hugo as he barges past anyone in his way. My heart is wildly beating, shaking my entire body with fear.

When I reach the double doors of the den, my breath hitches, and tears prick my eyes. Decked out in his full military uniform is Hawke. He is standing in the den with a duffle bag in one hand and a bunch of flowers in the other. A tear rolls down my cheek when Jorgie squeals again before rushing to her soon-to-be husband to throw her arms around his neck.

Hawke dumps his bag and flowers onto the floor so he can spin Jorgie around the room. Her excited squeals project over the jukebox playing in the corner of the room. When Hawke kneels in front of her to caress the curve of her belly, my heart painfully clenches.

That is what I want.

I want a relationship like Hawke and Jorgie's.

I want a man who has no qualms about showing his affection, even with a house full of spectators—a man devoted solely and entirely to me.

That is what I want and crave.

That is what I deserve.

I fling a tear off my cheek before drifting my eyes to Hugo. He, along with many others, are watching the exchange between Hawke and Jorgie with a broad grin on his face. I stare at him while pondering if he will be that man for me.

Will he love me above all others?

Cherish me as if I'm his most valued possession?

Like he can sense me watching him, Hugo's head shifts to the side, and he stares me straight in the eyes. He looks at me as if he's seeing me for the first time. My heart squeezes when the corners of his mouth carve into an illustrious, panty-clenching smile. It adds potency to my every hope and dream that one day he will be that man for me.

After paying an exorbitant fee, Jorgie and I enter a bustling nightclub crammed to the brim with patrons out enjoying their Saturday night. Half-moon suede chairs line three of the outer walls of the club, leaving the core of the space devoted to a glass dance floor. A black steel and glass bar is suspended midair by thick steel ropes on my right along with an area devoted to VIP clientele and a hallway leading to the bathroom is on the left.

The vibe at the club is invigorating, and the mood is sensual.

A gorgeous male host greets Jorgie and me with kisses on the cheek before he leads us to the roped-off VIP section of the club. A space screaming of ambiance, intrigue, and sexuality envelops me from all sides. A broad grin stretches across my face, and my excitement about spending the night dancing with my best friend is evident on my face.

I wobble in my stilettos when the hostess guides us to a black leather booth, and my eyes connect with Hugo. This is the first time I've seen him since our heartfelt connection in his kitchen last week. We live in the same apartment building, and our best friends are marrying each other, but I still haven't seen hide nor hair of him.

Putting two and two together, I assumed he was avoiding me.

Even annoyed by his lack of contact, my eyes can't help but drink in his deliciousness. As always, he looks deliriously handsome. The darkness of his black cotton dress shirt with printed cuffs makes his eyes even more effervescent and his boyish grin prominent. His hair has been recently trimmed, and his face is clean-shaven. He looks both classy and roughish at the same time.

My heartbeat kicks up when his eyes drop to adsorb the Lovers + Friends Revolve Riviera strapless dress I purchased specifically because of the asymmetrical hem. The daring cut of the coral material means the dress rides extremely high on my left thigh. With a heart-shaped bustier and a high slit, I knew it would be the perfect cock-teasing ensemble for a man fascinated with legs.

My nipples tighten when Hugo's heavy-hooded gaze scorches every inch of my skin as his eyes run over my body. After he finishes his avid assessment, his eyes return to my face. The shift of air between us is so noticeable the ground moves beneath my feet. Reaching out, I grab Jorgie's arm to steady myself before taking the final steps into the VIP section of the club.

In the corner of my eye, I spot Hawke leaning against the bar, raking his eyes over his soon-to-be wife.

"Who invites their brother and husband-to-be to their bachelorette party?"

Jorgie glances at me with impertinent eyes. "Did I forget to mention we are having joint bachelor and bachelorette parties?"

Her eyes soften when she tries to make her face appear innocent.

It's a futile attempt.

She grins when I say, "No, you didn't. Must be those pregnancy hormones playing up again."

After placing a kiss on Hawke's cheek and being introduced to three of his ex-frat brothers and two of Jorgie's work colleagues, I slide into the booth as instructed by Jorgie.

By the time everyone takes a seat, I'm practically sitting on Hugo's lap.

"Ava," he greets me in his deep, rumbling drawl.

"Hi." I'm breathless from his closeness, but I try to act unaffected. "Did you know it was a joint party?"

He shakes his head. "First I heard about it was when I saw Arthur and Martha walk through the club doors."

I gawk at him in surprise. "Who?"

He smirks against the rim of his whiskey glass before taking a large gulp. "Sorry, you probably know them as Kerri and Kirsty."

The light bulb in my head switches on when he nudges his head to Jorgie's work companions. Although they appear similar in age and are wearing matching black and white polka dot dresses, I didn't realize they were related.

"Are they twins?"

When Hugo throws his head back and chuckles, I glare at him, more confused than ever. "No, they're not twins, but their racks are a good set of twin peaks."

Like a perfectly timed skit, Kerri leans over the table, and I'm blinded by more than an eyeful of her generous twin peaks.

I dart my eyes in all directions, unsure of exactly where to look. Upon noticing my horror, Hugo laughs even louder. His vivacious chuckles make my womb clench. Just hearing his laugh incites my happiness.

Once his laughter dies down, I ask, "Does this bother you? Having me here?"

He adjusts his position so he can look me in the eyes. "As long as a group of strippers arriving when the clock strikes twelve doesn't bother you, we're all good."

I huff and cross my arms, embittered by his words.

"I'm joking, Ava." He gulps his beverage. "Besides, I prefer my nuts attached to my body. I'm pretty sure Jorgie would castrate me if I took Hawke to a strip club."

He coughs, splattering whiskey over the mahogany table when I rib him with my elbow, pretending to be offended by his comment. In all honesty, I'm loving his playfulness. He's the most relaxed and carefree I've ever seen. His cheeky disposition has me doubting my initial reaction to his lack of contact. Maybe he hasn't been avoiding me. Perhaps he's just been busy?

A waitress in a black mini skirt, crisp white blouse, and a top hat saunters to our group with a wide smile. "Hi, guys, welcome to The Chapel. My name is Keke, and I'll be your server today. Some platters will be arriving shortly, but how about we start you all with a few drinks?"

Loud hollering bellows out of Hawke's frat brothers. They bang their hands on the table, throw their heads back, and howl like wolves on a full moon night.

My eyes snap to Hugo in anticipation of seeing him undertake the same ritual since he pledged at the same fraternity. I'm taken aback when I discover his eyes are focused on me instead of his rowdy frat brothers. His passionate gaze has my pulse quickening, but I return my eyes to Keke when she says, "I'm not even going to take your orders. I'm going to keep it a *big* surprise." After snatching the drinks menu off the polished black tabletop, she saunters to the private VIP bar.

"Ava, is it?" asks the cute blond sitting next to me.

I believe Hawke introduced him as Aspen, but I've never been good with names. Aspen has charmingly handsome good looks, a lean-built body, and wholesome eyes.

"Yes, nice to meet you," I say, offering him my hand.

"Is Ava short for anything, or is it just Ava?" he queries while accepting my handshake.

"Just Ava." I intertwine my fingers and rest them in my lap, inwardly battling not to squirm. The instant Aspen spoke, Hugo's fingertips brushed the exposed skin on my back, sending a bolt of pleasure straight to my core. "My dad didn't want me to have a nickname, so he picked a name that didn't have one." I smile, relieved my voice doesn't give any indication of the hammering of my heart.

Aspen smiles before he nods. "Well, it's a beautiful name. Very fitting."

"Thank you," I reply softly.

When he scoots across the bench, filling the minuscule space between us, the refreshing scent of sand and coconuts filters through my nostrils. Whenever I smell coconuts, it reminds me of weekends at the beach with Jorgie and Hugo. "Can I buy you a drink, Ava?" Aspen overemphasizes my name by drawing out the last A in a long husky drawl.

Any reply I am planning to give is cut off when Hugo places his whiskey glass onto the table. Its loud clang gains us the attention of everyone in our booth and several surrounding it. "All drinks are on the house, Aspen. No one needs to *buy* Ava's drinks."

Aspen glances past my shoulder to Hugo. They don't speak, but their silent conversation creates a misting of sweat on my skin.

"Then perhaps Ava will do me the honor of saving me the first dance?" Aspen suggests after returning his unique greenish-gray eyes to me.

I nearly vault off my chair when Hugo places his hand on my knee and squeezes. At first, I take it as a silent warning to be attentive to my surroundings after what occurred the last time I went out dancing, but when his hand glides upward, only stopping once it's high on my thigh, I realize it has nothing to do with being attentive and everything to do with possession.

Not all women like jealous, possessive men, but I love them. Every book I devour is about hot, possessive men claiming their women. Just the thought of being possessed by Hugo has my thighs pressing together and my stomach quivering with butterflies.

I drag my eyes to Aspen when he coughs, wordlessly demanding my attention. He stares at me, waiting for a reply to his question. I can hardly breathe, let alone formulate a response. I'm unable to focus on anything but Hugo's fingers tapping along to the beat of the music blasting out of the speakers. His simplest touch has my every nerve paying careful attention to him and my womb coiling tight.

When Aspen's head slants to the side, and he eyes me curiously, I squeak out, "Maybe?" I try to keep my tone neutral, feigning that I'm not affected by Hugo's simple touch, but the smallest shudder is still heard in my voice, giving away my deceit.

Happy with my response, Aspen grins and nods before turning his attention to Hawke, then Hugo removes his hand from my thigh.

After gathering my dignity off the floor, I ask Hugo, "What was that?"

"What?" he replies with a shrug, acting innocent.

He can't fool me. The smugness is written all over his face.

"The hand on my thigh."

My stomach muscles bunch when he tilts in close to my side and his delicious woodsy scent hits my senses. "Aspen is only twenty-six and already on wife number two."

Oh.

I snap my eyes back to Aspen in just enough time to catch him slipping off his wedding ring and sliding it into his pocket. Although I have nothing to be ashamed of, guilt swamps me. I've never been *that* girl. I won't even socialize with married men in places like this because that's simply asking for trouble.

I flick my humiliated eyes back to Hugo. "You couldn't have just whispered that in my ear?"

He brushes the back of his fingers over my inflamed cheek. "Nah. It wouldn't have been as much fun that way."

He can say that because he isn't the one panting like a dog in heat.

Hugo adjusts his position, snagging my devotion when he leans intimately into my side. "Does it bother you? Having me here?" he questions, quoting me from earlier, his eyes smoldering.

"No." When a condescending smirk stretches across his face, I add, "Unless you're planning on cockblocking every guy who gets within a ten-mile radius of me."

He smiles, revealing his perfectly straight teeth. I blame him for my career choice. A beautiful smile is one of the most captivating features a person can have. With a bit of effort, everyone has the chance to achieve a smile almost as alluring as Hugo's. Wanting to make people feel as good as I did when I was graced with his heart-fluttering smile is the reason I became a dentist. When I see the smile on my patients' mouths after orthodontics, it makes the less stellar parts of my job less painful.

"And if I was planning on cockblocking every guy?"

I lean into Hugo's side. We're sitting so close his warm breath dries my already parched lips when I answer, "Then I have no problems with you being here."

There's only one man's devotion I want to secure.

He's sitting right next to me.

Sheepishly, I float my eyes to Hugo, desperate to gauge his reaction to my boldness. His smile that greets me is crass and smug. A tingle races down my spine, too turned on to control my body's response to his smirk. I stick out my tongue before scooting across the bench seat. My excitement is evident when my thigh clings to the leather seat. I move far enough away from Hugo so my body gets a small moment of reprieve from his alluring pull, but not far enough that Aspen will misinterpret my closeness as an open invitation.

SEVENTEEN
HUGO

Fuck me! I nearly died when Ava sauntered into the VIP section of the club. After spending my week wading my way through my new job, my mood was anything but pleasant. Add that on top of the guilt I felt knowing I was the cause of Ava's sudden decision to attend a university across the country, and my temper turned downright deadly.

I was riddled with guilt when I found out Ava was forced to leave her hometown because of *my* foolishness. I stupidly marked her skin, hopeful it would warn my competitors that she was taken, even when she wasn't. Jealousy was already hitting me fairly in the gut from the number of men ogling her when she stripped after I threw her into the pool, but it turned potent after I left her in Jorgie's room to get dressed.

What Jorgie said that night was true. Ava's seductive strip tease had guys crawling out of the woodwork, vying for her attention. None of them were worthy of her time, and I was determined to make sure they were aware of that fact.

It was only after a night without sleep did I realize I can't change the past, but I can shape the future. I woke up the morning after my housewarming party more spirited than ever. I was determined never to be parted from Ava again. Little did I know at the time, my new job would do exactly that.

For the past week, I've worked from when the sun set until it rose. Ava worked daylight hours. The realization of our situation had my mind scrambled for a way to fix it, but all that worry dissipated the instant I spotted Ava walking into the VIP section of the club.

Her beautiful face assured me she'd be worth weathering any storm for. The muscles in my thighs strained when my eyes raked her delicious body. There's no hiding the fact I'm a legs man. My expertise in my field of choice is extremely high because I've studied many pairs of beautiful legs, but not one pair I've assessed have been as spellbinding as Ava's.

Throw together a pair of ball-constricting legs, a captivating face, a seductive body, and a tight, strapless dress, and what do you get?

A drop-to-your-knees combination.

I've never been more ready to fall to my knees and crawl to a pair of feet as I was when Ava walked into the nightclub in a ravishing dress. No woman has ever beckoned me to drop to my knees the way she does.

When my eyes lifted from her captivating body to her face, a jolt of heaviness slammed into my chest, maiming my heart. It was in that instant I realized Ava was going to own me. Not slightly but completely and utterly consume me. No doubt about it.

For the past six years, I tried to act like I'd forgotten about our intense connection, but in reality, I had simply pushed it to the background of my mind, deciding that pursuing her was a fruitless endeavor. Now, I wish I'd been more stubborn to learn the reason Ava chose a university on the other side of the country instead of making assumptions.

I shake off the thoughts that will have my foul mood returning before pricking my ears. When I realize it is the song booming out of the main part of the nightclub is what I thought, I nudge Aspen with my elbow. I put a little extra power into my ribbing for his earlier exchange with Ava.

When he openly flirted with Ava, jealousy clawed at my chest, shredding my heart. I gripped my whiskey glass so tight, it nearly shattered.

Jealousy has never been a curse of mine...

... until it comes to Ava.

Then, it's blinding.

As soon as a man shows a slight interest in her, I become a bull in a china shop. I charge first and ask questions later.

"Move out," I request when Aspen peers at me, looking confused.

Cozy booths seem like an ideal setup for any club, but unless you're a couple looking to get intimate, they're more of a hindrance than an aid. Three people have to leave their seat just to let me out.

Once I'm released from the booth, I band my arm around Ava's waist and hoist her into my chest. Her laugh is only just drowned out by Jorgie's excited squeal. I hold her close while striding with urgency to the regular section of the club. My chest puffs high, proud that Ava doesn't put up an objection to my hold.

When we enter the sweat-smelling space, Ava's head shoots off my chest. "No," she whispers with a shake of her head.

I waggle my brows and nod. "Time to dust off your *Gangnam Style* moves."

Being forthright, half of my mood is teasing, and the other half is aroused. Visions of dancing with Ava weeks ago still occupy my dreams. Although I teased her the last time she danced, she's a skilled dancer. She moves with grace and ease while also being innately sexual.

Watching her dance is like foreplay, teasing and stimulating while leaving you desiring for more. I've always found the club scene a provocative hot box of lust and desire. Dancing with Ava beats that tenfold.

By the time we reach the middle of the dance floor, the song is halfway through. I place Ava onto her feet and circle my arms around her, protecting her from the mass of people surrounding us.

I failed to protect her last time.

That will never happen again.

Her chest expands with every breath she takes. She looks worried, but when she stares into my wild, heavily dilated eyes, the concern on her face vanishes. The pounding of my heart increases when she flashes her killer smile before she starts ponying on the spot. Although she follows the dance moves she did last week, she adds an edge of seductiveness to them, sparking my dick to harden.

When it reaches the part of the song that requires her to bend over and flick her knee, she spins in my protective circle and attaches her backside to my crotch. Even the deafening hum of people surrounding us doesn't have me missing the hiss that seeps from her lips when she brushes past my thickening cock.

Acting nonchalant, she braces her hands on my legs, digs her nails into my tense muscles, and then bows forward so she can grind herself against me. When she straightens her spine, her hair flicks my chin, engulfing me with her sweet smell. I find it amusing that someone who is a dentist smells so sweet. Ava's lips taste like candy apples, and her scent is even sweeter than that.

I grip her hips then swing them in rhythm to mine, swaying to the beat of the new song playing. Ava dances around me, staying within the invisible safety bubble but also relishing her newfound freedom.

Over time, the mass gathering of bodies in the compact space has my body temperature rising. Sweat glistens on my skin, and my throat dries from spending the past hour dancing.

A new type of thirst awakens in me when Ava pivots around to face me. Her cheeks are flushed, and her nape is dripping with sweat, giving her the alluring look of someone who is sexually sated.

She runs her tongue along the seam of her mouth as her smoky gaze lifts to mine. No longer capable of holding back my desire to taste her lips again, I tilt down and enclose my mouth over hers. Her husky moan fans my lips with strawberry-scented lip gloss. I groan as her delicious flavor hits my taste buds. Her mouth is an intoxicating mix of candy mingled with the fruity cocktails she's been drinking tonight.

I cup her ass, yanking her closer to me, not leaving an ounce of air between us, then I fist her hair. When I tilt her head back, demanding control of her mouth, her shuddering moan rumbles through my lips. She gives me complete control without a single protest.

I kiss her violently, stealing every moan whimpering from her mouth while also making up for the years we missed. For the past two years, my mom has regularly said, "One day, the right woman will knock you on your ass."

Little did she know, she already had.

Catcalls pelt through my ears when Ava curls her legs around my waist so she can rub her pussy against the rock my jeans are failing to conceal. Taunts about "getting a room" and "give it to her" continue when I stroll through the writhing bodies grooving on the dance floor with Ava still plastered to my front.

When we enter the corridor, she inches back and slings her eyes around the space, gathering her bearings. Still striding, I enter the office at the end of the hall. When we enter, Ava's eyes dance around the office with eagerness.

I place her on her feet before pulling a strand of hair off her sweat-drenched neck. While tucking it behind her ear, I ignore the tremor of my hands. My heart is beating fitfully, and my palms are sweaty. I'm the most nervous I've ever been.

I cough, clearing the frog in my throat before asking, "Did you want to go out?"

Fuck, that sounded nothing like I'd envisioned in my head.

"To the movies or something?" I blurt out, trying to save myself from an embarrassing situation.

EIGHTEEN

AVA

When Hugo asks me out, my eyes rocket to his, certain I heard him wrong. When he finalizes his question, I inwardly sigh. I thought my every wish was about to be fulfilled. Hugo curses under his breath while running his shaky hand over the top of his head. I remain quiet, studying his posture. A nervous twitch is hindering his jaw, his brows are furrowed, grooving a line between his eyes, and his posture is stiff. He's clearly nervous.

I smile. I've never seen Hugo nervous before, and I find it endearing that asking me out has made him this way. When he mumbles something about not listening to Jorgie's relationship advice, lucidity forms in my skewed brain.

I mask my excitement with a neutral tone. "Are you asking me out on a date or to be your girlfriend?"

His eyes missile to mine. When he spots the excitement I'm unable to contain, his eyes fire with his regular cheekiness. "I guess that'll depend on what your answer is going to be?"

"Is there a maybe box?" I'm pretending as if I'm not in the midst of a panic attack. I swear if my heart keeps thrashing like it is, it will burst out of my chest.

My insides clench when an angry growl rumbles through Hugo's chest. "You need time to consider?" Even though he's asking a question, his eyes expose it's a statement.

I stand on my tippy toes so I can peer into his eyes. "No, but it's not entirely fair to give a girl a mind-blowing kiss then expect her to answer a life-altering question."

He smiles a pussy-clenching smile. "Mind-blowing, hey?" His brows waggle. Cockiness is oozing out of him.

I shrug my shoulders. "It was okay."

Our kiss was *way* beyond okay. Fireworks exploding in the sky, I'm going to have nothing but smut dreams for a week is what our kiss was. I can barely stand as my thighs are shaking so much, but there's no way I can tell Hugo that.

All playfulness vanishes, and a new type of friskiness develops when Hugo's fire-sparked eyes glare down at me. While returning his stare, I scan his face, drinking in every spectacular detail. He truly is a beautiful man—a straight, sculptured nose, plump lips that taste as delicious as they look, and dark, thick hair that frames his ruggedly handsome face with perfection.

The intense pull I've always felt tugging between us strengthens, tethering my heart to him even more than it already is as we stand across from each other, staring but not speaking.

After several long seconds of silence, he cups my jaw and stares into my longing eyes. "I'm going to kiss you, Ava." He pulls me nearer to him. "There are kisses, and then there are *kisses*. Yours are the latter. I could kiss you for hours and still not get enough."

Not wanting to give him a chance to recant his statement, I propel myself onto my tippy toes and seal my mouth over his. A rough groan tears from his throat when my tongue plunges into his mouth. When he tugs me in closer, I feel how hard he is. He's hot, thick, and long.

Unlike the last handful of times we've kissed, this one is more controlled—sweet and tender.

"Hugo," I whimper when he pulls his sultry lips away from mine.

He peppers my jawline with feathery kisses while muttering, "I've been wanting to do that since the moment I saw you in that dress."

My skin prickles from the coolness of the washroom door when I lean against it, stabilizing my sways from his breathtaking kiss. Ardor sparks through me when he nibbles on my neck while tugging me even closer. His lust-filled eyes bore into mine as his index finger traces the clingy material sitting at the edge of my cleavage.

When his eyes seek my permission, I brazenly nod.

My head flops back when he pulls down the damp material so he can enclose his warm mouth over my pebbled nipple. I exhale a shaky moan when a jolt of pleasure gushes through my body before clustering in my core. My hand shoots out, seeking something to grab when his tongue teases my nipple into a tight, constricted bud. My search comes up empty-handed.

"You have beautiful nipples, Ava," Hugo says breathlessly, staring at my taut buds.

Surprisingly, my nipples harden even more. He smiles, loving my body's reaction to his touch. While staring up at me, he gently bites on my nipple before sucking it into his mouth.

"Oh god," I cry out when the power of his suck overwhelms me. I rake my fingers through his thick hair, securing his mouth to my breast. The tension in my womb rapidly builds with every perfect flick of his tongue and tweak of his fingers. "I... I..."

Any words about to spill from my mouth lodge in my throat when he slithers his spare hand to my backside to squeeze it. His hand is so large, the tips of his fingers graze the uncontrollable throb between my legs. A moan I've never heard before rumbles through my lips when his fingers lightly brush my pussy's weeping folds.

After slipping my panties to the side, he glides his finger inside me. My knees buckle, and my nails dig into his shoulder. He waits a beat for me to encourage him to continue before he pumps his finger in and out of me. The walls of my pussy massage his digit with every gentle thrust he does.

Between his mouth teasing my nipples and his finger finding the spot inside me many men can't, I shamefully moan like I'm starring in an adult film production.

My knees shake when the pad of Hugo's thumb rolls over my stiff clit.

"Please... I... umm."

The ability to form a sentence is beyond me as a toe-curling sensation sets off fireworks before my very eyes.

One, two, three strokes, and I'm done.

My knees buckle, and Hugo's name tears from my throat as an ear-piercing scream without the slightest bit of concern about the people milling only mere feet from us.

Hugo slowly guides me down from the earth-shattering orgasm by easing the pace of his thrusts. Once the tremors lessen to a shudder, he removes his finger from my pulsating pussy then pops it into his mouth.

My breath hitches when he sucks the evidence of my arousal from his glistening digit, then I'm more than ready for round two when he mumbles, "Your pussy tastes even sweeter than your mouth."

I can taste my excitement on his mouth when he seals his lips over mine. Even just enduring a mind-hazing climax, a hot trickle of desire reforms in my womb.

I comb my fingers through his hair before playfully tugging on the damp tips. The thump of my heart increases when a throaty growl seeps from his mouth. He likes having his hair tugged as much as I do.

I pull him closer, deepening our kiss at the same time a door being open clatters through my ears. A whimper leaks from my swollen lips when Hugo yanks back. Although I am trapped in a lust haze, I'm still thankful his large build conceals me from our intruder.

"Is everything okay in here?" questions a male voice with a thick drawl.

As I adjust my dress back to a more suitable position, Hugo replies, "Everything is fine, Roger. We'll be out in a minute."

The ruggedness of his reply sends tingles zapping down my spine. After a beat, the office door closes, and Hugo's focus returns to me. His eyes float over my face, absorbing my flushed expression before a breathtaking smile crosses his face. "What is it with us always being interrupted?"

With a smile, I shrug. "Cursed?"

When his tongue delves out to lick his lips so he can crack them into a smile, his eyes flare. "If Roger weren't outside that door, waiting for us, I'd be feasting on your pussy until the sun is hanging high in the sky."

My panties cling to my pussy when I press my legs together, futilely trying to lessen the throb begging for his attention. The raw hunger in his eyes steals my ability to breathe, not to mention the smile he flashes before he unpins me from the washroom door.

Too engrossed by an overactive imagination, I'm vaguely aware of Hugo moving around me, gathering articles and rearranging my clothing. But my thoughts only snap back to the present when he guides me out of the office.

The gentleman with a thick silver mustache I now know as Roger greets us with a curt nod and a set of straight-lined lips. Hugo dips his chin in greeting before briskly striding down the hallway. His speed is so fast I struggle to keep up with his lengthy strides.

I swallow the dryness in my throat before asking, "Was that Roger's office?"

Hugo smiles then shakes his head. "Nope." He guides me out of the corridor. "That was my office."

My mouth gapes open nearly as wide as Jorgie's when we enter the main section of the sweat-infused dance club hand in hand. I try to wipe the I-just-climaxed look off my face, but she notices before I can suffocate it.

Hugo's grip on my hand firms the closer we walk to the group. When we reach the booth, it dawns on me why he's clutching my hand so possessively. It has nothing to do with Jorgie's shocked expression and everything to do with the look of contempt on Aspen's face. He looks like a kid whose candy bag was confiscated on Halloween night by his parents.

When we arrive at the booth, Hawke whispers something into Hugo's ear. Hugo nods before sliding his eyes to me. "Hawke has arranged to meet a few guys from his squadron at a club on the other side of town. Did you want to come with me or stay with Jorgie?"

My eyes shift to Jorgie in just enough time to catch the end of a big yawn. "You guys go. I think Jorgie has had enough entertainment for one night."

Hugo chuckles. "All right. I'll see you tomorrow?"

Smiling broadly, I nod. Excitement is beaming out of me that Jorgie and Hawke are finally getting married tomorrow afternoon, but it has nothing on what I'm hit with when Hugo places a kiss directly on my lips.

NINETEEN
HUGO

"I'll grab my tux and be right out."

I slam Hawke's car door shut then bolt up the stairs of my parents' home. With everything hammering my mind the past few weeks, I forgot to collect my tuxedo from my mom's house earlier today. Since it's almost eleven, Hawke is refusing to come inside, claiming some shit about it being bad luck to see the bride on the day of the wedding.

I take the stairs two at a time. Even with half a bottle of whiskey sitting in my gut, my steps are unimpeded. My eager strides down the hallway of my childhood home slow when I notice a light creeping out of my bedroom. An inane grin carves on my lips when I spot Ava walking around my room, absorbing the scene.

I prop my shoulder onto the doorjamb and take my time drinking her in.

Fuck, she's beautiful.

She's the unique mix of innocence and seduction—sharp, intelligent eyes, full curvy lips, a little button nose, and a sexy tight body that molds against the hard ridges in mine like she was crafted especially for me.

She is no doubt the sexiest woman alive.

There were women as far as my eye could see at the strip club tonight, but I wasn't interested in any of them. Ava's husky moans, perfectly round nipples, and the way she tasted when I licked her sweetness off my finger kept my cock as hard as steel the entire night.

No matter how many propositions I received, my cock is only interested in filling one pussy. Ava's. I've never tasted a sweeter pussy. If Roger hadn't interrupted us, I would have spent the rest of my night devouring it on my desk.

I hadn't meant to be so crass when I told Ava I wanted to spend the night feasting on her pussy, but the tactlessness of my statement became a forgotten memory when she stared up at me, open-mouthed and eager.

Our time together in my office was riveting, but I felt like a slack-jawed idiot when I attempted to ask her out. I don't know why I bothered adhering to Jorgie's advice. Not once has she given solid relationship advice, but for some reason, this week, I stupidly listened to her.

I'll admit it, my attempts to woo Ava have been pitiful, worse than any fifth grader could have managed, but in my defense, I have a solid explanation for my lack of skills.

Before tonight, I'd never asked a girl out.

Not once.

Not to a school dance or a movie.

Nothing.

So just like Ava is my one and *only* crush, she's also the only girl I've asked out.

Although she didn't respond to my question, her eyes relayed the answer I wanted to hear. I don't know where we go from here, but no matter what happens, I'm sure it will be one hell of a ride.

Upon hearing my bedroom door creak, Ava's neck cranks to the side, and she peers at me. "Hey," she greets as her lips curl into a lascivious smile.

"Hey." I try to keep my voice steady, but my attempts are borderline.

After placing a photo frame onto my bedside table, she spins around to face me. "What are you doing here?"

I nudge my head to a tux bag hanging on the bathroom door. "I forgot my suit."

"Oh."

Even with disappointment shaking her vocal cords, I don't miss the slight slur of her words. "Have you been drinking?"

A husky laugh spills from her lips as she nods. "I played truth or dare with Kirsty and Kerri. Every question I refused to answer saw me taking a nip of vodka." Her eyes float from the floor to me. My cock, now hard, strains against my jeans' zipper when I see the hankering beaming from her rich eyes. "Most of their questions were about you." She licks her lips as her eyes drop to my crotch. "And the accuracy of your nickname in high school." When her eyes drift back to mine, it takes all my strength to remain glued to my spot. Her savage smile tells me she didn't miss the hardness in my jeans. "It's true, isn't it?"

The quiver in my words displays how badly my restraint is wavering. "You'll have to wait to find out."

"When?" she asks, unashamed.

I peer into her eyes. "When you haven't been drinking."

When her huff makes me even harder, I collect my tuxedo bag, no longer trusting myself around her. I spent half my night reminiscing about the sweet taste of her pussy, so there's no way I'll restrain myself if we're alone. I need to leave before all my inhibitions gravely falter.

I want Ava.

I want her urgently.

More than my next breath.

But I don't want our first time together to be a consequence of the alcohol lacing her veins.

My chance of a quick getaway is foiled when Ava asks, "Can I ask a favor?"

After swallowing the brick in my throat, I nod, approving her request.

I've never could deny her.

The stiffness of my cock turns painful when she asks, "Can you unzip my dress? I can't reach the hook, and Jorgie is passed out in the middle of her bed."

I grin, stifling a chuckle before shuffling across the room to dump my tux bag onto my bed. The closer I walk to Ava, the wider her eyes become. She stares at me but remains completely silent. I'd assume she had passed out if it weren't for the occasional blink.

Once I stop in front of her, she gathers her hair to one side before pivoting around, giving me access to the hidden zipper resting beneath her shoulder blades. It could be my overactive imagination, but I swear a faint moan escapes her lips when my fingertips brush the bare skin on her back.

Desperate to unearth if my simple touch caused her reaction, I run my index finger along her shoulder blade.

What I heard the first time was accurate.

There's no doubt in my mind when a lust-filled moan spills from her lips.

My stiffened shaft pitches a tent in my trousers when I lower her zipper. Once it's resting at the curve of her backside, she clasps her dress to her chest then spins to face me. "Thank you," she whispers faintly while peering up at me with her beautifully unique eyes.

I smile, accepting her praise before taking a step back. From the way she's staring at me, hungry-eyed and eager, I need distance between us, and I need it now.

My eyes bulge when Ava releases her grip on her dress. It plummets to the floor, crinkling around her stiletto-covered feet in less than half a second. Although my brain screams at me to leave, my eyes rake her barely covered body, not once, but twice.

Fuck me!

There are two types of people in the world. The first are the ones who use clothes to accentuate their beauty. Their garment selections are made purely to enhance their god-gifted assets. Then there's the second group —a very small, carefully selected group of people who should wander the earth as naked as the day they were born just to allow mere mortals the opportunity to witness perfection at least once in their lifetimes.

Ava belongs in that group.

Her beauty goes above and beyond what I could have ever envisioned when I was picturing her in nothing but a pair of heels and panties. She's too perfect to formulate an accurate description. Go to a dictionary and look up the definition of 'beauty' and 'perfection.' Those are the words I'd use to describe Ava as she stands before me now.

A gold cross sits between her pert, lush tits. Her frame is slender but seductive with curves in all the right places. From the sheer panties she's wearing and what I felt earlier tonight, her pussy is bare and erotically exposing her arousal.

She is a fucking goddess.

My eyes rocket to hers when she takes a step closer to me. I shake my head, pleading with her to stay where she is. My inhibitions on making her mine are severely wavering, meaning her closeness will only end one way.

"I want this," she mutters before stepping even closer. "I want you."

Stick me with a fork, I'm fucking done.

TWENTY
AVA

Although my mind is hazy, the alcohol strumming through my veins isn't the cause of my giddiness. Hugo is. I've spent most of my night floating on cloud nine after almost every desire, wish, and want I've ever craved was fulfilled beyond my greatest expectations. My every whim was satisfied—all except one.

I plan on correcting that misconception now.

Anticipation buzzes through me as the indecisiveness hampering Hugo's eyes fades with every step I take. The energy crackling between us is electric, spurring on my desire to seduce him. The ache weighing down my breasts increases when I stop to stand in front of him. His eyes are lusty and firmly planted on me.

"I'm not drunk," I assure him before bridging the final step between us.

My heart stops beating when an ostentatious smirk stretches across his face. Warmth floods my nether regions when he chews on his lower lip as his eyes rake my body. When his hooded gaze returns to my face, I swallow.

Any apprehension in his eyes has completely vanished, replaced with a new fervent look.

I cup his twitching jaw before saying on a purr, "Unless you count being drunk on you? If so, you better ship me off to rehab as I haven't been sober in over ten years."

My breath snags halfway up my windpipe when a greedy grin stretches across his mouth. Wetness puddles in my lower regions as his passionate eyes bore into mine. The yearning in them sends heat sliding through my veins, and it has my anticipation sitting on the edge of a very steep cliff.

"Hawke's outside—"

"We'll be quick."

My knees curve inward from the smirk carving on his mouth. Just his smile alone exposes he doesn't know the meaning of a quickie.

"Are you sure you can handle this, Ava?"

His coaxing tone makes me shudder with anticipation, but I nod, nonetheless. "I'll use two hands if I have to." I smile, delighted my voice comes out in the husky, rich purr I was aiming for.

Hugo's chuckle rumbles through my body, clustering in my womb. It makes my pussy throb. When I brace my shaking hands on his thrusting chest, his gaze sweet-talks me with no words leaving his mouth. The heat in the room turns roasting when I lower my hand to his impressively large cock.

Air violently leaves his mouth when I squeeze him hard, kneading him through his jeans.

My core clenches, loving the heaviness of his cock in my hand.

"The office was foreplay. Now it's time to finish what you started," I tease while staring into his vivacious eyes.

With a growl, he seals his lips over mine. My knees weaken when his tongue slips into my mouth, then I gasp when he pins me to the wall before he drops his focus to my aching-with-need breasts. While he sucks and licks my nipples, I fiddle with the buttons of his dress shirt. My movements are frantic and hurried as every dream I've ever imagined transpires.

When his hand slips inside my panties, and he feels how

drenched I am, my toes curl. The dampness between my legs hasn't lessened any since our time together in his office.

"You're so fucking wet," he hisses against my kiss-swollen mouth.

I don't answer him. Even if I wanted to grace him with a reply, I wouldn't be able to. I am speechless but extremely horny.

I yank at his zipper, hating that I'm standing before him in only a meager pair of panties while he's still fully clothed.

My breath hitches when I tug his jeans down his thighs, and his cock springs free. "You go commando now?"

When he laughs, I realize I said my private thoughts out loud.

I gasp for a second time when his cock twitches. *Jesus!* His penis is even larger than I remembered. My mouth salivates as my eyes absorb every spectacular inch of him. His cock is jutted, thick, and long. His balls are heavy and hanging on his thighs, and he's man-scaped—not in a gross, weird way, but in a hot I-can't-wait-to-taste-every-inch-of-him way.

I've seen a handful of naked men in my life, but none of their appendages have been as stellar as Hugo's. I'm honestly unsure if he'll fit inside me.

Desire floods my veins when my avid gaze of his body causes pre-cum to glisten on the tip of his cock. If my pussy wasn't throbbing with eagerness, begging to be filled by him, and Hawke wasn't waiting, I'd be falling to my knees and licking up every drop of his no doubt delicious cum, but for now, that will have to wait.

I swallow hard, relieving my scorched throat when Hugo's jeans gather around his ankles. He hoists me against the wall, holding me with ease with one hand while guiding his cock toward my heated entrance with the other.

My insides clench when he pulls my panties to the side and braces the crown of his cock against my pussy's entrance. "You need to relax, babe, or I'll tear you in half."

My heart warms over his term of endearment. It's the first time he's referred to me by a nickname.

After unclenching my vaginal walls, I spear my tongue into his mouth. I kiss him with so much aggression, his lips will be bruised in the morning. The wetness of my pussy increases when he guides the crown of his cock through my dripping folds. He coats himself with my excitement, sending spasms from my womb to my throbbing clit.

Tears swarm my eyes when he bends his knees before he thrusts upward, filling me with one fluid thrust. A burning sensation shreds through my pussy, stealing my ability to breathe. Although accommodating his girth is more painful than a root canal, there's also an element of excitement attached to it. It undoubtedly proves there's a very fine line between pleasure and pain.

"You not only have the sweetest pussy I've ever tasted, but you also have the tightest," Hugo grunts before slowly gliding his fat cock out of my stinging pussy.

My pussy ripples around him, coaxing him to stay, not willing to relinquish the feeling of him so deep inside me. When every inch of his cock is out of me, I feel hollow and completely empty. But before I can protest the loss of his contact, he slams back in. My head dips forward before my teeth gnaw on his shoulder. I battle through a range of emotions bombarding me while he pumps into me hard and fast.

Over time, the burning pain dampening my excitement shifts to a pleasurable tingle. The hot pants of Hugo's heavy breaths flutter my drenched neck when he mutters, "Fuck. I'm losing my damn mind. Do you have any idea how good you feel? Your tight pussy wrapped around my cock, squeezing me greedily."

The crudeness of his statement intensifies my pleasure. I lift my head from his sweat-drenched neck to brace it on the wall he has me pinned against. He stares at me with wild, crazy eyes as he slows the tempo of his thrusts. He watches me for several long seconds before he pulls me off the wall so he can have complete control of my body.

He carries me with ease, not the slightest bit impeded by my weight. Sweat rolls down his face when his licks a droplet on my budded nipple. I've never seen anything more erotic than his ecstasy-riddled face as he fucks me into oblivion while adoring my breasts like he's the best thing since sliced bread.

"This is better than any dream I've had of you," he grunts out between big, commanding pumps.

I moan a long, voluptuous groan that has every nerve in my body prickling. Any previous discomfort is a distant memory when Hugo slithers his hand from my hip to my pulsating clit. Dizziness clusters in my head when he rolls my clit with the pad of his thumb. My knees wobble as my race to climax gains momentum.

"I want you to come on my cock, Ava." He increases the quickness of his strokes. "I want to feel what my cock does to you. How it makes you feel."

When my eyes catch sight of his core-demolishing gaze, I lose all rational thoughts. Grunted and incoherent words tear from my throat as a climax rips through me so hard and fast that stars form in front of my eyes.

"God, yes! Milk my cock, babe. Show me how much you love it."

The tightening of my pussy during my orgasm sets Hugo off. His cock flexes, and he groans before his seed adds even more magnitude to my already soul-shattering climax. I shimmer and shake for several long minutes before absolute exhaustion kicks in.

That was amazing.

After a handful more pumps to ensure every drop of his cum is expelled, Hugo's movements still. He rests his sweat-drenched forehead against mine as we endeavor to get our breathing under control. The piquant aroma of sex mingled with sweat-slicked skin filters through the air. It is an intoxicating aroma that could be bottled up and sold for millions.

After a beat, Hugo's eyes slowly flutter open, and he stares down at me. "That was..." He stops talking, seemingly at a loss for words.

"Perfect," I fill in, panting heavily.

An exhausted smile carves on his face before he nods. "You're perfect." He seals his mouth over mine, once again stealing my ability to breathe. His lips taste salty from the sweat that ran over them during our ignitable exchange. "Everything about you is perfect," he mutters against my lips before peppering my jawline with kisses.

His attention compels a new wave of excitement to form, but this time, it isn't in my pussy.

It is in my heart.

As Hugo lavishes my neck, heavy footsteps thud through my ears. Panic floods me when the handle on Hugo's childhood bedroom door lowers. A thankful sigh spills from my parched mouth when the intruder's attempt to open the door is fruitless.

Hugo must have locked the door at some stage between entering and now.

"Hugo, you better not be a-fucking-sleep." Hawke's abrupt tone bellows through the door. "It's nearly midnight. Hurry the fuck up."

The rattling of the door handle stops when Hugo answers, "I'll be out in a minute."

I moan when his hum vibrates through me since his cock is still inside me. My lips curve high when he places a kiss on the edge of my swollen mouth before he slowly withdraws his half-masted penis. I'm not going to lie. Even knowing Hawke is outside waiting for him and being exhausted beyond comprehension, I'd happily go another round with Hugo. That was above and beyond anything I've ever experienced in my life.

When Hugo places me back on my feet, I lean my back against the wall and close my eyes. I need to fill my lungs with air before I faint. When air whistles through Hugo's teeth, I flutter my eyes back open. My stomach tenses when I drink in the look on his face. Saying he's horrified would be an understatement. He looks truly mortified.

"Fuck." He runs his hand over the top of his head. "Fuck, fuck, fuck," he curses some more with his eyes arrested on something lower than my stomach.

When I follow his gaze, fresh tears prick my eyes. A trail of blood has run down my inner left thigh, puddling near my knee. My heart clutches as my eyes dart around the room, looking for an article of clothing to cover myself. Standing before him naked while he's looking at me mortified is a brutal knock to my already low self-esteem.

Upon noticing Hugo's undershirt on the floor, I bob down to pick it up. On the way, I notice Hugo's rapidly deflating cock also has blood on it.

Hugo's voice is a cross between mortified and angry when he pleads, "Please tell me that's because you've only been with guys like Pencil Dick."

I straighten my spine and peer into his repentant eyes before shaking my head.

"You're a virgin?"

While cringing at the loudness of his voice, my eyes shoot to his bedroom door, praying Hawke isn't still behind it. This situation is already embarrassing, but having an additional witness will make it ten times worse.

Satisfied the door handle isn't moving, I return my eyes to Hugo. "Was," I squeak out, the hammering of my heart heard in my trembling word.

A stretch of silence crosses between us. It is awkward and heavy. My heart sinks to my stomach when regret forms in Hugo's eyes. I take a step toward him, wanting him to recall the affection displayed during our combustible exchange. There should be no regret—the moment should be treasured and explored, not lamented.

My heart crashes into my stomach when Hugo shakes his head before taking a giant step back.

I never thought I'd endure a greater pain than the rejection of my father, but this hurts ten times more.

Ignoring the tear spilling down my cheeks, I wipe the blood off my thigh. My movements are rushed as embarrassment festers in my heart. After throwing his legs into his jeans and tucking away his deflated cock, Hugo enters the bathroom.

Hawke's frantic bangs on the door return when the grandfather clock in the hallway chimes through the house, advising it's midnight. My tear-drenched eyes lock with Hugo when he ambles back into the room, holding a washcloth. I bite the inside of my cheek, refusing to let any more tears fall from my eyes when the cloth makes quick work of the blood smearing my leg.

I grimace when my knees curve inward. Not because Hugo is being rough but because even while dying of embarrassment, my body relishes his closeness.

My neck cranks to the side when Hawke's deep voice barrels through the door. "Hugo, hurry the fuck up. I don't want my marriage cursed."

Hugo's remorse-filled eyes drift to mine when I still his hand that's cleaning my leg. He is trembling so much a shudder vibrates the length of my arm. "Go." I nudge my head to the door. "I've got this." My eyelids twitch as I fight to hold in my tears.

"It's fine. Hawke can fuckin' wait."

Gritting my teeth at the hurt swamping his tone, I snatch the washcloth out of his hand. The room shrinks in size when he stands from his crouched position, filling it with his broad frame. My heart physically aches when I notice his shaking hands have spread to his entire body.

"They've waited years for this day, Hugo. Please don't ruin it for them." Surprisingly, my tone comes out stronger than I'm expecting.

He stares at me while he runs his hand over the top of his head. After a beat, he says. "Are you sure?"

After absorbing his clenched fist and standoffish demeanor, I nod. "I'll see you tomorrow."

When I hand him the shirt I collected from the floor, his brows furrow, and he shakes his head. "Keep it."

His twitching mouth tingles my lips when he presses a kiss on the edge of my mouth. When he walks toward the door, his steps are urgent and quick. He reaches it in two heart-thrashing seconds. Hawke's loud bangs stop the instant he unlatches the door lock.

Just before he exits, Hugo's head cranks back, and he peers at me. I muster up a fake smile, pretending the devastation in his eyes isn't shredding my heart into pieces.

Once the bedroom door closes with Hugo standing behind it, I crumble to the floor. Gathering my legs within my arms, I rest my tear-soaked cheek on my knees. Tonight was better than any fantasy I could have fathomed, but I never predicted the aftermath of finally handing in my v-card.

I never intended to stay a virgin until the age of twenty-four. Life just happened, and sex never did. Growing up, I regularly used the excuse of my grandmother's trust for why I'd never go further than third base. When my father refused to let me go to prom, my grandmother trusted me enough to drop me off at the dance without a single qualm firing from her lips. Unlike my father, she didn't believe spending time with her should overrule my need for social interaction.

Because she trusted me so much, I did everything in my power to keep her trust. When she passed away the year I began college, I thought my v-card would soon expire.

It never did.

It was only after a third date with a guy I'd been lusting over in Bio-Chem did I realize it wasn't just my grandmother's trust I was striving to keep. It was also Hugo's.

No man ever held a candle to him. Even though I've always denied it, I compared every man I dated to him. When they failed to withstand my stringent Hugo test, my interest in them waned.

This, ladies and gentlemen, is why until forty minutes ago, I was a twenty-four-year-old virgin.

I glance at Jorgie, who is eyeing me dubiously. She's been eyeballing me with the same suspicious look since I entered the kitchen this morning. Her narrowed eyes have the same glimmer Chase's held when he topped off my champagne flute with a mimosa during breakfast.

Obviously, the giant stamp on your forehead announcing to the world that you're a virgin disappears the instant you hand in your purity credentials.

"Is it good having Hawke home?" I ask, using any tactic I can to shift the focus off myself. "It's only for a week, and you won't get to go on your honeymoon until after the baby is born, but it must be nice waking up to a warm body each morning."

The smile Jorgie's been wearing all day widens. "Yes! You'd swear we're already on our honeymoon... if you know what I mean," she says with a wiggle of her brows.

I laugh before taking a sip of the fruity wine in my champagne flute. Even though my heart hurts from my exchange with Hugo last night, I refuse to let anything ruin my best friend's day. This is her day, and she deserves the focus to be solely on her.

"See, I told you your worries wouldn't amount to anything. Even if Hawke wasn't a fan of your basketball belly, you could have gotten on all fours because from your backend, you can't even tell you're pregnant."

Jorgie's gorgeous giggle bounces around our elaborate surroundings. I love seeing her happy. All the worry fretting her beautiful face the past two weeks instantly vanished when Hawke walked in the door a day earlier than she was expecting.

When he was deployed, Jorgie was only a few months pregnant, so she wasn't showing. She was petrified about Hawke's reaction when he saw her the first time with an expanded stomach. I was somewhat shocked by her admission. They have a relationship every couple should strive to achieve. There are no two souls better matched than them.

"Are you ready?" questions Pierre, the eccentric hairdresser who spent the last hour wrangling my unruly hair into smooth, straight locks.

After placing my flute on the counter, I chew on my lip before nodding. Only people who have African American heritage like mine would understand the complexity of maintaining my hair.

Because my hair is a mass of ringlet curls, I've never had it colored, and it most certainly never sat above my shoulders. I always envisioned that a shorter hairstyle would make it look like I stuck my finger into an electrical socket, or even worse, like a poodle. Feeling daring, and with a gentle push from Pierre and Jorgie, I agreed to cut my hair into a wispy wave design for the wedding. Pierre guarantees it will enhance my facial features while also being easier for me to maintain during the work week.

After exhaling a shaky breath, I flutter my eyes open.

"Wow," is the only word I can formulate, so it's what I use. I swivel in my chair to face Jorgie. "What do you think?" *Or better yet, what will your brother think?*

Jorgie's painted lips twist as she absorbs every inch of my hair and made-up face. My heart thrashes against my ribs, eagerly awaiting her reply.

"Remind me to hide a stick in my wedding dress," she says playfully several long seconds later.

I arch my brow, clearly confused.

"To beat all the men away with," she adds with a wink.

The first genuine smile of the day morphs onto my face.

"Are you ready?" I ask Jorgie. From the butterflies fluttering in my stomach, anyone would swear it's me about to get married. I've never been more nervous.

"More ready than I've ever been," she replies, smiling broadly.

After ensuring the tulle on her dress has been ruffled and her veil is sitting right, I accept my bouquet of irises and white roses from Kerri and take my spot in front of Jorgie. When "Everything" by Lighthouse filters through the air, Kirsty moseys down the church aisle. Because we're hidden by a curved alcove of the church, I can't see any of the guests, but a smile curves on my lips when I hear Mrs. Marshall shushing them, demanding quiet as the wedding ceremony begins.

Once Kerri, bridesmaid number two, is halfway down the aisle, the wedding organizer gestures for me to go. I run a shaking hand down the purple satin dress, roll my shoulders, then walk around the corner. When my eyes lift from the floor, the first person they lock onto is Hugo.

My breath hitches when I absorb how incredibly handsome he looks in a black tuxedo with tails. His hair has been cut into a shorter, sexed-up style, his face is freshly shaven, and he fills out every inch of his tuxedo with perfection. The visual of him at the end of a church aisle is so stimulating, the throbbing of my pussy overtakes the beating of my heart.

As his eyes vigorously assess the bridesmaid dress Jorgie selected for me to wear, Hugo's lips part. Thankfully, Jorgie selected a dress more suitable for a cocktail party than a wedding. It's gorgeous and more daring than anything I've ever worn before. There's a side split that's seductive but not trashy, and the back of the dress curves into a dovetail point. The silk material continues into a train that fans out behind me as I glide across the white carpeted aisle.

When Hugo's eyes return to my face, an inhibited smile curves on his mouth. It isn't his normal cheeky grin. It's reserved and surprisingly shy.

I return his smile before taking my spot at the side of the altar. When my eyes float over the congregation of wedding attendees, I witness Mrs. Marshall dabbing her eyes with a tissue. My heart squeezes, pleased as punch that she's so proud.

When the music switches to "Marry Me" by Train, Mrs. Marshall returns her tissues to her clutch purse then stands. Tears well in my eyes when Jorgie and Mr. Marshall step into the alcove at the end of the aisle. The crowd gasps at how beautiful Jorgie looks. I agree with their assessment. She looks exquisite in her wedding gown, but it's the joy invisibly radiating from her that makes her even more stunning.

She is also the happiest I've ever seen her.

After angling my head to the side, I discreetly dab my eyes with a tissue wrapped around my floral bouquet stem. Pierre will curse my head if his hard work is ruined before the professional photos are taken. When I shift my gaze back to Jorgie, a flurry of blonde catches my eye. The veins in my neck thrum when my eyes lock in on the Queen of Bitches herself, Victoria Avenke. She's sitting in the second row, wearing a killer body-hugging teal blue dress, a seductive smirk, and a rampant spark of lust is firing in her eyes.

The grinding of my teeth overtakes my pulse thumping in my ears when I discover who her lust-riddled eyes are drinking in. *Hugo.* He must have invited her. It's the only logical reason as to why she would be here. I sure as hell know Jorgie would *never* invite her to her wedding. She hates her even more than me.

Anger overwhelms me when Hugo smiles at Victoria. Unlike the smile he issued me, hers isn't laced with unease and apprehension. Refusing to allow childish jealousy to ruin my happiness at watching my best friend marry the love of her life, I stray my eyes back to Jorgie. The anger boiling my blood simmers when I see the love projecting out of Hawke's eyes when he glances down at his soon-to-be-wife. Nothing but admiration spills from his eyes when he looks at her.

There's barely a dry eye in the house by the time the wedding ceremony is over. After placing a quick peck on Jorgie's cheek, I hand back her floral bouquet before gathering her train. Rose petals and rice float through the air as the newly wedded couple make their way outside the church. The anger hampering me evaporates when I see the happiness in Jorgie's love-sparked eyes. I stand to her side, proud as punch to be her Maid of Honor while she greets her wedding guests in the hundreds.

By the time the wedding photographer finishes capturing the bridal party in a range of professional shots, my heart is hurting more than my blistered feet. I thought enduring Victoria's gawk the thirty minutes of the wedding ceremony was bad, but she beat that tenfold when she had the audacity to follow the wedding party around the church grounds as we had professional shoots taken.

God forbid she was required to leave her date's side for forty minutes.

Not only did she indiscreetly ogle Hugo the entire time, but she also openly flirted with him as well.

I hope the wedding photographer has good Photoshop skills, as it will take him a lot of work to turn my frown into a smile.

I plop into an empty chair at the side of the ballroom Jorgie's wedding reception is being held in, desperately needing a few minutes to gather my composure. Even though I've spent the past three hours in Jorgie's loved-filled bubble, nothing has doused the fury blackening my veins. My Maid of Honor title necessitates that I ensure Jorgie's every whim is taken care of, but I've been using it more as an avoidance tactic against Hugo.

The closer I stand to Jorgie, the more Hugo stays away.

I jab a fork into the piece of fruit cake, pretending the damage being inflicted is being done to certain parts of Hugo's body instead of the poor, defenseless cake. Mrs. Mable, Jorgie's neighbor, sits in the spare seat next to me.

After roaming her eyes over my face, she pats the top of my hand. "Too drunk to remember? Or regretting a drunk decision?"

My eyes rocket to hers. "I beg your pardon?"

Ms. Mable rolls her rheumy eyes. "Young kids these days. Anyone would think you invented moonshine from the way you're acting." She leans in close to my side. "These crinkles you see on my face, they aren't wrinkles you're seeing."

"No, of course not," I confirm, shaking my head to hide my lie.

Mrs. Mable would easily be in her eighties.

Her face is well beyond wrinkled.

Her penciled brows hit the tight ringlets of her silver hair. "They're life lines. My life map showing I've lived my life to the fullest. Years of smiling, laughing, and crying. You won't see me prancing into a surgeon's office to get my face pumped with god-knows-what chemicals just so I can walk around looking like a sour-puss too scared to crack a smile for fear of getting a new wrinkle."

Even in my woeful mood, I can't help but laugh at her statement. "Life lines or not, that doesn't explain how you reached your conclusion," I reply while placing the mutilated cake onto the table in front of me.

"Sheesh, I'm getting there." She waves her hand into the air as if she's swatting a fly. "Keep your panties on. You're not the one with your foot halfway in the grave."

Grinning, she places her teacup on the table. The floral-printed china rattles in the saucer from her shaky movements. After dabbing her lips with a napkin to ensure there's no spilled tea on her mouth, she turns her eyes to me. I'd be lying if I said my insides weren't flipping like an Olympic gymnast. Other than Mrs. Marshall and Jorgie, I don't have any female companions I can talk to, and although neither of the aforementioned would judge me, I can't discuss the details of this situation with them. That would be too awkward.

"Even with your pretty little mouth sagging downward for a majority of the night, it can't hide the glimmer in your eyes. A glimmer that only happens after...." Mrs. Mable coughs, clearing her throat. "*Certain events.*"

I shyly smile and nod, acknowledging I understand her metaphor while also confirming her suspicion.

"When Hugo came sauntering into the church, he looked like he'd been thrown under the bus, but his eyes still had the same glimmer yours do. Putting two and two together, I gathered you two young'uns had an enjoyable night."

My cheeks get a rush of heat to them.

"I knew it!" she declares loudly when she sees my flushed expression.

After peering down at the thick gold band on her translucent-skinned hand, she spins the band around her wedding ring finger. "You should consider yourself lucky. My first too-drunk-to-remember encounter saw me waking up married to a stranger."

My eyes bulge. "Oh, wow. Did you get the marriage annulled?"

"Heavens, no." Her eyes get a glossy sheen. "A blessed sixty-five years of marriage I had to my darling Henry."

I smile at the adorable shimmer in her eyes.

"Don't let my happiness deceive you," she adds, noticing my smile. "I gave my husband hell for months. Only once he proved his worth did I let him back into my bed." The tears in her eyes dry when a rascally glimmer forms in them. "That was a hard feat as that boy knew how to shake the sheets, but by treating him mean, I kept him keen."

A genuine smile tugs my lips high. I don't know if you can legally adopt a grandmother, but if you can, I'm claiming this one.

She pats my knee. "Give him hell, sweetie. The meaner, the better."

My focus diverts from Mrs. Mable when a dark shadow envelops the white cotton tablecloth. I don't need to lift my eyes to know who is standing before me. His woodsy smell gives him away.

After exhaling a nerve-eradicating breath, I raise my eyes to Hugo. He has removed his tuxedo jacket, and his bowtie is unknotted and hanging around his neck. Even with a heavy groove indented between his eyes, he looks scrumptious.

His eyes flick between mine for several heart-thrashing seconds before he gestures his head to the foyer at the front of the ballroom. "Can we talk?" He tries to mask the nervousness in his voice, but the fast pace of his pulse bulging the veins in his neck hampers his tone.

Although anger has never been a mood I can hold for long, today is an exception to that rule. Because it's not just anger I'm harboring. It's downright fury.

"No." My reply is swift and precise.

Hugo balks before staring at me like I've grown a second head. His eyes drift to Mrs. Mable as he crouches down in front of me. He tilts in close to my side, vainly trying to get a snippet of privacy in a room filled with hundreds of wedding attendees.

The hairs in my nose tingle when the heavy scent of the alcohol bounds out of his mouth when he pleads, "Please, Ava." He stares into my eyes. "We need to talk."

I cross my arms in front of my chest then shake my head. "We have *nothing* to discuss."

Mrs. Mable pats my knee, encouraging my take-no-prisoners

stance that's slipping from my grasp with every second I glance into Hugo's glistening baby blues.

The hairs on the nape prickle when Hugo's breath flutters my earlobe. "You either come with me willingly, or I'll throw you over my shoulder and drag you out of here, kicking and screaming."

My mouth gapes. "You wouldn't dare."

My heart beats double-time when a boyish grin etches onto his sinful mouth. "I've never backed away from a dare, Ava. Today won't be any different."

I huff before strengthening my stance. When I look at anything but Hugo's sinfully gorgeous face, I realize our little spectacle has gained us the attention of a handful of eyes, including Mrs. Marshall.

"You have to the count of three, Ava," Hugo warns. "One, two—"

"What am I, five years old?" I retaliate after snapping my eyes back to his.

"If you're going to act like a child, I'll treat you like one."

My mouth forms an O as my face reddens with anger, but before any response can escape my lips, the wedding MC announces it's time for the bridal waltz. I inwardly sigh, grateful for the distraction.

My pleasure doesn't last long when the MC requests the attendance of the wedding party to dance alongside the bride and groom.

A grin carves on Hugo's mouth as he stands from his crouched position and cocks his elbow. "May I have this dance?"

Even with my insides quivering from the seductiveness in his tone, I don't allow my outer shell to exhibit my excitement. The rugged grin on his face vanishes when I stand from my chair, sidestep him, and storm toward the dance floor.

I only just hit the edge of the mahogany floor when Hugo's long strides catch up to me. When Hugo pulls me in close to his body, preparing to dance, I keep my eyes on Jorgie and Hawke, remembering this day is about them.

Even fuming with anger, my body melts into his embrace within seconds.

I huff when "I Don't Wanna Miss a Thing" by Aerosmith booms out of the speakers.

Of course, Jorgie would pick the longest song in the history of songs for the bridal waltz.

My eyes rocket to Hugo when he mutters, "What the fuck is wrong with you today?" only loud enough for me to hear. "Jorgie has an excuse for her erratic mood swings, but what possible excuse could you have?"

Assholes who have sex with you then turn up to the next day with a date is what I want to say, but instead, I keep my mouth clamped.

Hugo's eyes shift between mine for several awkward seconds before his spine straightens. "Are you on your period?" When anger boils my blood, I try to pull away from him, but he strengthens his grip, foiling my quick getaway. "Nice try, but you still have *well* over four minutes before you're going anywhere."

I glare into his eyes, delivering every obscenity running through my brain but without words.

He returns my stare, minus my blatant fury.

By the time the song reaches halfway, I'm exhausted. Not just physically but emotionally as well. I hardly slept a wink last night, and spending the past several hours dodging Hugo has been exhaustive, but the crippled ache in my heart is more from dancing with him the past two minutes. We've danced previously, but it was to gritty club music, not a love song. Every word Steven Tyler sings adds to the constrictive hold Hugo has on my heart.

"Why did you bring her?" I ask, no longer able to harbor my anger.

My nails dig into Hugo's shoulders when he says, "Who?"

Gritting my teeth, I nudge my head to Victoria entering the dance floor on the arm of an older man with strands of silver hair on his temples. Fury unlike anything I've ever experienced before shreds through me when Hugo follows the direction of my gaze then has the absurdity to laugh.

I'm glad he finds the situation amusing.

I'm anything but amused.

"You've been avoiding me because you're jealous?"

Snarling, I slap his heaving-with-laughter chest before slipping out of his embrace. He snags my wrist and drags me back to him before I get two steps away. My nipples bud when my breasts press against his firm pectoral muscles.

Battling to keep my tears at bay, I dart my eyes between the people surrounding us.

When Hugo catches my disarrayed face, he mutters, "Vicky is Hawke's stepsister."

My eyes snap to his so quickly, I make myself dizzy. My heart recommences beating when I see the honesty in his eyes.

"I didn't invite her," he confirms while staring into my eyes.

Oh.

A bucket of water is thrown on the raging fire in my stomach, suffocating my anger in one quick swoop. I try to say something, to apologize for my appalling behavior, but my mouth refuses to relinquish my words, so instead of begging for clemency, I peer into his eyes, silently relaying my apologies.

When the bridal waltz is over, wedding attendees congregate onto the dance floor while the bridal party couples separate so they can return to their respective partners.

Excitement surges through me when Hugo doesn't release me from his hold. He pulls me in closer, and any embarrassment about last night dissipates when he swings his hips in sync with the music. The dynamic between us is as intense as ever—fire sparking and combustible.

But two seconds later, Hugo stiffens.

"Excuse me. I'm cutting in."

Turning my eyes, I catch the amused face of Marvin. He's decked out in a black suit with a light blue dress shirt. His hair is gelled in a side part, and his eyes are hazy, but the most notable feature is his arrogant grin.

"Back off, Marvin," Hugo mutters, beyond annoyed about being interrupted.

Marvin scoffs. "I'm not allowed to dance with my date?"

Pain spasms through my hip when Hugo strengthens his grip on my body. When his eyes lower to mine, I take a step backward. They're crammed with irritation. "Is Marvin your date?"

His angry snarl has my heart rate racing, but it isn't in fear. It's in excitement.

Cowardly, I nod.

Air blasts out of Hugo's nose before he relinquishes me from his hold. A shiver courses through me when he steps back, taking his warmth with him. "Please, don't let me stop you from dancing with your *date*."

With that, he stalks to the bar without a backward glance. I stand frozen, unable to determine what to do in a situation like this. Yes, unfortunately, Marvin is here as my date, but in my defense, I asked him to come weeks ago, way before I knew he had too many of my father's characteristics and long before Hugo was back in the picture.

No woman in their right mind wants to attend a wedding without a plus one, so I asked Marvin to come with me. When he failed to show up at the wedding ceremony, I assumed he wasn't coming.

My skin crawls when Marvin yanks me into his chest. "You look beautiful, Ava," he praises while his hooded eyes rake my body. He plants a kiss right on my lips before I have the chance to object.

Even with music blasting my eardrums, I swear I hear Hugo's furious growl boom across the room. It quickens my pulse, and the increase is heard in my reply, "Hi Marvin. I must have missed you at the ceremony?"

His face scrunches. "I didn't go to the ceremony. Snooze fest."

"I thought it was lovely service. Very romantic."

"You would say that. You have a cunt."

I balk, disgusted at his use of the 'C-word.'

When the song ends, I politely excuse myself before attempting to walk away from Marvin. I need to find Hugo and explain the circumstances of Marvin's arrival because I know what it felt like when I thought he'd brought Victoria as his date, so I can understand his angry response.

Marvin clutches onto my wrist. "Just one more dance," he requests, pleading into my eyes. In his inebriated state, he stumbles, bumping into Kerri and her dance partner. "Sorry," he apologizes, half-chuckling.

I wrap my arms around him to steady his heavy sways. "Have you eaten anything tonight?"

Air seeps from my lips when he shakes his head. Taking my aide in keeping him on his feet as an open invitation, Marvin pulls my body flush with his. My stomach heaves when he taps his fingers on the curve in my lower back. One inch lower, and he'd be touching my backside.

"Thank you for the dance," I say before once again pulling away from his embrace. "But I have somewhere I need to be."

My brisk strides halt when Marvin says, "Did you know my dad is considering giving my partnership to Daniel?"

Pain squeezes my heart. As much as Marvin irks me, we do have some similarities with our family situation, but there's one big difference between us. He still craves the approval of his dad, whereas I learned years ago I'll never get my dad's seal of approval.

I peer into Marvin's downcast eyes. "I'm sure he doesn't mean it, Marvin. You're his son. He will always support you."

When he stumbles again, I re-secure my grip around his waist before I guide him to the bar at the side of the kitchen. I need to get him away from Jorgie's guests before he makes a fool of himself, or even worse, me.

It takes several tedious minutes to assist Marvin across the expansive ballroom. Although my gaze remains planted on the floor to ensure I don't trip over Marvin's stumbling feet, I feel Hugo's eyes on me the entire time.

When I reach the bar, I sit Marvin on a stool before heading for the kitchen. It appears empty.

"Hello?" I call out, pacing further inside.

A lady with a tight bun pops out of a walk-in refrigerator and greets me with a smile.

"Umm... I have a friend a little drunk outside. I was hoping you might have something that could help absorb the alcohol sloshing in his stomach?"

Her smile enlarges before she moves toward a massive walk-in pantry at the back of the kitchen. My stomach rumbles when the smell of cranberry sauce filters through my nose. Since I was fuming with anger, I didn't touch the confit stuffed duck leg they served at dinner. It smelled delicious, but my stomach was swirling so much, I couldn't risk placing food in it.

My lips curve upward when the lady heads back to me with a bag of bread in one hand and a plate of the confit stuffed duck leg in another. "For your friend," she says in a thick, heavy accent while gesturing to the bread. "For you."

My mouth salivates when she hands me the overflowing plate of food. "Thank you so much," I say as graciously as possible, my insides beaming with excitement.

My eager steps back to Marvin falter when my eyes lock in on Hugo. He's sitting at the end of the bar, slamming down shots of whiskey as if they're soda water. *I hope it's an open bar, or his bank account will be hurting in the morning from the fifteen-dollar-a-nip whiskey he's guzzling.*

My hackles bristle when Victoria prances toward Hugo. Snarling at me, she leans into Hugo's side to whisper something in his ear.

Ignoring the desire to peg a roll at Victoria's head, I place my plate on the countertop and plop my backside onto the spare stool next to Marvin.

"Ava, you're a doll." He snags the duck leg off my plate and devours it as if he's never been fed.

After rolling my eyes at his rudeness, I rip off chunks of the bread and dip it into the cranberry sauce. I endeavor to keep my eyes off

Hugo, but no matter how hard I fight, they incessantly steer in his direction.

I can't help it.

He's a magnet, and I'm attracted to him.

Although he continues to exchange words with Victoria, his body language gives no indication that he appreciates her attention. If anything, he looks annoyed.

Once Marvin has consumed every smidgen of food on my plate, he locks his eyes to mine. The concept of filling his belly with food instead of alcohol seems to have worked. His eyes are no longer glassy and bloodshot. They appear clear even with a slight hint of arrogance tainting them.

"Did you want to get out of here?"

Bile scorches my throat when I can't miss the ambiguity in his tone.

Without hesitation, I shake my head. "It's my best friend's wedding. I'm her Maid of Honor." *I also don't want to go anywhere with you.*

He shrugs like nothing I said is a big deal. "So?"

I talk through gritted teeth. "It's rude to leave a wedding before the bride and groom."

"So?" he replies again, chuckling.

He either can't read the signs I'm giving or is choosing to ignore them. Either way, my patience is wearing thin. "How about I call you a taxi?" I suggest, slipping off the barstool.

He waggles his brows. "Sure, you can call *us* a taxi."

Inwardly gagging from the abhorrent gleam in his eyes, I enter the coatroom in the foyer to retrieve my cell phone from my handbag.

Thankfully, since it's Sunday, the cab company advises a taxi should arrive within the next ten minutes. I store my phone in my clutch and place it under my arm before moseying out of the coatroom. Upon entering the foyer, I spot Marvin standing at the side. When he notices my approach, he stuffs his hands into his pockets and rocks on his heels. I can't miss the suggestive look on his face. He looks like a man about to go on a hunt.

Little does he know he has his sight set on the wrong target.

My hesitant steps freeze when Hugo charges across the room. His fists are balled at his side, and the veins in his neck are throbbing.

Upon noticing my panicked expression, Marvin's eyes follow the direction of my wide gaze. When he spots Hugo's furious composure racing his way, his throat works hard to swallow.

Hugo's steps are unbridled when he slams into Marvin. He rams him to the floor with a stomach-churning thud. I stumble back, sickened by the harshness of their impact on the cold marble. When Hugo's fist connects with Marvin's chin before they lower to pummel his ribs over and over again, my hand shoots up to cover my gaped mouth.

Marvin attempts to fight back, but he's no match against a man of Hugo's size, much less his fury.

"Hugo, stop!" I scream when Marvin's painful grunt echoes in the silence of the foyer.

My panicked squeals gain the attention of the wedding attendees inside the ballroom. Hawke rushes out of the double wooden doors. His face is white, and his pupils are massive.

Tears slip down my face when Marvin's wildly flying fist connects with Hugo's right cheek before Hawke can break them up. Even after copping a hard blow, Hugo continues to wallop the living hell out of Marvin. He relentlessly pounds his fists into him with so much force, I'm sure Marvin will sustain broken bones.

Hawke's eyes dart from Hugo and Marvin wrestling on the floor to me. "What the fuck is going on?"

More tears escape my eyes when I timidly shake my head, advising him I'm unaware of what has caused Hugo's anger. Although he's always had an edge of jealousy when it comes to me, it's never been so full of wrath.

Relief engulfs me when Hawke drags a red-faced Hugo off Marvin. My stomach churns when Marvin lurches to his feet before spitting on Hugo's chest. His face is as red as Hugo's, but his coloring isn't from anger. It's from the pounding of Hugo's fists.

"Stay the fuck away from her!" Hugo's angry voice reverberates off the walls. "If you go near her, I'll—"

"Get some of your crim buddies to teach me a lessen?" Marvin interrupts, his lips forming a vicious snarl.

Hugo balks, surprised by Marvin's taunt.

I'm also taken aback. *Crims?*

"You didn't think I knew?" Marvin sneers while glaring at Hugo. "I know everything."

The pompousness of his tone fuels Hugo's annoyance back to an unrestrained level. He pulls out of Hawke's grasp and throws a fist into Marvin's face before Hawke can stop him. "You know fucking nothing." His voice is the deepest I've ever heard. "You're that stupid you can't even tell she isn't pure anymore."

My heart plummets into my swirling stomach, but a menacing grin carves onto Hugo's face when he notices the shocked expression on Marvin's face. Loving that he's wiped his arrogant smirk right off his face, he continues to taunt, "I beat you to the punch. I already fucked her. Hard and fast against the wall. She loved every goddamn minute of it."

Oh god. I'm going to be sick.

My stomach swirls as my eyes bounce between the people watching the spectacle between Marvin and Hugo. I inwardly sigh, eternally grateful that other than Mrs. Mable watching me with vigilance, no one is none the wiser that Hugo's statement refers to me. All eyes remain on Hugo and Marvin.

Not even five seconds later, the rug is pulled out from underneath my feet when Marvin swings his narrowed gaze to me. "Is it true?" he questions, staring straight at me. "Did you fuck Hugo?"

Every set of eyes in the foyer snaps to me. I feel physically ill when I notice within the numerous pairs of eyes glaring at me are Hugo's and my parents.

I don't need to answer Marvin's question. My flushed cheeks and tear-welling eyes answer on my behalf.

"Fuck," Hugo curses under his breath when he spots me standing at the side, vainly trying to ignore all the gawks directed at me.

When he takes a step toward me, I angrily shake my head.

I've never been more mortified.

My chin quivers when I sling my eyes to Mrs. Marshall. Out of everyone here, she deserves my sincerest apology. I not only ruined her daughter's wedding, but I also disrespected her by sleeping with her son under her roof.

"I'm sorry," I mumble shakily.

A tear rolls down her cheek when she nods, accepting my apology with a sincerity I don't deserve. After one last glance at the hundreds of people staring at me, I dash for the hotel's double revolving doors.

Gratitude floods me when I spot the taxi I ordered for Marvin idling on the curb.

"The corner of Marcia and Trate," I request the cab driver when I dive into the back seat.

Hugo charges out of the hotel as the taxi pulls away from the curb.

"Did you want me to stop?" asks the taxi driver with his dark eyes peering at me in the rearview mirror.

After wiping my hand under my nose, I shake my head. My heart hammers my ribs, its beat no doubt matching Hugo's as he chases the taxi halfway down the street and around the corner.

TWENTY-TWO
HUGO

"I'm sorry, sir. This bar has a strict policy on limiting the drinks of intoxicated patrons."

"Are you kidding me?" I stand from the wooden barstool my half-drunk ass is precariously sitting on. "I'm not even close to drunk." The hiccup sounding from my mouth douses the strength of my statement and don't even get me started on my inability to stand straight.

After guzzling enough whiskey to make most men slip into an alcohol-induced coma, my body is only just registering a warm buzz. Since alcohol was the only thing supporting me through the debacle of my life the past year, it takes a lot for me to get drunk.

"Give him the bottle." Turning my eyes, I spot Isaac standing in the middle of the out-of-date bar I'm drowning my sorrows in. His hand rests on the button of his suit jacket as his eyes glare at the bartender. "If I'm required to voice my request again, I won't use words the second time around."

The bartender's eyes shift between Isaac and me before he leaves the half-empty bottle of whiskey on the counter and stands at the far end of the bar.

Isaac removes his black suit jacket and slings it over the countertop while muttering, "Good choice."

"This one of your clubs?" I ask, my words slurred when the alcohol I've been downing seeps into my veins. A chuckle escapes my mouth when Isaac shakes his head. "Then what are you doing here?"

He doesn't answer my question. He merely sits quietly on the vacant stool next to me then drops his eyes to my busted knuckles.

Once his silence becomes too much for me to bear, I ask, "Want to play a game?" His brow arches high on his face, seemingly unimpressed by my suggestion. "Come on. You want me to be your right-hand man, don't you?" A smirk carves on his mouth before he curtly nods. "Well, the right hand can't operate without knowing what's going on with the left hand."

After a beat, he asks, "What type of game?"

I nearly vault out of my chair, shocked he finally spoke. "Twenty questions," I reply, grinning.

Isaac's furious growl makes the bartender's thighs quake.

"Not your standard schoolyard game. Let's up the ante."

"I'm listening," he interrupts, his tone stern.

"Every time one of us shares something *shocking*, we take a drink of whiskey."

His lips purse as he considers my suggestion.

After a short period of silence, he gestures for the bartender to bring him a bottle of whiskey from the top shelf. When the bartender begrudgingly does as instructed, Isaac snags a shot glass from the wire rack in front of us. Once our glasses are full to the brim with whiskey, he says. "You go first."

An hour later, we've consumed more liquor than a drunken sailor on shore leave.

"That guy I saw leaving your office after our first meeting, is he a mob boss?"

Isaac's dark eyes drift to the bartender. When he discovers he's more interested in watching a rerun of a Red Sox game than us, his eyes turn back to me. "Yes," he replies, his voice unwavering. "Is that a good or a bad thing?" he adds when neither of us reaches for our shot glass.

"Fuck'd if I know, but I am thirsty," I say before downing my nip.

Isaac smirks before lifting the shot glass to his mouth. Glass clanging onto a wooden counter sound over my laughter when he slams his glass down and grimaces.

The whiskey he selected is expensive, but it tastes like shit.

"You couldn't have gotten drunk at one of my clubs?" He cringes as the bile flavor slides down his throat to settle in his gut.

I laugh and shake my head. "Your whiskey is too expensive for my blood."

He doesn't attempt to refute the accuracy of my statement.

"Your turn," I say.

"Why haven't you cashed the check I gave you?"

My eyes snap to his. "Because you said I had to talk to a shrink."

He shakes his head. "So until I remove that stipulation from your contract, you'll keep working for me for free?"

Air whizzes from my nose. "Dreaming."

We both laugh, then I drink my nip. There couldn't be anything more *shocking* than finding out I have to talk to a shrink as a requirement of my employment.

A grin tugs my lips high when Isaac also downs his nip. "Not a fan of therapists?"

He shakes his head then replenishes our drinks.

Once I have it in my hot hand, I ask, "Why are you sitting so gingerly in your chair?"

Isaac's eyes rocket to mine. Although his exterior is one of the hardest I've ever seen, a wince crossed his face when he sat down earlier tonight.

Just when I think he won't answer, he mutters, "I had an operation..." He coughs, clearing his throat, "*Down there.*"

My wish to secure a shot glass spills fragrant whiskey over the bar.

I recant my previous response.

Having your manhood operated on would beat talking to a shrink tenfold.

"Should you be drinking if you just had an operation?" I ask when Isaac refills our glasses.

"Probably not, but do you think I care?" After downing his latest serving, he drags the back of his hand over his mouth then asks, "Why are you getting drunk in this shitty pub instead of celebrating your sister's wedding across the street?"

You'd think I'd be surprised he knows about Jorgie's wedding. I'm not. I learned early on that Isaac knows everything. If he doesn't know, he'll find someone who does.

"I snatched the virginity of the only girl I've ever cared about."

I down my nip of whiskey, but Isaac's remains untouched.

"Come on," I say in a long drawl. "That deserves a drink."

"Not necessarily," he responds with a smirk. "I could think of far worse things than the woman I love only being with me."

"It's not that," I reply. "It's the fact I fucked her against the wall in my childhood bedroom without preparing her first. I hurt her." Even with a thick slur impeding my voice, I can't miss the shaky rattle inhibiting my vocal cords. Although I previously said I never want to have sex with a virgin, I'm not upset Ava was a virgin. I'm angry that I hurt her.

Isaac peers into my eyes before he downs his nip.

"You think that's bad, wait until you hear the rest." I huff. "I announced her impurity to a room full of people that included both sets of our parents."

Isaac snags two full-sized glasses off a wire rack. Remaining quiet, he fills them to the brim, emptying the three-hundred-dollar bottle of whiskey. "Is that the reason you have busted knuckles?"

I jerk up my chin. "The guy she brought to my sister's wedding is a fucking douche. I was already struggling to keep a rational head when they were dancing, so when the bartender told me he was bragging about taking Ava home to *pop her cherry*, it fucking killed me. I didn't want him to touch her. I hate the idea of anyone touching her. I want to be the only one who gets to touch her," I slur as the heaviness on my chest turns lethal.

"'Then be the only one," Isaac says, making me realize I rambled some of my quiet thoughts out loud instead of keeping them in my head. "If she's truly the girl you want, don't wait. Because if you lose her, you'll regret it every day of your life."

When Isaac guzzles down a large portion of his whiskey, my brain signals for my hand to reach for my glass, but no matter how many times I stretch out my arm, my hand refuses to grasp the glass.

Nothing Isaac said was shocking.

Ava has *always* been who I've wanted.

She *will always* be who I want.

Our connection is so strong, it couldn't even be broken with years of absence.

I just hope I can get her to forgive me.

TWENTY-THREE
HUGO

I shake my head when Hawke waves a beer in front of my face. "I'm good."

He places the bottle on the table in front of me. "In case you change your mind." His ass fills the empty spot next to me in the double-seater love swing in his backyard. "What's the deal? I've never seen you turn down free beer before."

My nose scrunches as I shrug. "I learned the hard way that drinking makes you do stupid things."

"Stupid things or people?"

I barge him with my shoulder. "Do you need a reminder about the number of times I saved you from chewing your arm off in the morning? You have the worst pair of beer goggles I've ever seen a drunk man wear. When you're drunk, you think Betty White is hot."

Hawke chuckles a full-hearted laugh. "Come on, even if I weren't drunk, I'd tap that. She's a silver fox." When he catches my furious glare, he adds, "Would have tapped that. *Would have.*" He smirks against the rim of his beer before taking another swig. "I'm starting to wonder if I've been transported to an alternative universe."

"It's the pregnancy hormones running through her body. You'll soon adjust."

He smiles. "I'm not talking about Jorgie, I'm talking about you and Ava."

My heart freezes at the mention of Ava's name, but thankfully, my outward appearance gives no sign of my heart's betrayal. I haven't seen Ava the past week but don't think that's from a lack of trying. After leaving Isaac in the desolate bar, I hailed a cab and headed straight to our apartment building. I don't know if Ava was inside her apartment, but she refused to open the door even with me threatening to kick it in.

For a woman who gains the attention of every man when she enters the room, when she wants to remain hidden, she becomes the invisible woman. I've stalked her apartment, her workplace, and Jorgie's house numerous times the past week, yet I still haven't seen her.

All I want is the opportunity to apologize for my appalling behavior. I'm man enough to admit when I make a mistake, and I was in the wrong for the way I behaved at the wedding. In my drunken state, I reacted first and sought questions later. Even if Ava never wants to see me again, I still want the chance to say I'm sorry. I thought a hangover was the worst thing you could wake up with after a heavy night of drinking, but the guilt of knowing I caused Ava's tears beats that tenfold.

I grip the cup tighter, trying to ignore the tremor shaking my hand when I ask, "Is Ava coming tonight?"

With Hawke returning to Iraq tomorrow, Jorgie threw him an impromptu going away party. I'm hoping Ava's admiration for him will entice her out of hiding.

"I wanna hope so, considering she's already here."

My eyes rocket to his so fast, there's no chance in hell he missed the eagerness in my reaction. "Where is she?"

He smirks against the rim of his beer. "In the kitchen, slamming down tequila shots like they're lemonade."

I bound out of my chair and am halfway across the deck before the word 'kitchen' fully escapes his lips.

I hear Ava's laugh before I see her, a soulful giggle echoing down the hall. When I enter the kitchen, she acts like she doesn't notice my presence, but I didn't miss her posture straightening and her breathing altering.

My pulse lowers, and for the first time in my life, panic grips my heart when Ava tosses back a shot of tequila without licking the salt on her hand or sucking on a wedge of lemon. My eyes shoot to the half-empty bottle at her right. *I hope that wasn't full. If it was, she'll feel like rat shit in the morning.*

Jorgie's eyes drift between Ava and me for several terrifying seconds. After making an excuse to leave, she scurries out of the kitchen without formulating an excuse, leaving me alone with Ava. It took Jorgie four days to talk to me after her wedding—that was a new record. If I didn't agree to give her the CD from her twenty-first birthday party, I have no doubt her radio silence would still be in effect.

When Ava realizes we're alone, she snatches the bottle of tequila off the counter then heads for the door. My hand shoots out to seize her wrist before she can exit. Although she remains facing the door, she doesn't attempt to pull away from my embrace. "I just want a chance to tell you how s—"

Before I can issue my apology, Hawke's cousin and ex-frat brother, Aspen, enters the kitchen. He smirks a greeting at Ava and me before he heads to the refrigerator to help himself to a bottle of beer.

My jaw ticks as I impatiently wait for him to leave, my agitation provoked by his eager assessment of Ava's body.

Once the kitchen door swings shut with Aspen behind it, I return my attention to Ava.

Two seconds after Aspen leaves, another frat brother enters the kitchen.

Fuck my life!

When we're joined in the kitchen by another body, I realize the room housing the only refrigerator in Hawke's residence isn't a suitable location for a deep and meaningful.

The hairs on Ava's neck prickle when I lean in close to her side. I'm not going to lie, my chest puffs high at her reaction. "We'll finish this conversation later... in private."

"I'm not going anywhere with you," she sneers.

A faint moan spills from her lips when I flatten my palm across her stomach and pull her back until her back is flush with the front of my body. My cock stirs, stimulated by her closeness. "I'm sorry for what I did, Ava, but until you hear me out, I'm going to become your new best friend."

She peers up at me to gauge the truth of my threat. "Fine," she huffs, intuiting that I have every intention of following through with my threat. "But not here. Not now."

"When?"

She pats her hands on her dress. "Oh, darn it, I forgot to bring my planner with me." Her lips twist before she inhales a dramatic breath. "I'll have my people call your people. We'll do lunch."

I smirk. Even pissed, she can still make me laugh. That's an incredibly rare find in a woman these days.

Her sassy prima-donna attitude dulls when I raise my pinkie in the air. "Promise?" I ask, knowing she'll never renege on a pinkie promise.

Through gritted teeth, she says, "I promise."

As hard as it is for me to do, I let her go.

Hawke takes the spare seat next to me while muttering, "Don't do anything you'll regret in the morning."

I glance down at my swollen knuckles. "Who said I'll regret it?"

I certainly don't regret teaching Marvin a lesson.

My eyes lift from my knuckles when Jorgie frolics across the room to sit on Hawke's lap. When her lips seal over his mouth, I return my eyes to Ava. For the past two hours, she's been downing liquor as if it is soda, batting her lashes, and openly flirting with every one of my single ex-frat brothers.

As if that isn't bad enough, for the past thirty minutes, she's been dancing with Rhys Motherfucking Tagget.

Yes, that's his real middle name.

Well, it's what I've christened him anyway.

"You don't think you should say something to Ava?" I suggest, nudging Jorgie with my elbow.

Jorgie stops sucking face with Hawke before she snaps her furious eyes to me. "And what exactly should I say? Hey, Ava, you're nearly twenty-five years old, you don't have to work in the morning, and you look smoking hot in that sexy little number, but can you please go home because my brother is about to burst a vein in his temple over you dancing with another guy?"

The tick hammering my jaw the past two hours gains a new spasm. "If that will stop her from making a fool of herself, yeah, say that."

Jorgie scoffs. "I'm not going to kick her in the shins when she's finally having a bit of fun. Besides, she could do far worse than snag a man like Rhys Tagget."

"Snag a man? She needs you to save her from his clutches, not throw her toward him. She deserves better than him!"

Jorgie's brow cocks. "Keep lying to yourself, Hugo, because you know as well as I do, Rhys is one of the rare good guys in this town. A gifted surgeon with an extremely large heart."

"Good guy or not, he's looking at Ava like she's a dessert menu," I yell as the heaviness plaguing my chest the past week amplifies.

"She's safe with Rhys. He won't do anything to her that Ava doesn't want him to do."

Jorgie's reassuring words don't offer me any comfort. If anything, they agitate me more.

"Maybe Ava doesn't want him to touch her," I interject, my jealousy building even faster than my temper.

Jorgie scoffs. "Get your head out of the clouds. Every girl in this town wants a slice of the Rhys Tagget pie, Ava included."

Our heated argument ends when a growl rumbles from Hawke's stern, shut mouth. Jorgie's cheeks go a shade of pink as her eyes drift back to her husband. She looks like a kid who got caught with her hand in the cookie jar.

Hawke's jaw muscle is tense, and he glares at Rhys with the same I-want-to-rip-your-head-off-and- stick-it-up-your-ass look I've been giving him the past thirty minutes.

"Every girl but me, baby." Jorgie's tone is super girly as she tries to pacify Hawke's furious wrath. "I'll never want anyone but you." She cups his cheeks. "I'm all yours."

Hawke's gaze softens when his eyes lock with Jorgie's. I suppress a gag when he doesn't attempt to hide the sexual undertone in his voice when he says, "You better come show me then."

My wish for alcohol has never been more paramount when a spark of lust ignites in my baby sister's eyes. With a smile that makes my stomach churn, Jorgie wiggles in Hawke's lap before she saunters to the stairwell.

Hawke gestures that he'll be with her in a minute before he locks his eyes with mine. "If you don't like what Ava is doing, stop her from doing it."

"How am I supposed to do that?" My words come out in quick succession as anger takes control of my vocal cords. "Drag her out of here kicking and screaming?"

Hawke smiles. "It might be the first, but it certainly won't be the last," he says before stalking to the stairwell.

When Jorgie notices him prowling toward her like a panther on the hunt, she squeals before darting up the stairs. Hawke is on her heels before she hits the second step.

My gaze drops to the red plastic cup of Coca-Cola as my mind works to unjumble the riddle issued in Hawke's statement. I've heard it before, but I can't recall where.

Before my brain can contemplate what Hawke meant, Ava's husky laugh sounds through my ears. Lifting my eyes, I am met with her being dipped by Rhys. Her ponytail is loose and hanging halfway down her head, her skin is flushed and covered with a misting of sweat, and her eyes are bloodshot and glassy from the copious amount of liquor she's downed, but she can still stop traffic. And from the gleam in Rhys's eyes, he fucking knows it.

The instant Rhys flips Ava up and her exquisite eyes lock with mine, the meaning behind Hawke's statement crashes into me hard and fast. It wasn't something I heard before—it was something I said to him. It was the very first time he dragged Jorgie out of a sorority party kicking and wailing over his shoulder.

They weren't even a couple at that stage but seeing him have enough gall to go up against a girl as stubborn as Jorgie, I realized in an instant Jorgie had met her match. They've been inseparable since that night.

I don't know if Hawke is saying he thinks the same about Ava and me, but I'm no longer willing to stand by and watch Ava make a headless mistake because I pissed her off.

The vein in Ava's neck thrums when I push off my chair and stride toward her. Her pupils dilate more with every stride I take. Without a word seeping from my lips, I clasp her wrist, yank her away from Rhys, then throw her onto my shoulder. The pounding of her fists on my back matches the whacking of my heart as I make my way to my truck.

Her wailing halts at the exact moment a garbage compactor and a washing machine going to battle sounds from her stomach. One of her hands shoots up to cover her mouth while the other secures a rigid grip on my jeans.

"I'm going to be sick," she squeaks out.

Her warning comes too late.

My teeth crunch together when splashes of vomit spilling

through her fingers is absorbed by my shirt. My shoulders stiffen, and a low, dangerous growl ripples from my lips.

I move to the rose bushes at the front of Mrs. Mable's house before placing Ava onto her feet. As she expels the bottle of tequila she drank into the bushes, I comb my fingers through her sweat-drenched hair to secure it into a braid.

I swear, I've never seen someone spew so much. The bottle of tequila was a fifth in size, but Ava pukes more than double that.

Once her stomach is void of liquid, I scoop her into my arms then continue walking to my truck parked half a block down. Carefully, I place her in the passenger seat and secure her belt before bolting around to the driver's side.

While grumbling to myself, I remove my vomit-stained shirt and throw it into the bed of my truck before jumping into the cab and kicking over the engine. Ava tries to be discreet, but I feel her eyes running over my body when I pull my truck into the car-lined street.

After she's finished her avid assessment, she fans her cheeks and then shifts her gaze to the pitch-black sky.

"Don't you dare vomit in my truck," I warn, my tone deadly serious. "It's bad enough you hurled all over my favorite shirt, but if you vomit in my baby, I'll spank your ass."

My statement is not an idle threat. If she fails to adhere to my warning, I will spank her ass. It took me hours of scrubbing to get her Skittle spit marks off the leather on my dash, but at least that smelled refreshing. I'll never get rid of the smell of vomit.

When a chill runs down Ava's spine, I adjust the air-conditioning temperature. She flashes me a quick smirk in gratitude but remains quiet.

The short four-mile trip from Jorgie's house to our apartment building is made in complete silence, and thankfully, it's vomit-free. After throwing my key to the parking valet, I run around my truck to help Ava down. She mumbles something about her not being a child before she jumps down unaided.

Any further protests halt when the heel of her shoe gets caught in the crack of the concrete, and she stumbles onto her knees. Seeing that her knees are bruised and bloody, I scoop her into my arms and walk through the double glass revolving doors while Ava hides her tear-stained face in my bare chest.

When Patty absorbs my shirtless frame approaching with Ava in my arms, he rushes to the elevator bank and hits the call button. Because of the late hour, the elevator immediately dings open.

"Thanks," I say, pacing into the empty car. "Can you push the penthouse button?"

Patty's worldly eyes lock with mine. His gaze is apprehensive, and his genuine concern for Ava is beaming out of his eyes.

"I'll look after her."

His eyes bounce between mine for a short while before he says, "Damn straight you will."

"My security access code is 3156," I advise after he hits the P as requested.

By the time the elevator arrives on the top floor, Ava is fast asleep, cradled in my arms. My heart pounding is the only noise heard as I move through my penthouse to the guest bedrooms located in the hallway. The desire to take Ava into my room is overwhelming, but until I've had the chance to apologize, I don't need another imprudent decision added to my long list of mistakes.

I tug down the pastel pink comforter on the bed then gently lay Ava down. The darkness of her hair is even more striking against the pale color of the sheets. She groans before rolling on her side, curling her legs up near her chest. Although I'm certain she has no liquid left in her stomach, I remove the plastic lining from the waste bin and place it beside the bed.

Once I've removed her shoes, I make my way to the bathroom, hoping my mom purchased some iodine and Band-Aids when she stocked my refrigerator and pantry earlier this week.

I send a quiet blessing to God for my mom when I find all the supplies I need to patch up the grazes on Ava's knees. She winces when the iodine is rubbed over the gash on her knee, but other than that, she's unaware of the medical procedure being undertaken while she's asleep.

After tucking her in, I switch off the light and take my position in the chair in the corner of the room. I don't trust that I'll hear Ava if she wakes from the other side of my apartment.

As her breathing shallows, my eyes flutter shut, and my memories drift.

When I wake the next morning, Ava is gone.

"I'm so sorry I'm late." I rush into the office Patty and I have brunch at every Sunday. "I slept in."

I step into the compact space, wrangling with bags of breakfast foods I picked up at the corner café. Normally, I'd prepare most of the food we eat, but with a horrific hangover and a pounding head, I purchased our breakfast instead.

I dump the bags onto the glass desk then move to the cupboard at the side to grab the plates and cutlery. My heart leaps out of my chest when I crash into a solid chest. Even though I don't need to lift my eyes to know who it is, I do.

"Good morning, Ava," Hugo greets, staring down at me. "What's for breakfast?"

Snarling, I sidestep him. "I didn't buy enough for three."

That's a lie. I have enough food to feed an army, but I refuse to tell him that. Prior to my drunken spectacle, today is the first time I've seen Hugo in a week. I've gone out of my way to ensure I don't have to associate with him.

My desire was so vicious that when he turned up unannounced

at Jorgie's house, I scaled the fence between Jorgie and Mrs. Mable's property just to avoid him.

Mrs. Mable was both shocked and delighted by my impromptu visit.

Although she may not be next time when she realizes who added extra fertilizer to her award-winning rose garden.

I even went as far as sharing my aunt's couch with her cats so I didn't have to go back to my apartment and face him. Avoidance isn't the solution in any situation, but it's the only defense I have against Hugo and his alluring pull, so I've been using it to my full advantage.

After pinching the bridge of my nose to lessen my pounding headache, I head to the cupboard to remove the cutlery and plates. The dishware clangs together when I aggressively throw it on the desk. Having the enormity of Hugo in this small space is too much for me to bear. There's nowhere I can escape from his familiar scent that makes my heart clutch every time I smell it.

"Where's Patty?"

If he doesn't arrive soon, I need to leave. Being so close to Hugo hurts.

"It took a lot of convincing, but Patty agreed to give me five minutes alone with you."

My eyes rocket to Hugo's. "You need a lot more than five minutes to fix the mistakes you've made," I sneer. "Do you have any idea how embarrassed I was having my personal life broadcasted to hundreds of people? I've never been more mortified!"

Hugo stands at the side of the room as I unpack the array of food. His arms are crossed in front of his chest, and his remorseful eyes track my every movement, but he remains so quiet you could hear a pin dropping.

My eyes continually dart to the clock on the wall so I can count down the seconds I have left to be subjected to the torture of smelling his intoxicating scent. Endeavoring to get through the pain of having him stand so close but not being able to touch him, I suck in a big breath. The crippling pain in my chest strengthens when I realize I'll probably never get to touch him again.

You can do this, Ava.

Grow a backbone!

Be strong!

"Your five minutes are up," I say once the clock strikes noon.

For the briefest second, I pray he'll ignore my request and demand to stay because even being furiously angry at him, my stupid body craves his attention no matter how minute it is.

My prayers are left unanswered when he smiles before he ambles to the door, passing Patty on his way in.

When I slouch into the office chair and bury my head into my shaking hands, Patty runs his wrinkle-covered hand down my back. "Did you give him the chance to explain?"

I raise my welling eyes. "No," I say with a shake of my head.

Patty's mature eyes peer straight through to my soul when he says, "You might want to listen to what the boy has to say. He's not a bad man, Ava. He cares for you."

"He hurt me, Patty."

"Trying to protect you."

My brows furrow, unable to grasp what he means by his statement.

Hugo was fighting with Marvin because of his jealousy.

Wasn't he?

The remainder of my time with Patty is in silence. It's the quietest we've ever been.

After placing a farewell kiss on his cheek, I walk to the elevator banks. The heaviness of my heart weighs down my shoulders, making my steps slow and lazy.

When the elevator dings open, my wrist is seized, and I'm hauled into the elevator car. My heart hammers against my ribs when Hugo stuffs a key into the lock on the dashboard. My anger that was slowly subsiding returns full pelt when the elevator doors snap shut tighter than a vault.

Gritting my teeth, I push every button available on the elevator panel. My efforts are fruitless, and the doors remain closed.

I knew Hugo living in my building would be a bad idea.

After rolling back my shoulders, I spin to face him. "Let me out."

He shakes his head. "No can do."

Fuming with anger, I cross my arms under my chest while pacing to the furthest corner of the elevator. I put as much distance between us as possible.

"You agreed to talk to me last night."

"I lied," I sneer. "There's nothing you could say that will make me forgive you, so you may as well save your breath."

"Luckily, I've always believed actions speak louder than words."

He snatches my wrist then yanks me toward him before his mouth crashes into mine so furiously, my lips feel bruised. I yank away from him, pushing hard on his chest. He firms his grip on the nape then plunges into my mouth. I clench down my teeth, gnawing on the very thing that caused most of my pain—his vindictive tongue.

My knees shake when his deep growl rumbles through my heaving chest. My disloyal nipples pebble, turned on by the roughness of his kiss, but guilt swamps me when the bitter tang of blood mingles with the sweet cinnamon taste of his mouth.

I didn't mean to hurt him. The buildup of anger was just too much for me to inhibit a second longer.

Even injured, Hugo continues to kiss the living hell out of me. He kisses me like a man starved of my taste.

Warm slickness coats my panties when I stop thrashing against him, no longer having the strength to fight off a man I've craved for years. My nipples tighten with pleasure as my fingers rake through his hair. When he realizes I'm no longer fighting him, Hugo adjusts the intensity of our kiss, switching it from a raw, primitive embrace to a sweet, heart-combusting one.

His tongue coaxes into my mouth, sweeping inside in slow, core-clenching strokes. He pulls me in close to his body, allowing me to feel how aroused he is by our kiss. A whimper escapes my lips when he grips my thighs to hoist me up the wall so I can grind against his thick, hard cock.

My heart clenches when he pulls back so he can peer into my eyes. His are full of remorse, and they're beaming with silent apologies.

"It killed me, Ava," he breathes heavily before dropping his lips to my neck. "Hearing him say he was going to touch you fucking killed me."

My brows scrunch, confused by his statement, but the crinkle between my brows smooths when he sucks on the skin of my neck, marking me with his mouth. "He was bragging to anyone who would listen that he only turned up to the wedding to take you home." He pulls his wicked mouth away from my tingling neck. "To fuck you and make you his."

When he stops talking to inspect the mark he created on my skin, his cock twitches, seemingly pleased with his effort. Arousal tingles down my spine when he sucks my erect nipple into his mouth through my shirt. I grip his hair as pleasure jolts through my pleading pussy.

My cotton shirt clings to my chest when Hugo releases my nipple from his gifted mouth with a loud pop. They peak even more when he blows air onto the moist material, then my breath hitches when he strays his eyes to mine. "When I saw you gathering your coat, preparing to leave with him, I lost it. I didn't want him to touch you. I *hated* the idea of him touching you. I want to be the only man who gets to touch you."

I gasp in a sharp breath while staring into his wild eyes. Even with his heart hammering his ribs so fast, I feel it pulse through my body, his eyes open and raw. They expose the cyclone of emotions surging through him.

Hugo has always been a communicator, but his eyes relay more than his words ever could.

I cup his jaw. "I wasn't leaving with Marvin. I was calling him a taxi," I explain while staring into a pair of eyes that have captured my soul. "There was only one man I wanted to leave with that night. That man was you."

A hiss seeps from his lips, fanning my heated cheeks. As I stare into his eyes, the ice that formed around my heart the past week thaws. The past seven days have been the hardest week of my life. I've barely functioned.

It's scary how quickly Hugo stole my heart. I shouldn't be surprised, though. He's been the only man occupying it the past ten years, so it was easy for me to relinquish its care to him.

I've always said my crush on Hugo was childish and immature, but in all honesty, I loved him from the moment I tackled him to the floor and straddled his hips.

"Do you have time to talk now?"

Smiling, I nod.

My heart stutters when he puts me back onto my feet before he stuffs the key into the elevator panel then jabs the penthouse button.

"How did you get a key for the elevator?" My voice is croaky from the roughness of our kiss.

"My boss owns the building."

I gasp. Now I know why I'd thought I had seen him before. He was the young man sitting in the corner of the room when I entrusted my money to the company building my apartment.

"Does your boss have a name, or are you just going to keep calling him 'boss?'"

My pulse flutters when a broad grin stretches across Hugo's sinfully handsome face. "I might just call him boss. It has a nice ring to it."

I roll my eyes, pretending I'm not loving his playfulness.

When the elevator arrives at Hugo's floor, he encloses his hand around mine then guides me out. The erratic beat of my heart starts up again as we stroll toward his door. When we reach it, he gathers a key from the top lip of the door. I huff while shaking my head. No matter how many times I advised the Marshall family that it isn't a safe practice, they continue to store their keys on the lip of the door frame.

Hugo unlocks his apartment door before he gestures for me to enter first.

"Why did it make you angry?" I question while kicking off my shoes and placing them at the side of the entryway table.

He throws his keys and cell phone into a crystal bowl on the table. "Did what make me angry?"

I lick my tingling lips before breathing out the words, "That I was a virgin."

Hugo freezes dead in his tracks. I mimic his frozen posture as a frenzy of emotions twists my stomach. When he spins to face me, I'm taken aback. I was expecting anger to reflect in his eyes, not remorse. "It didn't make me angry, Ava. I just wish you would have told me."

"And how exactly should I have done that? Had business cards made up to hand to dates, warning them they were in the presence of a naïve virgin?" I try to keep the bitchiness out of my tone, but I fail miserably.

Why is it anytime someone mentions the word 'virgin,' guys run for the hill? I could think of far worse words that could be used when referencing a women's sexual experience.

Hugo smirks at my witty comment, but his heart isn't fully into it. "I would have happily accepted a card if it avoided me hurting you."

"You didn't hurt me."

His appearance pales. "You bled, Ava."

"That's normal. That happens all the time." I stare into his remorseful eyes. "Have you never slept with a virgin before?"

His eyes widen before he shakes his head. I smile, loving that although I'm not the first woman he's slept with, I am his first something.

"Well, I guess you'll just have to take my word for it then. You didn't hurt me. I'm perfectly fine."

The veins in my neck strum when he crowds closer to me. "I don't have to take your word. You could prove it to me."

"How?" My overly girly voice echoes in the foyer of his apartment.

Agitated excitement spurs through me when hunger forms in his eyes. "You can show me."

Eagerness builds when he places his hand on the small of my back to lead me through his residence. Because his apartment is the exact replica of mine, only ten times bigger, I know where he's taking me.

My aching muscles from a lack of sleep the past week loosen when I surrender to the gentleness of his touch as he guides me toward the master suite of his penthouse. An array of emotions hit me at once when he swings open his bedroom door. Standing on shaky legs, my eyes absorb the grandeur of the room. A king-size bed covered in dark, rich material sits in the middle, a walk-in closet Carrie from *Sex and the City* would die for is on my right, and rich material covers the floor-to-ceiling windows on my left. The room is impressive and very manly.

Desire runs rampantly through my veins when the scent of Hugo's aftershave activating my senses is closely followed by the smell of his skin. I swallow hard when he walks me to the side of the bed, unbuttoning my blouse on the way. The material sags off my shoulders before it topples to the floor.

I inhale a quick, sharp breath when his hooded gaze drops to absorb my body. It is predatory and hungry, and it has my pulse thrumming.

His hands make quick work of my jeans. He yanks them down my quaking thighs until I am once again standing before him in nothing but a pair of panties and a lace bra.

"Lay down on the bed," Hugo instructs, nudging his head to the monstrous bed.

My unease about following his instructions fades when he pulls his shirt over his head, exposing inches upon inches of his delicious skin. As my eyes absorb every hard ridge of his muscles, I scoot across his king-size bed. It won't matter how many times I see his perfect body, it will never be enough—wide, broad shoulders bulked with muscles, drool-worthy biceps, a tight, lean waist, and legs that go for miles.

His body has been the cause of many self-induced orgasms the last eight years.

Unfortunately, since he only has two articles of clothing to remove, his seductive striptease doesn't take long.

I can't wait for winter.

The muscles in his arms flex when he yanks me down the bed. Any laughter preparing to escape my lips halts when his heated eyes burn into mine. While kneeling at the end of the bed, he hooks his thumbs into my panties and glides them down my quivering thighs, exposing me to his rapacious gaze. He stares unashamedly at my bare mound. My pussy aches, begging to be consumed by him, and excitement scorches my veins when he places his hands on my thighs to gently pry them open.

"Keep them there."

I bite my lip and nod, unable to secure an entire breath.

My thighs shake when he runs his index finger down my labia. "Does it hurt here?"

I shake my head. "No."

My breathing excites when he spreads my vagina open with his fingers, fully exposing me.

"Here?" The tip of his finger brushes my inner labia.

God no!

My body is thrumming with excitement.

"No," I breathe out huskily when his eyes wordlessly demand a verbal response.

When he rubs the pad of his thumb over the hood of my clit, I snap my eyes shut. "Here?"

I try to force the word 'no' out of my mouth, but my brain is too occupied with rampant horniness to relinquish words.

Taking my silence as a yes, Hugo mutters, "I better kiss it better then."

When his lips press a gentle kiss to my throbbing clit, I swivel my hips, shamelessly begging for more contact.

My pleas fall on deaf ears when he lifts his eyes to mine. "Is it better?"

Embarrassingly, I shake my head. I've never been one for deceit, but if a little lie forces him to touch me there again, I'm willing to bend the rules.

Hugo smiles, aware I'm lying, but thankfully, he lets my little white lie slip.

My back arches when his mouth encloses over my aching-with-desire clit. I gasp when he tongues my clit with quick-fired hits. Both my mind and my insides coil as husky moans seep from my lips. My eyes squeeze shut, and my body tingles, overwhelmed by how quickly my release is building.

"Fuck, you taste sweet. I've never eaten a sweeter pussy."

Hugo's dirty words send a tidal wave of desire gushing through my body. He's never had any trouble communicating, and I love that even in the bedroom, there is no exception.

As my race to climax hits momentum, I weave my fingers through his hair. He continues to lick, suck, and devour every inch of me, slurping up every drop of my excitement with a thirst of a man lost in the Sahara.

When the intensity becomes too much for me to bear, I grip his hair and yank him away from me.

"No, Ava," he murmurs against my clit. "That was dinner. Now give me my dessert."

My grip on his hair tightens. "I can't. I've never..." *climaxed on a man's face before.*

Although I was a virgin, I've taken part in other sexual activities. My primary goal during those exchanges was to ensure my partner's every whim was taken care of. I learned early on if they were thoroughly satisfied, they never cared that we didn't have sexual intercourse. All they cared about was getting off. So even though I have experience in this aspect of sexual encounters, I've never done *that* on a man's face.

"Then I'll once again be your first, babe, because I'm going to eat your pussy until you come on my face."

My body shakes, aroused by his determination, as his big hand slithers up my stomach to grope my breasts. With the combination of his tongue lavishing my clit and his talented fingers tweaking my nipples, all concerns vanish, and exhilaration takes over.

I groan and rock against him, my body coiled and ready to release.

"That's it, babe, give it to me."

His voice vibrating through my core sets me off. My body quakes when I splinter into a glass-shattering orgasm.

Hugo increases the speed of his lashes, forcing me to ride the wave of my climax instead of fighting against it. It is a crazy and wild out-of-body experience.

I've barely recovered from the earth-shattering aftermath when a condom wrapper being torn open sounds through my ears. I moan when the crown of Hugo's fat cock braces the entrance of my pussy. Anticipation about being filled to the brim by him heats my blood.

It turns to frustration when a delay stretches between us.

Surprised by the holdup, my head lifts off the bed, wondering why he hasn't plunged his thick cock inside me. Hugo's eyes are drifting around the room, seeking something. When he notices my curious glance, he says, "We need to change positions, or I'll hurt you again."

Before I can announce that he didn't hurt me the first time, he leaps off the bed. I crank my elbows to watch his naked retreat out of the room. I use the pause in proceedings to my advantage. I run my hands down my hair, de-fluffing the crazy mess then scrub at the mascara under my eyes.

My hands drop when Hugo walks back into the room, carrying a dining room chair. My mouth waters when my eyes zoom in on his rock-hard condom-covered cock.

After placing the chair in the middle of the room, he locks his eyes to mine. The raw, primal look in his eyes spears me in place. With a lift of his chin, he requests that I join him. Through shaking legs, I slide across the bed and saunter toward him. His eyes run the length of my body with as much eagerness as mine absorb him.

When I reach him, he sits down on the chair then offers me his hand. Excitement dashes through me when his thick shaft brushes my drenched folds when I straddle his lap.

"This way, you can guide the pace, only taking as much of my cock as you can handle."

When I nod, with his hands on my hips, he guides me upward until the entrance of my pussy is hovering over his thick, throbbing crown. The sting of both pleasure and pain jolts through my womb when I lower down, taking in the first inch of his cock.

"Go slower, Ava. You may be wet, but your body needs time to adjust."

My breathing stops when he raises his eyes from our fire-combusting connection to me. No apprehension. No concern. Nothing but admiration is sparked in his eyes.

He groans, and a swear word seeps from his lips when I slam down hard, taking every inch of his cock in one quick motion.

"Fuck, Ava," he growls, his fingertips bending as he obtains a tight grip on my hips to secure me to his pelvis. "I said to take it slow."

I shake my head. "You said to only take as much of your cock as I can handle." My words are breathless as my body relishes being stretched so wide.

"Because I didn't want to hurt you."

I stare into his narrowed eyes. "There's a very fine line between pleasure and pain."

Pleasure rockets through my body when he slaps my backside with enough force, fiery heat spreads across both cheeks. He stares into my eyes while soothing the sting of his slap with a gentle rub of his hand. "There's a very fine line between pleasure and pain, but there are other ways you can achieve that thrill than using my cock."

"But I like your cock." I breathe out heavily.

A meow purrs through my lips when his cock twitches, stretching me even wider.

"I take that back. I *love* your cock." *I've never felt so whole.*

The smile stretching across his face almost makes me come. My god, he is beautiful. A flawless specimen hand-crafted by God himself. I could stay like this forever. Our bodies are connected in the most intimate way, and his heart is felt through my palm resting on his chest as I stare dotingly into his eyes. It's perfect. Better than any dream I've ever had.

It's a memory I'll cherish forever—until the end of eternity.

TWENTY-FIVE

AVA

My eyes pop open when a tormented moan ripples through my ears. A strange, unknown environment surrounds me. Rich, dark coloring and a manly feel make my concern even more noticeable.

When another pained sound resonates through the quiet, I realize why I've awoken. It wasn't the thumping of my head from a lack of sleep or the thrumming of my pulse from experiencing countless orgasms overnight. It's someone in the midst of a nightmare.

I gingerly rise from the bed just as Hugo screams, "Get off!" at the top of his lungs. His leg kicks out, and his fists curl into tight, constricted balls. As he thrashes against the mattress, his face contorts with pain. "Stop it! Stop it! Get off!" he screams before a tormented cry shreds from his throat.

I scamper across the bed on my hands and knees. My hands shake when I raise them to his face, but before I can get them anywhere near him, he snatches up my wrist.

My face winces when a sharp pain jolts up my arm from his rigid hold. "Get off!" he screams again.

Ice-cold fear chills my veins when he tightens his grip. An

animalistic groan tears from his stern, shut lips as he shoves me away from him. From the brutal force of his throw, I sail off the bed and land halfway across the room.

Tears prick my eyes. Not from the pain of my wrist jarring against the carpeted floor but from the terrified mask hampering Hugo's face. His eyes rapidly move under his eyelids as his nightmare continues to wreak havoc on his usually cheeky nature.

He needs to wake up.

I need to wake him up.

"Hugo, wake up!" I shout from a distance, too scared to go near him but still wanting to ease him out of his nightmare.

His violent thrashing stills, but his face remains contorted with pain.

"Wake up!" I scream again as the first lot of tears spill from my eyes.

Abruptly, his eyes pop open.

His chest heaves up and down.

His pupils are the size of dinner plates.

His body is covered with a dense layer of sweat.

While panting hard, his panicked eyes dart around the room. When he notices me sprawled on the floor, the sternness on his face dissipates, and a new, unreadable shield slips in its place. "Ava?" His voice is extra hoarse from the tormented screams released during his nightmare.

I can tell the instant the reality hits him. The pain in his eyes firms as he climbs off the bed to kneel before me. Because of how much he's sweating, his woodsy scent is even more alluring than normal.

"Did I hurt you? Are you hurt?" he asks as his eyes assess my face and body.

The rapid shake of my head sends tears flying off my cheeks.

"Then why are you crying?" His eyes drift to the bed several feet from me. "And why are you on the floor?"

I try to construct a response, but with the combination of the events that just transpired and my restless night, I'm at a loss for words.

"Fuck." He sits on the balls of his feet before he runs a trembling hand over his head. His body is rigid, and the aftermath of his nightmare reflects in his clouded eyes.

After a short stretch of silence, he stands from his crouched position and stalks out of the room. I want to go after him but stay kneeling. My brain is too fried to force my legs to move, and a surge of emotions is crashing into me.

Once I've gathered my composure, I scamper off the floor and go after him. My heart races as I make my way out of the main bedroom and down the hall. The trickling of freshly brewed coffee in a percolator changes the course of my direction. The strong, heavenly scent activates my senses when I enter the kitchen, waking me more from my agitated state.

As tempting as a hot brew is right now, I exit the kitchen when I discover it is void of Hugo. After checking the den, dining room, and living areas, I make my way to the master bathroom on the other side of the apartment.

The sound of running water amplifies the further I walk down the hall. I knock on the partially cracked-open door before pushing it open. Through the billowing steam, I see Hugo standing under a double shower head. His feet are planted wide, his head is bowed, and the heavy pressure of the shower head is blasting hot water onto the nape of his neck.

When he senses my presence, he slants his head to the side. My heart cracks when I see the bleakness in his eyes. They appear almost lifeless. Utterly broken.

When his eyes return to the dark gray tiles, I strip out of my clothes, leaving them where they fall. Cold sweat clings to my skin when I open the glass door and slip into the steam-filled space. The muscles in Hugo's back flex when I run my hand down his spine, soothing him while also hopeful my touch will free him from the aftermath of his nightmare.

"I'm sorry if I hurt you, Ava." The brokenness in his voice breaks my heart.

"You didn't hurt me."

He angles his head to the side and stares into my eyes, calling out my deceit without words.

My heart slithers into my gut. "You scared me, but you didn't hurt me."

I slip under his arm bracing against the wall then wrap my arms around his waist. His racing heart pounds through my ear when I rest my head on his chest. "You're not capable of physically hurting me," I mumble against his chest.

He runs his trembling hand down my back before pulling me in closer.

Several long seconds later, I pop my head off his torso and peer into his downcast eyes. The furious beat of his heart pulverizes my hand when I press my palm to it and say, "This is the only thing that can hurt me. Not you."

"That's the most fucked up part of me," he says as his heavily dilated eyes dance between mine.

Lifting my hand, I cradle his sweat-drenched jaw. The blood coursing through his veins throbs against my palm. "Why? Because you had a nightmare?"

His eyes relay the words his mouth cannot speak.

He feels ashamed.

"Don't be ashamed of something you can't help. Nightmares in adults are generally caused by a psychological trigger. You have no control over them."

A rumble escapes Hugo's parted lips. "You sound like my therapist."

My eyes rocket to his. "You're seeing a therapist?"

"Not exactly," he grumbles. "My boss included it as a requirement of my employment, but I haven't turned up to a session yet."

My brows scrunch, wondering why that stipulation would be included in an employment contract. I've never heard of such a requirement before. Hugo watches me, soundlessly gauging my reaction to his confession he needs to see a therapist. I'm not concerned. There's no shame in seeking help during a crisis. Many men are embarrassed to admit they're struggling, but to me, acknowledging that you need help is one of the bravest things you can do.

I place a quick kiss on the edge of his mouth before squashing my cheek back against his chest. I don't want him to share anything he isn't willing to divulge.

Although his heart is still pounding forcefully, it isn't as intense as it was earlier.

A stretch of silence passes between us. It isn't long enough that the water cools, and it also isn't uncomfortable or weird. It actually feels right.

I run my hand over the small of his back, supporting him while his index finger traces the veins in my neck. With the heat of the water and the closeness of his body, any agitation hampering my mind soothes.

I can only hope it's the same for Hugo.

After a beat, he mutters, "I reacted the way I did because when I saw the blood running down your leg, I thought I'd hurt you."

I shake my head, denying his statement, but remain quiet, happy he's chosen to talk instead of keeping quiet.

"I wasn't angry at you. I was furious at myself. If I'd known you were a virgin, I would have ensured that you and your body were prepared. I wouldn't have done it the way I did."

"I'm glad you didn't know then." I lift my head off his chest so I can look into his eyes. "That night was better than anything I could have dreamed. Because you didn't know I was a virgin, it was void of the awkwardness I was prepared for. The fact you didn't treat me like a porcelain doll made it so much better. I couldn't have entrusted a better man with the task. Not many virgins get knocked-it-out-of-the-park sex on their first try. I not only got that, but I also orgasmed too."

I become lightheaded from the broad grin etching on Hugo's face. "That just proves I fucked up."

My brow arches high into the air. "How?"

He waggles his brows. "You can't get any better than a home run, so I've got no chance of topping that."

I laugh. "I'm sure you'll find a way."

After stretching onto my tippy toes, I seal my mouth over his.

He found a way to beat it.

Not once, but twice.

TWENTY-SIX
HUGO

Two weeks later...

"Come on in, Hugo."

My eyes lift from the outdated magazine to where the voice is coming from. A lady with short brown hair offers me a reassuring smile while gesturing for me to join her at the end of the hall.

"Avery Clarke. It's a pleasure to finally meet you in person, Hugo," she introduces before gesturing for me to enter her cramped office with a wave of her hand.

I run my sweaty palms down my trousers before entering the space. Bland, whitewashed walls, a cream shrink couch, and a large blind-covered window make her new office one of the most boring spaces I've ever encountered.

"A little bit of color wouldn't go astray," I mumble under my breath, my mood surly at being forced to attend therapy against my wishes.

"Sorry? What did you say?" Avery questions, closing the door behind her.

I shrug my shoulders. "I didn't say anything."

She smiles a tight grin before gesturing for me to sit. My eyes drift around the room. Other than a clinical-looking shrink bed in the middle of the space, there's a wooden desk and a leather chair squashed in the far corner of the room.

"I'll be back in a minute," I say, rushing to the door.

Not giving her the chance to reply, I dash into the even more outdated foyer of her office building to collect an empty chair. Avery's brow arches when I walk back into the room, carrying the chair in my arms.

After placing the chair down in the middle of the space, I drag her faded leather chair to sit across from it. Once I have the space set up in a less depressing configuration, I take a seat.

Air whizzes out of Avery's nostrils before she gathers a yellow-lined notepad from her briefcase and sits in the leather chair. She stares into my eyes while asking, "Are you comfortable?"

I cross my arms in front of my chest. I'm not trying to intimidate her, I just want to ensure she knows I'm not here of my own free will. "I am now."

"Before we get started, I want you to be aware that anything you say within these four walls—"

"Will remain in these four walls," I interrupt, not needing the same rundown I'd been given in Afghanistan.

She smiles, seemingly pleased by my response. "Is there anything you'd like to discuss today?" She tries to keep optimism out of her voice, but I didn't miss the increase of huskiness in her tone.

I shift my gaze to the window displaying the sun hanging high in the sky. It's rare for me to see the midday sun anymore. With my new job, I'm normally arriving home as the sun is rising. I wake Ava up with a mug of coffee and a few kisses, see her off to work, then I crawl into bed, where I stay until the sun is setting.

The past few weeks with Ava have been staggering—the best

time of my life. I've never felt as content as I have the past few weeks. I always said I wasn't interested in a relationship, but knowing Ava is waiting for me when I come home is the only thing keeping me going.

We have a vigorous, sexually-sparked relationship, but it's the quiet times when I watch her sleep that I realize it isn't the only connection we have. She's the anchor tethering me down during a storm—the yin to my yang. And as much as this makes it sound like I've awoken with a vagina, she stole my heart.

To be honest, after our first weekend together, I was worried my nightmare would have scared her away, but surprisingly, the twinkle her eyes get every time she looks at me didn't dampen at all. If anything, it grew stronger.

Although I knew my nightmares would eventually return—I hadn't had one in months—I was unprepared for how hard they would rattle me once they did return. That nightmare was by far the worst one I've endured because no matter how much Ava denies it, I didn't just scare her that night, I hurt her.

My nightmares are the reason I've stuck to my exhausting schedule of working from sundown to sunup seven days a week. Although Isaac is adamant I can choose my own schedule, I can't risk falling asleep with Ava next to me. That nightmare wasn't the only one I've had the past two weeks. I've had them numerous times, some more violent than the first.

By sticking with my current arrangement, I can see Ava while also keeping her safe.

I'll do everything in my power to keep her safe.

I shift my eyes back to Avery. She's watching me cautiously but stays quiet.

The fact she doesn't push me to talk eases my agitation.

"Is there anything I can do to stop nightmares?"

Although my arrangement with Ava is working fine as it is now, I eventually want to wake up with her sleeping in my arms.

Avery's brows furrow. "Are you having nightmares?"

Gritting my teeth, I nod. There's no harm in seeking help during a crisis, but this is different. My nightmares are based on real-life events, not because I watched a scary movie before going to bed.

"Are your nightmares about what happened in Afghanistan?"

My eyes snap to her. "You know about what happened there?"

Her throat works hard to swallow. "Yes." Her eyes are void of the judgment I was expecting to see. "Isaac supplied me with your details in the hope that I could help you through this, Hugo."

Unable to maintain her eye contact, my eyes shift around the room.

"How long have you been having nightmares?" She angles her head to the side, requesting my focus. She has eyes like Ava—inviting and warm.

They see me opening up.

"They stopped a few months after the incident, but they returned stronger than ever three weeks ago," I reply, my tone short.

Avery sits on the edge of her chair and peers deeply into my eyes. "Was there a significant change in your life that triggered their return?"

A grin twitches my lips. "I have a girlfriend," I say with a laugh, mortified by using a term only middle school kids should use.

A genuine smile spreads across Avery's face. "That's pretty significant."

I chuckle and uncross my arms, loosening my arrogant stance. I know if I give Avery a chance, I'll like her. She also doesn't deserve the wrath of anger I've shown her the past six weeks when she calls to do phone consultations with me. Although her career path is horrible, so is Ava's, and I *really* like Ava, even if she's the equivalent of every child's worst nightmare.

Avery's smile sags when I say, "I also stopped drinking."

She stares at me while nodding. "Alcohol can seem like an easy fix, but eventually, it isn't even enough anymore. Until you work through the underlying issue causing your nightmares, they'll never fully disappear."

I nod before turning my eyes back to the window. I'll never forget what happened in Afghanistan, so I guess I'll never stop having nightmares.

Avery places her hand over my clenched fist. "Something may have happened that triggered the return of your nightmares. Do you know what that may have been?"

I dump my purse in my desk drawer and dash out of my office. With summer arriving early, my free-flowing cotton dress is accentuated by the pair of rosy cheeks I've been wearing the past three weeks. There's no doubt my v-card has been well and truly handed in. I've had more sex the past few weeks than most women achieve by the time they're thirty. My sex life is so vigorous I'm rarely seen without an aroused appearance, but even with my excitement being embarrassingly exposed, I wouldn't change a single thing.

My relationship with Hugo has been going great—almost too perfectly. He greets me every morning with a hot brew before seeing me off with a kiss on the lips, then I arrive at his office every evening for an early dinner. We've had sex at nearly every location we've visited. His truck. His office. The storeroom at a bustling nightclub. Even the den at Jorgie's house.

Unsurprisingly, the only place we haven't slept together is at my work. Hugo is adamant he'll never step foot inside my office, let alone sit in my dentist chair.

Smiling at the mortified look on his face when I suggested he drop in for a quick check-up today, I enter the reception area to call in my first patient of the day. My eager steps falter when Marvin exits his office. Although his fight with Hugo was weeks ago, his face is still sporting some faded bruises. He's spent the past few weeks ignoring me, which suits me just fine. I have no intention of talking to him ever again anyway.

When sidestepping Marvin, my cell phone in the pocket of my white coat vibrates. Quickly, I slip it out of my pocket then peer down at the message on the screen.

JORGIE

Lunch?

I smile while typing a reply.

ME

Sounds great. I'll meet you at Capers at noon.

An ellipsis trickles across the screen as Jorgie types a response.

JORGIE

Yes! I was hoping you'd say Capers. I'm dying for their Caesar salad and cheeseburgers. See you at twelve.

Smiling at her excitement, I return my phone to my pocket, then call in Mrs. Roach and her son, Xavier, into the examination room attached to my office.

By the time midday rolls around, I'm starving. Not just for food, but Hugo as well. He's my addiction, and I'm beyond saving when it comes to him.

After slinging off my coat, I hang it on the coat rack in my office then dash down the corridor. Mrs. Gardner bids me farewell with a nod when I rush past her in the parking lot at the back of the office. A blast of hot air smashes my face when I enter my car. It's only mid-May, but the temperature has been hovering around the mid-eighties.

Jorgie greets me with a smile and numerous plates of food when I enter the restaurant twenty minutes later. "Hey, sorry I'm late. A mother's paranoia about a clean stretched my schedule thin." I lean in to place a kiss on her cheek.

"That's okay. It's not like I have anything better to do," she replies, her tone cheeky.

"How is the maternity leave going?" I steal a couple of French fries off her plate before signaling for a waiter.

Jorgie waits for him to jot down my order for two iced raspberry teas before replying, "It's as boring as hell. It's only been a week. I have no clue how I'll survive the next six months."

"You won't be saying that when you're juggling diapers, bottles, and a screaming baby in five weeks."

A large grin stretches across her face. "He'll be worth it," she mumbles while rubbing her expanded stomach.

"Yes, he will."

Jorgie huffs while adjusting her position before she lifts her eyes to me. "Well, enough about me and my watermelon. How are things with you and Hugo?"

I bite the inside of my cheek, internally battling to hide my excitement.

One glance into Jorgie's mist-filled eyes tells me she isn't buying my attempts at candor, so I spill the beans. "It's really good. I wake up every morning and pinch myself just to make sure I'm not dreaming."

I try to keep my tone neutral but miserably fail. I've never been happier. Hugo and I have only been officially together for a couple of weeks, but we have a lifetime of memories we share.

"I'm hardly sleeping because I don't want to wake up and find out it was all a dream. I also don't want to miss a single moment."

Now it's Jorgie's turn for tears to prick her eyes. "Oh, stop it," she demands while using a napkin to dab the rogue tears threatening to escape her eyes.

I pinch my thigh, sighing when I don't wake up from the dream I'm living.

After flinging my immature tears off my cheeks, I lean in close to Jorgie's side and whisper, "The rumors are true. Hugo's nickname you're trying to pretend doesn't exist... it is one hundred percent true!"

When my excited squeal gains us the attention of a handful of patrons, Jorgie gags. I laugh at her repulsed expression before taking a bite out of one of the many cheeseburgers in front of me.

After devouring enough food to feed a small community, I signal the server to bring us the bill.

"I'm paying," I declare when Jorgie collects her purse from her handbag. "It's the least I can do."

She looks at me, confused by my statement.

"If it weren't for you, I'd still be fighting fate."

When a large grin stretches across her face, my heart skips a beat. She and Hugo have many similarities. A heart-stopping smile is one of them.

After paying the bill, Jorgie and I walk out of the restaurant arm in arm. My eyes shoot to hers when she fails to suppress a big yawn. "Are you not sleeping?"

She shakes her head. "If having a watermelon strapped to your belly isn't bad enough, I can't sleep without Hawke next to me."

As my heart painfully squeezes, I pull Jorgie in for a hug. "He'll be home soon," I promise as a surge of emotions pummel into me.

I miss Hugo when I'm away from him for a few hours, so I can understand Jorgie's dilemma about not seeing Hawke for months. Thankfully, their absence this time around is only a matter of weeks. Hawke's squadron is returning home the week Jorgie is due.

"Do you want to join Hugo and me for dinner tonight?" Jorgie's nose scrunches as her face whitens. "I promise I'll keep my hands to myself at all times," I say after crossing my fingers behind my back.

She eyes me dubiously, but in her tired state, she doesn't spot my lie. "Alright, but if I see one thing that makes me gag, your lunch schedule for the next five weeks is booked out." She bumps me with her hip. "I've missed you a lot the past few weeks."

My heart warms. I've missed her too, more than she'll ever know.

"Deal," I say, raising my pinkie into the air.

Giggling, she accepts my pinkie promise.

"Where are you parked?" I ask while seeking her beat-up Honda in the street.

She peers past my shoulder. "Across the street."

I gasp when I spot Baby parked a couple of spots up. "You got Baby on the road?"

She smiles. "Yep." The 'P' pops from her mouth. "She still needs a bit of work, but she's drivable."

Her head cranks to the right before she shifts it to the left. "Where are you parked?"

"Halfway down the block," I grumble. "I went around the block three times, and I still couldn't find an empty spot."

Smiling, Jorgie wraps her arms around my neck and hugs me goodbye.

"Bye," I murmur in her ear.

"You don't say goodbye, you say, I'll see you later," she reminds me.

I pull back from her embrace and peer into her glistening eyes. "And that I will," I reply with a smile. "I'll see you tonight."

She nods before returning my grin. After running my hand down her arm, I pivot on my heels and stalk away. The sun warms my arms as I stroll to my car, but it has nothing on the heat that treks through me when my rummage for my keys in my handbag announces I have a new text message.

My heart races when I read the message.

HUGO

I cleaned out the storeroom in anticipation
of your visit. I can't wait to see you.

Grinning like the cat watching the canary, I press the speed dial for Hugo's number then press my phone to my ear.

My smile fades when my call is directed to his voicemail. "Hey, you've reached Hugo. Leave a message."

"Hey," I say breathlessly, my excitement heard in my voice. "We have a special guest for dinn—"

I stop talking when tires skidding across asphalt boom into my ears. Fear clutches my heart from the awful sound. When my neck cranks toward the noise, distress surges through my blood, turning it black. As my heart breaks, my phone slips from my hand and tumbles to the ground. The screen cracks when it connects with the sidewalk. It shatters into a million pieces—just like my heart.

TWENTY-EIGHT
HUGO

"Mark, can you give Dane a hand unloading the supply truck, please?"

Mark waggles his brows before bolting out the back entrance of The Chapel.

"And don't break anything today," I yell with a roll of my eyes.

Mark is the newest bartender at The Chapel. If it weren't for his *GQ* magazine cover looks, I would have let him go his very first night, but even with him spilling more drinks than he serves, the female clientele loves him. Whenever he's on duty, they flock the club in droves. He's good for business and staff morale.

"We're not open for a few more hours," I advise when the entrance bell on the front door chimes.

I finish scribbling my signature at the bottom of a receipt before drifting my eyes to the door. I'm shocked when I spot Ava standing there, staring at me with wide eyes.

"Hey," I greet while pacing closer, wanting less space between us before my eyes ravish her skin. "You're early." I lean in to press a kiss on her mouth.

Normally, she doesn't arrive until a little after six. We have dinner together in my office before she occupies the remaining hour of my self-prescribed two-hour lunch break.

She must have got a little excited about my text message.

My brows scrunch at how cold Ava's mouth feels when my lips brush against it. Although we haven't hit summer yet, the temperatures the past week have been setting record highs. Pulling her to arm's length, I run my eyes over her face. Her pupils are massive, filling her corneas, her face is white and covered with a dense layer of sweat, but the most concerning feature is the devastation reflecting out of her beautiful eyes.

Her terrified look sets me on edge. "Ava, babe, are you okay?"

"Y-your phone," she stutters. My confused eyes bounce between hers, baffled by what my phone has to do with her frantic state. My stomach cramps with dread when she stammers out, "Y-y-you didn't answer your phone."

I run my hand down the front of my jeans, discovering my pockets are empty. "I must have left it in my truck after my appointment with Avery."

Despair slams into my chest when fresh tears spill down Ava's pale cheeks. A rock settles into my stomach, subjugated with confusion. My eyes dart from Ava to Isaac when he pushes off the doorframe of my office, and he moves to stand next to me.

"Ava, what's going on?" When I lower my eyes to the rest of her body, the air in my lungs is forcefully sucked out when I notice a bloodstain on her dress. "Did someone hurt you? Are you hurt?" My words come out in a frantic rush as fury blackens my veins, heating my body. "Who did this to you? Did Marvin do this?"

Tears fling off Ava's cheeks when she shakes her head. After running her hand under her nose, wiping away the contents spilling there, she whimpers, "There was an accident."

Her eyes are glancing past me. She looks like she's in a trance.

Carefully, I grip her chin then slant her head upward. "You were in an accident? Is that why you have blood on your dress?" I try to keep my tone neutral, but my panic makes it come out as abrupt.

Conscious I'm spiraling out of control, unable to grip the reality of the situation, I turn my bewildered eyes to Isaac. I stare at him, wordlessly questioning if he has any better understanding of the situation. He looks just as lost as I feel.

My eyes rocket back to Ava when she says, "Not me. Jorgie," through a barrage of hiccups.

Fear grips my heart. "Jorgie was in an accident?"

A painful sob tears from Ava's mouth before she nods.

"Where?"

Her pupils widen even more, but she remains silent.

"Where, Ava!" I yell, projecting my voice over the ringing of my pulse in my ears. "Where is she?"

When Ava stays quiet, Isaac grips the top of her arms and shakes her hard enough her teeth clang together. Normally, his type of rough handling would cause my blood to turn black, but I can tell from the look in his eyes, he isn't trying to hurt Ava. He's doing everything in his power to snap her out of her trance.

"Where is Jorgie, Ava?" Isaac's tone is demanding and clipped. "Tell Hugo where Jorgie is!"

Ava's massively dilated eyes lock with mine before she mumbles, "She's at the hospital."

I'm out the double doors before all her sentence escapes her cracked lips.

TWENTY-NINE
AVA

When Hugo's boss wraps his arm around my shoulders, I flinch.

"It's okay," he mutters, his voice shifting from the angry roar that pulled me out of my stupor to a soothing purr. As he guides me toward the door Hugo just bolted through, he says, "I'm going to take you to the hospital." Suddenly, he stops walking then peers down at me. The sincerity in his unique gray eyes causes new tears to form in mine. "Do you want to go to the hospital?"

My chin quivers as I nod. No matter how broken my heart is, I need to be there for Hugo.

Hugo's boss smirks in an attempt to ease the haze clouding my mind before he peers past my shoulder. "Roger, bring my car around."

The ten-minute trip to the hospital is made in silence. Although Hugo's boss doesn't seem the talkative type, he offers silent support the entire way. He grips my clammy hand while running his thumb over the veins bulging in my thumb.

Due to Roger breaking every possible traffic law, we enter the hospital emergency bay not long after Hugo. A crippling pain twists in my stomach when he throws open his truck door and rushes through the hospital's automatic glass doors. I unclasp my seat belt, toss it off my body, then take off after him.

I shake my head, begging for the images that will haunt my dreams to stop playing on repeat. Once the fog hampering my brain is clear, I increase my pace. My urgent steps are guided by the need to ensure both Jorgie and Hugo are safe.

Before she was carried off in an ambulance, she locked her pain-filled eyes with mine. "I'll see you soon," she whispered weakly before they slammed the ambulance doors shut.

When I round the corner of the emergency department, I spot Hugo at the nurses' station, frantically requesting information from the only nurse there. He runs his trembling hand through his hair, frustrated by the nurse's lack of knowledge. His posture shows his first emotion is fear. It is closely followed by anger.

His head cranks to the side when Rhys walks out a set of doors in scrubs. Hugo charges for him, reaching him in two heart-thrashing seconds. The concerned mask on Rhys's face causes my stomach to churn. He only began his surgical internship three weeks ago, but he already looks exhausted.

I can't hear any words they share, but their conversation looks heated. Hugo's clenched fists tighten with every second that passes. My hand darts up to clutch my neck when he grabs Rhys by the neck and throws him against the wall. As I stand still, frozen in shock, two security guards attempt to drag Hugo off Rhys. Their efforts are pointless. Hugo is too strong and too angry.

Rhys is only released from Hugo's deadly clutch when Hugo's boss drags him away. As Rhys falls to his knees, gasping for air, Hugo yanks away from his boss. When he storms for the emergency department exit doors, my heart is torn into shreds from the devastation on his face.

The broken look in his eyes after his nightmare was nothing compared to the soulless look they have now.

Air wafts my face when he storms past me, tossing over a medical equipment cart on the way by. Unable to secure a breath, I crumble to the floor in a heap.

When my devastation becomes too much to bear, I permit my tears to fall. Loud, howling sobs bounce off the hospital walls and jingle in my ears. My distressed cries become even louder when I realize the howling is coming from me.

When polished black shoes appear in my field of vision, I lift my tear-drenched face. The scent of expensive cologne engulfs my senses when Hugo's boss crouches down in front of me. After accepting the handkerchief he is offering, I wipe my tears and blow my nose.

A pain I've never experienced before rips my heart to pieces when his gray eyes stare into mine as he says, "You need to get Jorgie's family here. She isn't going to make it."

My eyes lift to the lettuce leaves in the sink to the treehouse in the backyard. A handful of the kids from the neighborhood, too young to understand the complexity of the situation, are climbing the rickety wooden ladder. Their bright smiles are amplified by the sun hanging in the sky.

That was the treehouse I sat in, quivering like a bag of nerves when I confessed my crush on Hugo to Jorgie. I'd expected her to take the news a lot worse than she did. Although she said it was "totally gross" that I'd ever find Hugo attractive, she also said she'd support me no matter what.

I'm going to miss her every day of my life.

Against the doctor's advice, the Marshall family kept Jorgie on life support for three days. It gave Hawke the opportunity to say goodbye to the love of his life. Three hours after he returned home, they switched off Jorgie's life support.

She passed away a few hours after that, surrounded by her family and friends.

She was buried this morning with her son, Malcolm, resting in her arms.

It was a beautiful service, packed with attendees as far as the eye could see. The Marshall family is a well-respected and much-loved entity in the Rochdale community and that shone through at Jorgie's funeral. No expense was spared to give her the heartfelt sendoff she deserved.

I run my hands down my black sheath dress, smoothing out the invisible crinkles I believe are there before pouring the washed lettuce into the salad bowl. Once Mrs. Mable places cherry tomatoes and cucumber slices on top of the lettuce, I walk the bowl into the dining room.

Making sure the food table stocked is helping to keep my mind off my grief.

Mrs. Hamilton, Jorgie's fourth-grade teacher, watches me as I cross the room. She doesn't speak, but her eyes relay her silent sympathies.

After placing the tossed salad on the table, I roam my eyes around the space. Everyone here had some significant part in Jorgie's life— either a family member, teacher, friend, or work colleague.

I was the only one lucky enough to class her as both my family and friend.

As I head back into the kitchen, I stop, frozen in my tracks, believing I saw Hugo's profile. Although I saw him at the funeral, I haven't *seen* him since the night they switched off Jorgie's life support. I don't have solid evidence, but I'm fairly certain he's sleeping at his office.

I want to help him through his grief, but I'm at a loss on how to do that while also dealing with my own anguish.

Through shaky steps, I move in the direction of where I thought I saw him. Several eyes stray to mine to issue silent sympathies as I skirt by.

Although I can't see Hugo, I know he's here somewhere. I can feel it in my bones.

When I turn down the hallway, I spot him and a flurry of blonde.

I shake my head, certain I haven't seen whom I think I've seen.

My heart thrashes against my chest as I walk down the hall and take a left at the end. I freeze at the back screen door of the Marshall residence, giving my eyes a chance to assess the situation so I don't make an irrational decision.

Once I'm certain I have the facts right, I storm out the screen door. Upon hearing the creak of the door, Hugo's eyes snap to mine. He tries to speak, but his words stay entombed in his throat. It's for the best. I sidestep him so I'm in front of the bitch deserving of the full severity of my wrath.

My palm sets on fire when I slap Victoria so viciously, her head flings to the side. "You're a piece of shit! Using his grief to dig your claws back into him." My tone is dangerously low as an absurd amount of anger crashes into me so hard and fast, I'm nearly sprawled onto my ass. "You're nothing but a motherfucking whore!"

An arm wraps around my waist and yanks me back. I thrash and kick wildly, fighting against Hugo's hold. When that doesn't work, I dig my nails into his arm so hard I draw blood.

I've never been a violent person, but that doesn't stop me from inflicting as much damage as I can to Hugo's shins and arms as he carries me down the deck stairs and further into the backyard.

When he places me onto my feet in the garage at the side of the Marshall residence, I violently yank away from him.

"Calm the fuck down." He stares at me with wild eyes. "That wasn't what it looked like."

I laugh a scary, menacing chuckle that displays what I've suspected the past five days.

I no longer have a beating heart in my chest.

"It wasn't?" I ask, my pitch smeared with bitchiness. When he shakes his head, I yell, "Then why do you have lipstick smeared on your damn mouth?"

Hugo's eyes widen before he runs the back of his hand over his lips, removing Victoria's fire-engine red lipstick from his mouth. A curse word sweeps from his lips when his eyes absorb the red stain marking his hand.

When he takes a step closer to me, I violently shake my head. "Stay away from me," I sneer through clenched teeth. "I don't want you to touch me!"

My words have more of an effect on him than any slap I could have inflicted. He stands across from me, staring but not speaking. Other than his jaw twitching, he remains perfectly still.

My gaze flicks to Victoria standing at the side entrance of the house. Her eyes are drifting around the surroundings, no doubt seeking out Hugo. I can barely breathe through the anger enveloping every fiber in my body.

I'm not just angry about them kissing.

I am fuming mad that Hugo left me to deal with my grief alone.

No support.

No backup.

He just left me to battle through my grief one tear at a time.

He wasn't the only one who lost Jorgie. I lost her too.

I straighten my shoulders before returning my eyes to Hugo. His fists are clenched, and his chest rises and falls with every breath he takes. "You can have her." I nudge my head to Victoria. "Because I deserve way more than you could ever give me."

With that, I pivot on my heels and exit the garage.

Hugo lets me go without a single protest.

And that... that hurts more than anything.

THIRTY
HUGO

Four weeks later...

"Are you sure you want to pack it all away? He may change his mind."

My mom's eyes lift from the box she's packing to me. The spark of life that usually fires in her eyes has been snuffed, replaced with a glimmer I don't recognize. They're full to the brim with turmoil and loss.

Even though it's been four weeks since Jorgie passed away, my family is still in the process of grieving. I honestly don't know if we'll ever come to terms with our loss.

"Hawke is never coming back, Hugo. I could see it in his eyes when he said goodbye," she whispers faintly.

I tried to convince Hawke to take some time to formulate a rational decision, but he re-enlisted in the military the day after Jorgie's funeral. He left for Iraq two days after that.

It almost killed me seeing the devastation of his loss in his eyes. I was struggling losing my baby sister and nephew, but he lost his wife and son in one devastatingly cruel blow.

That's more than any man should *ever* have to go through.

I shadowed Hawke from afar the days following Jorgie's death, making sure he didn't do anything to harm himself or anyone around him. Most of his time was spent at the bar on the outskirts of town that refused to hire me several months ago, stating there were no suitable positions for a man like me.

I wanted to talk to Hawke, to offer him my support, but when I looked into his eyes, I knew solitude was the only thing he wanted.

Silence is the one true friend that never betrays you.

I fold down the flap on a brown moving box and seal it with a strip of tape before placing it on the stack of boxes at my side. I've spent the last several hours aiding my mom in packing up Jorgie's house. It isn't a task I want to complete, but someone has to do it, and I couldn't leave that burden resting solely on my mom's shoulders.

Upon noticing that the kitchen and living room have been packed, I move to the main bedroom. Jorgie's room is untouched, left as it was the day she died. Her perfume bottle is sitting open on her dresser alongside a collection of souvenirs she amassed over the years.

A smile tugs on my lips when I spot a button pin for Lake George. Jorgie loved visiting that lake as much as I did. Every school break, my parents rented the same cabin on the water's edge. From the age of ten, Ava joined most of our family vacations. Like every young boy, I taunted my crush the entire break. Ava kept me thoroughly entertained.

Lake George is also where Jorgie met Hawke. If you asked Jorgie to explain how they met, she would say he was an angel who fell from heaven and landed in her canoe.

It sounded more extravagant than it was.

In reality, he was climbing a tree to get the clothes I'd thrown up there after he went on an impromptu skinny dip with a group of college girls. When a branch cracked under his heavy weight, he assumed the water would soften his fall. He never expected to crash into a wooden canoe.

He missed four games over the summer, waiting for the bruises on his back to heal and even more weeks than that chasing Jorgie.

I slip out of Jorgie's room, closing the door behind me.

I've done more packing than I can handle today.

"Do you think Ava would want this?" my mom asks when I enter the living room.

The first genuine smile in weeks crosses my face. Nodding, I remove the friendship rock from my mom's grasp. My smile enlarges when I see the difference in the size of the hands painted on the rock. Ava's handprint is much smaller than Jorgie's.

I haven't seen Ava since Jorgie's funeral. As much as what she said hurt me, it was true. I've always known she deserved a man much better than me. I was just hoping she was foolish enough not to care.

What she stumbled on at the back patio with Vicky wasn't as it seemed. Yes, I did have Victoria's lipstick smeared on my mouth, but that was only because she dove at me before I could register what she was doing.

I pulled away from her in an instant, fuming with anger. I had just buried my sister and nephew, and the last thing I was interested in was a quick fuck in the coatroom.

Even if I weren't attending a wake, I still wouldn't have been interested in what Victoria is offering. You can't spend weeks devouring a prime steak then go back to eating a pork chop.

I was in the process of removing Victoria from Jorgie's wake when Ava discovered us.

I'm going to be honest, seeing Ava finally stand up to Victoria was one of the most visually satisfying things I'd ever seen. Victoria taunted both Ava and Jorgie for years, so witnessing her being put in her place was a gratifying experience.

My eyes snap to my mom when a loud gasp escapes her lips. One hand is covering her mouth and the other is clutching a piece of paper. She's trembling so much, the paper shakes like a leaf.

When her eyes drift to mine, my steps falter. It's only the smallest spark, but it is the first time I've seen it in her eyes in weeks. It's happiness.

"What is it?"

When my mom remains quiet, I remove the paper from her hand. My brows scrunch when my eyes scan the document, speed reading the letter from the bank Jorgie worked at. "Jorgie and Hawke's mortgage was paid in full?"

As tears roll down my mom's cheek, she nods. "Do you think it's from the same company who paid Jorgie's medical expenses and funeral?"

My eyes rocket from the letter to my mom. I was unaware someone had paid for Jorgie's funeral expenses. Up until now, I didn't consider how my parents could afford those types of expenses. I was too focused on my grief to worry about those details.

"What was the name of the company?" I query, even though I'm certain I already know the answer to my question.

"Holt Enterprises," my mom replies.

When he perceives my presence, Isaac's gray eyes snap up from his desk covered in papers to me.

"Did you pay my sister's mortgage?" I question, pacing further into his office.

After standing from his chair, he buttons his suit jacket. "Yes."

"Why?"

His eyes bore into mine as he scratches his brow. Most men would be quaking in their boots from the fierce look he's hitting me with, but I can see behind the furious mask he wears that he is a man struggling as much as me.

His eyes drift to the open door of his office before he turns them back to me. "I understand what Hawke is going through." My brows furrow, but I remain silent, waiting for him to elaborate on his reply. He does a short time later. "Seven months ago, my girlfriend was killed in a traffic accident. She was pregnant with my baby."

I suck in a big breath, shocked by his response.

How is he functioning so well in such a short period?

I wonder if he can read minds when he mutters, "Everyone handles grief differently. I threw myself into building my empire."

I nod, finally understanding why Hawke left so quickly.

If he didn't occupy his mind, he would have gone mad.

"Although your stories are similar, it doesn't explain why you were so generous. You don't even know Hawke. He's a stranger to you."

"But I know you," Isaac interrupts. "When you joined my empire, you became family. I take care of my family." Even though his tone is stern, his eyes reflect nothing but genuine remorse.

I once again nod.

I spent my entire life protecting my sister, but the one time she needed me the most, I failed.

A shrilling cell phone echoes in the silence that has encroached Isaac's office. I shove my hand into my pocket when its vibration jingles through my thigh. I'm surprised when I notice it's my mom calling. I only left her ten minutes ago.

Hitting the connect button, I press the phone to my ear. "He's getting away with killing my baby," she yells down the line before I get the chance to issue a greeting. "The DA just called. He was released this morning. All charges have been dropped."

"What?" I reply, my mind spiraling.

The man driving the car that struck Jorgie was three times over the limit. He was arrested at the scene and charged with vehicular manslaughter.

How could he get away with this?

It makes no sense.

"There must be a mistake. It can't be true. He was arrested at the scene."

"The only mistake is that the bastard who killed my baby now gets to walk free," my mom sobs.

I clutch the phone so tightly my knuckles go white when my mom's howling sobs sound down the line. "I'll fix this. I'll make it right," I promise before disconnecting the call.

My brisk strides out of Isaac's office slow when he calls my name.

After cranking my neck, I stare into his stern eyes as he warns, "Haste decisions will cause unforgiving mistakes."

"And sitting around doing nothing will make me a coward." My jaw ticks as the wave of emotions hits me at once. "I failed to protect Jorgie, but I will *not* let her murderer walk free."

THIRTY-ONE
AVA

Two weeks later...

"**G**ood boy, Jarrod. Just one last swish of water, and you're good to go."

Jarrod's excited eyes dart to his mom sitting in the corner of the room, seeking praise for the bravery he showed while having his first filling done. I slide my swivel chair over to my desk to collect a roll of stickers I keep in the bottom drawer. A smile tugs on my mouth when I notice the first sticker is a gold sheriff's badge with 'Sheriff Brave' printed on it.

Jarrod squeals excitedly when I hand him the sticker before assisting him down from the dental chair.

"Now remember, no more yogurt before bed. Yogurt has calcium in it, but it also has a lot of nasty sugars your teeth don't want to sleep in," I say, rising from my chair.

Jarrod eagerly nods before he joins his mother. The fake smile on my face slips the instant they exit my office. I slump into my chair and swivel around to peer out my small office window. The room is completely silent, and I've never felt more alone. I not only lost my best friend when Jorgie passed away, but I also lost part of my soul. And the loss has been even more devastating since I lost Hugo as well.

Suffering the loss of two exceptionally important people in my life within days of each other was nearly more than I could bear. I barely functioned the days following Jorgie's death. If it weren't for Patty bringing me food and forcing me to eat, I would have perished on the bed I refused to leave.

I only returned to the land of the living when the two weeks' bereavement leave Mrs. Gardner kindly granted expired. For the past four weeks, I've thrown myself into my job. I arrive before the sun rises and leave once the sky is pitch black. Occupying my mind has been the only godsend in this horrible situation. Work is truly the only thing keeping my head above water.

After running the back of my hand over my cheeks, I remove a handful of stray tears that fell from my eyes before I gather my belongings from my desk in preparation to go to lunch. My stomach is swirling, but if I don't eat, I'll die.

Like that would be a bad thing.

I inhale a quick, sharp breath when my cell phone displays I have a voicemail. My shock isn't because no one has called my phone in weeks but because the voicemail is from Hugo.

I've missed him more than words can ever express, but I'm also angry at him... *and myself.* I'd give anything to see Jorgie again, but Hugo lives in my apartment building, and I still haven't worked up the courage to see him.

Jorgie's death should have brought us closer. It should have made us realize that life is too short, and we should cherish every moment, but instead of doing that, I'm letting stupid jealousy rule my heart.

My heart hammers against my ribs when I dial my voicemail and press my phone to my ear. Seconds feel like hours as I wait for the call to connect.

"Hey, Ava. It's Hugo." Tears prick my eyes from his dejected tone. Then they roll down my face when he says, "I've missed you so much, babe, more than you'll ever realize." I push the phone in close to my ear, ensuring I can hear his message over the furious pounding of my heart. "I didn't kiss Victoria at Jorgie's wake... I know what it looked like, but I swear on Jorgie's grave, it wasn't as it seemed. I'd never betray you like that, Ava. I could never... I love you. I have for years. Ever since you dove over the couch and tackled me to the ground." A loud sob tears from my parted lips. "I hope one day you'll find it in your heart to forgive me for what I've done."

When the line goes silent, I squash the phone in tightly to my ear, assuming the line has gone dead. It's only when I hear Hugo's pants of breath do I realize he hasn't hung up.

"Goodbye, Ava," he says a short time later before he disconnects the call.

My finger shakes as I redial my voicemail and listen to his message again, and again, and again, only stopping when a commotion outside the office draws my attention.

"Sir, you can't go in there," Belinda, the office receptionist, says as my office door swings open.

I stand from my chair, shocked when Hugo's boss enters my office unannounced. I haven't seen him since the afternoon at the hospital.

"Where would Hugo go if he didn't want anyone to find him?" he questions me, his words hurried and abrupt.

"What? I don't know. I haven't seen Hugo in weeks."

When I step toward him, my brisk strides halt, cut off by the furious glare he inflicts on me. "An isolated place he could go where no one would find him? He wouldn't have any fear of being seen?"

"I don't know." I shake my head as my voice gains an edge of fury behind it.

"Think, Ava, think!" he demands, stepping closer to me. "There has to be somewhere he could go for privacy?"

The concern in his eyes causes my stomach to twist in panic, but

I try to help him. It's the least I can do after what he did for Jorgie's family. "Lake George?"

The suit-clad man shakes his head. "No, it has to be closer. Somewhere local."

A range of addresses flurry in my mind, adding to the giddiness cluttering my brain. There's nowhere Hugo could go that he'd be alone. Every residence I can think of is occupied.

Suddenly, I freeze.

My eyes snap to Hugo's boss. He's watching me with a pleading look in his eyes.

"Jorgie's house?" I suggest, my tone flat.

His eyes widen, and his shoulders square. "Yes. Where did she live?"

"Umm... I don't know?"

"Please, Ava, this is very important."

"I honestly don't know." My eyes relay that I'm telling the truth, but just in case, I mutter, "I've only ever driven there."

His hand delves into his pocket to remove an ancient-looking cell phone. The urgency of his movements sets me on edge.

"I could show you where she lived?"

He nods before he houses his cell phone back into his pocket. "We need to hurry."

When he pivots on his heels and exits my office, I grab my handbag from my desk drawer then follow after him. Halfway down, Marvin steps into the hallway. His eyes flick between Hugo's boss and me before he warns, "If you leave, you'll risk your career. You will lose everything."

Without hesitation, I reply, "I don't care. He's worth it."

I sidestep Marvin with my head held high, pretending my heart isn't racing a million miles an hour. I slide into the back seat of a Lexus town car parked at the curb. Hugo's boss holds a conversation on a large brick cell phone as Roger weaves us through the streets of Rochdale. I don't hear any of the words he's speaking. The ringing of my pulse is too loud to hear anything.

We arrive at Jorgie's house in record time. Relief overwhelms me when I spot Hugo's truck parked half a block down.

It doesn't linger for long.

Why would Hugo not park his truck in Jorgie's driveway?

When I attempt to follow Hugo's boss down the sidewalk, he pivots around to face me. The sternness in his eyes causes my steps to falter and has my thighs quaking. Once he realizes I'm frozen in fear, he drifts his eyes to Roger, who is still exiting the car. "Make sure she stays here," he instructs, his tone firm.

My stomach flips as I watch his quick retreat into Jorgie's house. I swallow several times in a row, fighting to keep the bile in my stomach from surging up my throat.

Even in the humid, suffocating air, an icy chill darts down my spine.

No longer able to hold in my fear, I vomit in the gutter, narrowly missing Roger's polished shoes. Since I skipped lunch, my body only expels small portions of green bile.

After accepting a handkerchief from Roger, I dab my mouth, removing leftover smears of vomit before straightening my spine. After what feels like a lifetime, Hugo exits Jorgie's front door. His face is gaunt and pale, his shirt has flecks of blood on it, and his eyes are dark and lifeless.

He takes a step backward, hesitating when he notices me standing on the sidewalk.

I brush away a tear tracking down my face before staring at him. The pain in his eyes amplifies when he returns my stare. So many unspoken words drift between us as we stand across from each other, staring but not speaking.

Our searing staredown only stops when Hugo's boss emerges from Jorgie's house. His dark eyes drift between Hugo and me for several heart-clutching seconds before they lock with Hugo. Hugo's eyes snap to mine when his boss mutters something in his ear. Although I can't hear what his boss is saying, I know the news he's delivering isn't good because Hugo has the same look in his eyes he did when I stammered out that Jorgie had been in an accident.

My mind reels out of control when Hugo commences walking down the concrete sidewalk. I clutch my chest when he takes a left at the end of the path. I'm standing at his right. He walks three steps away before he suddenly stops. His shoulders rise and fall with every breath he takes, but he stays frozen with his back facing me.

As I pray for him to turn around, to have the courage to face me, the courage to fight for us, my heart wildly beats. Its twist hurts from his slumped, defeated posture. I try to think of something to force a reaction out of him, to stimulate him to remember our powerful connection.

When I recall his earlier voicemail message, I shout, "You don't say goodbye, you say, 'I'll see you later.'"

For once, my prayers are answered. He pivots on his heels and charges for me. His lips crash into mine with so much force, my feet lift from the ground. After bracing my back on his boss's town car, he kisses the living hell out of me.

I kiss him back with just as much passion, expressing everything I wanted to say to him the past six weeks—my sorrow, my apologies, my regret for my cruel words.

As his tongue strokes mine, tasting and absorbing every inch of my mouth, he steps closer, pinning me between his imposing body and the car door. Heat pools in my nether regions when his thick cock braces against my pussy and halfway up my stomach, but tears well in my eyes about the passion displayed in our kiss. Every stroke, nip, and gentle caress have my heart enlarging more.

He kisses me like a man who owns me because he does.

By the time he pulls away, my lips are nearly as swollen as my heart.

As Hugo's fire-sparked eyes dance between mine, he carefully places me back onto my feet. He removes the tears dripping down my cheeks, rubbing them away with a sense of urgency. Once he's satisfied all my tear stains are gone, he cups my face.

Air whistles out of my mouth when he stares lovingly into my eyes as he says, "Goodbye, Ava."

He races down the sidewalk even quicker than earlier. I don't take my eyes off him as he urgently strides to his truck and jumps inside. His tires squeal from his heavy compression of the accelerator, and the look on his face when he whizzes past me places a constrictive hold on my heart.

Once the smell of burning rubber no longer mingles in the air, Roger guides me into the back seat of the town car. When he pulls the Lexus away from the curb, I crank my neck in enough time to see Hugo's boss re-entering Jorgie's house.

Twenty minutes later, I walk into the foyer of my office building, more confused than ever. Mrs. Gardner's dark eyes drift to mine when I enter. My voice rattles when I blurt out the first excuse that enters my brain. "I'm back from lunch."

I don't know how I did it, but I finished all my patients' appointments, and I even took in an emergency case of a little boy whose front tooth was chipped by his brother's fast curveball.

By the time I'm leaving my office, it's a little after nine o'clock.

Patty greets me with an apprehensive smile when I enter the foyer of my apartment building. "Good evening, Ms. Westcott."

"Hi, Patty."

"Rough day?" he asks, already intuiting what my answer will be.

"I could really go for a glass of wine right now."

He chuckles before pushing the elevator button for me. I stare at the elevator doors, recalling the time the doors opened, and I discovered Hugo standing behind them.

I'd give anything for him to be standing behind them now, waiting for me.

I release the breath I'm holding in when the elevator doors ding open, and I discover the car is empty. After drifting my eyes to Patty, I ask, "Could you please put in the penthouse floor code for me? I... umm... left my coat in Hugo's apartment." I cringe at my pathetic excuse. It's nearly ten o'clock, and the temperature is still hovering around eighty degrees. A jacket is not needed.

After a beat, Patty says, "I did hear we were supposed to have rain tomorrow." My fingernails dig into my palms when he pushes the 'P' button on the elevator panel before inserting the four-digit security code for the penthouse floor. "I'd hate for you to catch a cold if a cool change comes through with the rain."

I issue my gratitude with a smile before stepping into the elevator. When the doors snap shut, I check my face in the mirror. I look as horrific as I feel.

The thrumming of my pulse increases with every level the elevator climbs.

By the time I reach Hugo's floor, I'm perspiring profusely.

My hand rattles when I knock on his door.

When Hugo fails to answer my knocks, I stand on my tippy toes and run my hand along the top seal of the door. A grin lifts my lips high when my fingers grasp the spare key the Marshall family members always hide there.

After placing the key into the lock, I swing open the front door.

My breath hitches halfway between my lungs and my throat. While moving deeper into the large space, my eyes frantically dart around, absorbing the enormity of the situation.

The apartment is empty.

Not partially empty.

Empty, *empty*.

Like no-one-has-ever-lived-here empty.

Fear overwhelms me as I make my way out of Hugo's apartment

and back down the hall. My mind is hazed, confused as to why Hugo would move out of his apartment only months after moving in.

When heavy footsteps boom through my ears, my eyes float up from my feet. Two gentlemen dressed in dark suits are briskly walking down the hall.

"Sorry," I apologize when I scoot past them.

My eyes rocket to the side when the gentleman's brisk movements reveal a black revolver holstered to his waist.

Maybe they're detectives working Jorgie's case?

I push the elevator button before drifting my eyes back down the hall. My interest piques when the strangers stop at the front of Hugo's apartment. I lean into the elevator doors, concealing myself in the nook when the gentleman carrying a gun kicks in Hugo's door. I tumble into the elevator when its doors pop open. I didn't hear it ding, announcing its arrival over the erratic beating of my heart.

I pop my head out of the elevator in just enough time to see the gun-carrying man exit Hugo's apartment. "I'm sorry, Mr. Petretti, he's gone," a man with a heavy set of wrinkles angrily snarls.

"Find him and anyone associated with him and find them *now!*"

I jump when his thunderous roar echoes down the corridor, then my heart stops beating when his head flings to the side, and he spots me spying on him. A squeal parts my lips as I stumble backward. I land on my backside with a sickening thud as the man shouts, "The elevator!"

Scampering off the floor, I rush to the elevator panel. My hand shakes as I frantically push the 'Close Door' button. Feet stomping on a carpeted floor overtakes the mad beat of my heart. I squeal when a man lunges for the door, but thankfully, he's too late. The doors close with him on the other side.

Stepping back, I rest my sweat-slicked skin on the back wall of the elevator. I gulp in air as the signs of a panic attack overcome me. I've never been more petrified.

Nothing but evil reflected from Mr. Petretti's eyes when he stared at me.

His eyes belong to the devil.

My thoughts snap back to the present when the elevator dings, announcing it has arrived at my floor. I exhale a shaky breath before stepping into the hallway. I dig my hand into my purse in the hunt for my keys as I walk to my apartment.

My brisk strides halt when I'm unexpectedly grabbed from the side.

"You need to come with me," says a raspy voice, dragging me further down the hall.

Don't fret.
Hugo's second book is already available!
Beneath the Sheets – Book 2

Join my Facebook page:
www.facebook.com/authorshandi

Join my READER's group:
https://www.facebook.com/groups/1740600836169853/

Join my newsletter to remain informed:
http://eepurl.com/cyEzNv

My Amazon Page:
https://www.amazon.com/Shandi-Boyes/e/B01D8C13WU

If you enjoyed this book - please leave a review.

ALSO BY SHANDI BOYES

** Denotes Standalone Books*

<u>Perception Series</u>

<u>Saving Noah</u> *

<u>Fighting Jacob</u> *

<u>Taming Nick</u> *

<u>Redeeming Slater</u> *

<u>Saving Emily</u>

<u>Wrapped Up with Rise Up</u>

<u>Protecting Nicole</u> *

Enigma

Enigma

<u>Unraveling an Enigma</u>

<u>Enigma The Mystery Unmasked</u>

<u>Enigma: The Final Chapter</u>

<u>Beneath The Secrets</u>

<u>Beneath The Sheets</u>

<u>Spy Thy Neighbor</u> *

<u>The Opposite Effect</u> *

<u>I Married a Mob Boss</u> *

<u>Second Shot</u> *

<u>The Way We Are</u>

<u>The Way We Were</u>

<u>Sugar and Spice</u> *

<u>Lady In Waiting</u>

<u>Man in Queue</u>

<u>Couple on Hold</u>

Enigma: The Wedding

Silent Vigilante

<u>Hushed Guardian</u>

<u>Quiet Protector</u>

Enigma: An Isaac Retelling

Twisted Lies *

Bound Series

Chains

Links

<u>Bound</u>

<u>Restrain</u>

<u>The Misfits</u> *

Nanny Dispute *

Russian Mob Chronicles

Nikolai: A Mafia Prince Romance

Nikolai: Taking Back What's Mine

<u>Nikolai: What's Left of Me</u>

<u>Nikolai: Mine to Protect</u>

<u>Asher: My Russian Revenge</u> *

Nikolai: Through the Devil's Eyes

Hotshot Neighbor *

<u>The Bobrov Bratva Series</u>

Wicked Intentions *

Sinful Intentions *

Devious Intentions *

Deadly Intentions *

www.ingramcontent.com/pod-product-compliance
Lightning Source LLC
Chambersburg PA
CBHW071135180726
48291CB00007B/2181